Out of the Fire

JUDITH BARRETT

Printed by Hurstbourne Publishing

First published under the pseudonym 'Millie Pearson' April 2017

ISBN 978-1-9998427-1-0

Cover image: Simon Mendez
Cover design: More Visual Ltd

For Laurie, who gave me both the story
and the time in which to write it

'The Lord spoke to you on the mountain out of the fire.'

Deuteronomy 5:4

CONTENTS

AUTHOR'S NOTE

The key events of this novel are matters of historical fact, recorded by Jewish and Christian twelfth century writers and elaborated on and interpreted by many subsequent historians. Many of the characters who appear on the pages that follow this were real people. However, my respect for them and those who have previously written about them has not prevented me from taking whatever liberties with the truth that I deemed necessary to tell a story that also talks to us about our lives now.

Judith Barrett
April 2023

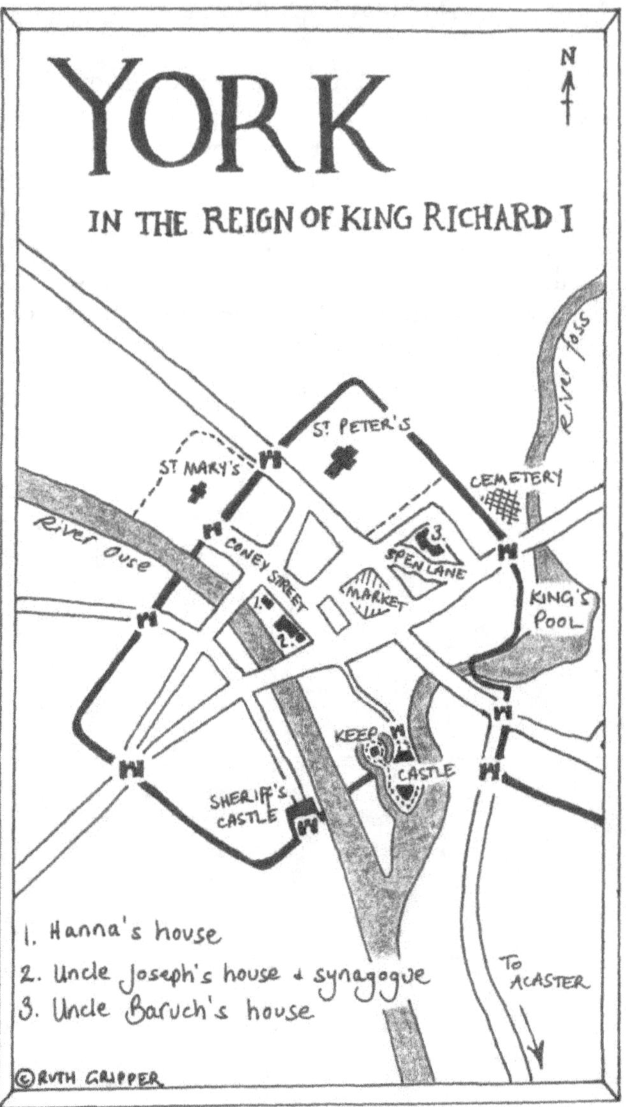

YORK
IN THE REIGN OF KING RICHARD I
N
River Foss
River Ouse
ST PETER'S
ST MARY'S
CEMETERY
CONEY STREET
SPEN LANE
3.
MARKET
KING'S POOL
1.
2.
KEEP
CASTLE
SHERIFF'S CASTLE
TO ACASTER
1. Hanna's house
2. Uncle Joseph's house & synagogue
3. Uncle Baruch's house
© RUTH GRIPPER

ISLES
OF THE
SEA
Dunfermline
N
River Ouse
York
Lincoln
Lynn
Norwich
Northampton
Oxford
St. Albans
LONDON
River Thames
Canterbury
Rouen
© Ruth Gripper

CHARACTERS

HANNA'S FAMILY
IN YORK

Hanna

Ben, *twin*

Abigail, *mother*

Moses/Moshe, *father*

Samuel the physician, *grandfather (widower of Miriam)*

Jessie, *servant*

Baruch, *uncle (Abigail's half-brother)*

Comtessa, *aunt (married to Baruch)*

Cresselin, *cousin (Baruch and Comtessa's son)*

Serlo, *Baruch's attendant*

Elias Quatrebouches, *Baruch's attendant*

IN LINCOLN

Sampson, *uncle (Abigail's half-brother, Baruch's brother)*

Margaret, *aunt (married to Sampson)*

Deulesault, *cousin (Sampson's son)*

IN NORTHAMPTON

Jacob, *uncle (Abigail's half-brother, Baruch's brother)*

Floria, *aunt (married to Jacob)*

OTHER YORK HOUSEHOLDS
MURIEL'S FAMILY

Muriel, *Abigail's friend and business partner*

Gentill, *Muriel's daughter-in-law*

Manasser, *Muriel's son, married to Gentill*

Leo, Hakelin and Flo, *Gentill and Manasser's children*

JOSEPH'S FAMILY AND HOUSEHOLD

Joseph, *Baruch's business partner*

Anna, *married to Joseph*

Mordecai, *Joseph's attendant*

Rabbi Yom Tov, *rabbi, scholar and poet*

Simeon, *Rabbi Yom Tov's nephew*

LEVI'S FAMILY

Levi, *carpenter*
Abe, *Levi's son*
Dinah, *married to Levi*
Leah, *married to Abe*
Little Levi, *Leah and Abe's son*

OTHERS
Caleb, *butcher*
Aaron, *Caleb's brother*

KING'S REPRESENTATIVES IN YORK
Ranulf de Granville, *sheriff (until 30 Sept 1189)*
Gospatric Fitzhorn, *constable*
Aelred, *king's man*

AT ST MARY'S ABBEY, YORK
Prior William, *prior of St Mary's Abbey*
Master Thomas, *monk at St Mary's Abbey*

(Abbot Roger of Dunfermline; Lambinus, *chaplain to Abbot
Roger – Benedictine monks travelling to London with Master
Thomas for the coronation of Richard I)*

THE MANOR HOUSE, ACASTER
Richard de Malebisse, *lord of the manor*
Emma, *daughter of Richard*
Hugh, *steward to Richard*
Will, *Hanna and Ben's friend, son of Hugh*
Marmaduke Darrell, *friend to Richard*
John Marshall, *friend to Richard*
De Cuckney, *squire to Richard*

IN LONDON
RABBI ABRAHAM'S HOUSEHOLD
Rabbi Abraham
Sarah, *married to Rabbi Abraham*
Reuben, *youngest child (of six)*

JEWISH COMMUNITY REPRESENTATIVES
Deulebene of Lynn
Haim of Lincoln
Isaac le Gros of Canterbury
Jurnet of Norwich
Benedict le Puncteur of Oxford
David, *son of Benedict le Puncteur*
Isaac le Docteur of Lynn
Crispin of Northampton

JOSEPH'S HOUSEHOLD
Elise, *daughter of Joseph of York*
Jacob of Orléans, *poet; married to Elise*

QUATREBOUCHES HOUSEHOLD
Ursell Quatrebouches, *brother of Elias*

PROLOGUE

Still the storm raged. The sky had been dark since morning and it was impossible to tell if it was day or evening. All the world was water. The cliff-top castle was lost in the rain as if it no longer existed; vanished, too, were the port buildings on the shore line. The wind blew in terrible squalls over and around the harbour walls, lashing its waters into a frenzy.

The hailstones hurled against him by the wind needled the boy's bare arms and legs and the cold burned them red raw. The salt spray stung his eyes. His dark hair clung to his head. His feet were numb. He knew Da was next to him, but both were too exhausted to speak.

He felt a hand on his shoulder, half-turned to see, and recognised the three-fingered grasp of a friend with a gold ring in his ear, wrapped in a black leather cloak. The boy smiled at him, a dimple flickering in his right cheek. Then the man was gone.

With the other passengers and crew, the father and son continued to bail out the water in which they sloshed shin deep, the bowls out of which they ate their daily ration pitted against the might of the storm. The water in the boat continued to rise. Yet another wave crashed over its bow, and the father and son clung to the ship's side, lest they be washed overboard.

It was impossible to hear what further orders the captain shouted at them above the roar of the sea and wind. The sails had long been furled, and anything that might move tightly secured.

Then there was a sudden, even stronger burst of wind and a cracking sound. The second mast had snapped, was falling. Some pushed out of the way. Too late, the boy turned.

Next, blackness, nothing.

1. HANNA

York, Tamuz 4949 / July 1189

Hanna shut the door and let her eyes adjust to the semi-darkness. Thin white lines of light marked the joins in the shutters across the windows at the far end of the room.

This time she wasn't scared of what was lurking in the shadows: it was her – just a tall, skinny girl with a deep dimple in her left cheek and a mass of dark curly hair; no ghouls or demons lying in wait (and anyway, she reminded herself, there were no such things – Granda said so).

But she could hear voices in the street outside, and laughter. She stood rigid, holding her breath until they passed. Her nose wrinkled at the room's familiar medicinal smells – sweet rosemary and cinnamon, the tang of thyme and cumin – and others, indistinguishable, smells of Da. She felt a sudden ache of longing – when would Da and Ben come back? Hanna pushed the feeling aside.

She hadn't got long. She needed to be back in her room, lying sick upon her bed, before Ma returned. Despite the gloom she knew where to find what she was looking for.

She felt her way around the large oak desk with its high-backed chair and then the heavy chest in which Granda stored his manuscripts. But she'd forgotten where she'd left her stool and stumbled against it, sent it crashing to the floor. The rugs underfoot and rich hangings on the wall dulled the noise, though it still sounded loud to Hanna. She'd caught her knee on the stool's sharp corner and she winced at the pain as she picked the stool up and put it back in its place.

Her heart was thumping and her hands clammy. She reached up to the shelf above her, third one up, and began to feel along its books' familiar shapes. Each was bound in soft leather, protection over the many miles and years since

"

they were taken from their – and Granda's – southern home: Cordova, jewel of Andalus, set in a fertile plain at the foot of mountains overlooking the Guadalqivir river, a place of paved streets, fruit trees and flowers ('Let's make such a city here in York,' said Da).

The books' strong pages of vellum contained knowledge accrued over centuries long past – ideas astrological, historical, medical, mathematical, magical – which had been translated and transcribed by Islamic, Jewish and Christian scholars. She'd return the book, when she'd finished with it, so it wasn't really stealing.

It was one that Granda said was worthless yet refused to lend. He said it was 'too dangerous'. Hanna and Ben had read it in surreptitious bursts, with no time to memorise its contents. It wasn't the book as such that Hanna wanted, or even the knowledge contained within its pages – but rather the fun that could be had with its magical combinations of letters and numbers and ancient spells and incantations. Magic was like tree-climbing or swimming – an activity that adults forbade you to take part in because you could hurt yourself – but only if you weren't any good at it.

Here the book was, in its allotted space – seventh one along, slightly shorter and thinner than those on either side. Just one, among so many, would surely not be missed. Hanna removed it from the shelf and placed it inside her tunic, then eased the other books along the shelf to fill the gap.

Then there was a thudding of horses' hooves outside the window, and shouting. She started, broke out in a sweat – who could that be? – turned to the door. No matter, the book was hers.

That night, Hanna kept her candle burning. Once sure Ma was asleep, she pulled the book out from where she'd hidden it, wrapped in a long-treasured scrap of soft leather, in the clothes chest at the end of the bed she'd shared with Ma since Ben and Da left.

The book was at least forty years old. That was how long ago Granda and his family had fled the fierce

Almohads from across the sea – but the knowledge it contained was far, far older. The ink was only slightly faded and its Hebrew script remained clear. Hanna began to read.

By the time she was so tired that she could read no longer, her head was a complete jumble of angels' names and the wonders they could help her to perform.

The book set out for her the seven firmaments, the angels powerful within each one, and which could help with what. Although the actions for each spell were not that complicated – *if any enemy has got hold of thee and wishes to kill thee, bend the little finger of the left hand, say the magic words and he will run away from thee like one who runs from his murderer* – the words were, often some fourteen angels' names to invoke.

There was a spell which promised to help her remember immediately all she had learnt: to write various angels' names on a new-laid egg, then wash the writing off with strong wine early in the morning and drink the wine, and not eat anything at all – but she wasn't sure she could fit all the names on just one egg, even if she had the book in front of her to copy from. The magical powers the book had promised her turned out to be long lists of names, invoking not just G–d but myriads of angels.

Ma told tales of a woman and her son expelled from the city in winter, accused of killing their neighbour and his cows with their magic powers, the mother and son found frozen in the snow next day outside the city walls; and of a young woman, stoned to death, for enchanting another's husband. But these spells weren't like that. What harm could experimenting with these do?

Ben could help her, and Will – and that would be the fun part. Only Ben was with Da and who knew where they were. Without Ben, on her own, she wasn't sure she could count on Will. She pushed the book under her mattress. The names of angels and thoughts of Ben and Da whirled around her head. She slept.

2. FISH

'Come on, Will – Ma needs the fish smoked before dark.'

The afternoon sun was warm on Hanna's back. Beaumon sat alert opposite her, eyes fixed on Hanna's face, tail wagging against the floor of the boat.

'All right, all right,' Will replied as he unhooked the rope from the tree stump to which the small boat was moored. He gave it a heave from the shore and then jumped in to sit next to his dog.

'Careful, you'll have us all in the water,' Hanna complained, steadying the boat with the oars before pulling strongly on them, directing the boat against the current into the midstream.

'You're no fun when Ben's away,' said Will, looking at her from under his floppy brown fringe and over the pile of willow baskets in the centre of the boat.

'Maybe that's because I have to do his chores and mine,' Hanna retorted. The effort of rowing prevented her from saying more. It was all very well for the family to send Ben away with Da to keep him out of trouble, but it felt like it was her, Hanna, who was the one being punished, with scarcely a minute to herself since they had left.

Will said nothing. They were well past the abbey's fisheries now and he concentrated on looking out for the wooden floats which marked out Mistress Abigail's traps. He wished Ben was there, too. When the three of them were together, emptying the traps didn't feel like work. He enjoyed the closeness of the twins, the way each seemed to know what the other was thinking and how one could often finish the other's sentence, the spooky occasions on which one had been hurting when the other, somewhere else entirely, sustained an injury – as when Ben, on the Acaster estate with Will, had clutched at his foot, writhing in pain, only to find, when they returned home, that Hanna had stepped barefoot into the still hot ash of a spent cooking fire. When the three of them were together, there was always teasing and laughter, and the seductive pull of Ben and Hanna's insistence on the possibilities of magic.

None of the three could remember a time when they hadn't been friends. Da and Granda's medical skill had saved Will's and his mother's lives at Will's birth, and the children had grown up together with the city of York and the estate of Acaster equally their playground – but Will could do without Hanna's ill humour today. He scratched his back under his shirt and felt the scars still jagged under his fingers, though it was many years since the whipping which had put them there. The man who'd then wielded the whip had this morning greeted him with a cheery smile.

Will spied a string of floats just up ahead.

'There's the first,' he cried, 'Take us into the bank here, if you can, under the willows.'

Hanna ducked under the drooping branches of the willow trees and held the boat steady with the oars while Will scrambled onto the bank to wind the rope around a tree trunk before knotting it. Next, back into the boat, and the two of them reached down into the water, four hands on the trap's rope. Beaumon, familiar with the routine, kept out of the way. Then, hand over hand over hand over hand, and out of the water came the basket spurting with water and a silver wriggling mass inside, which Hanna and Will landed with a wet thump into the boat.

'Not bad,' said Will. 'The weather might be warm, but there's plenty here.'

Hanna didn't reply, busy untying the wet rope and its floats from the basket and fixing it instead to one of the empty traps they'd brought with them. She checked its bait and weights, then lowered it into the water.

'Your turn to row,' she said to Will, as she clambered up onto the bank to untie the boat. She jumped lightly back in, at last smiling at him. She took her place on the other side of the baskets and pushed damp curls of dark hair behind her ears. The familiar dimple appeared in her left cheek, Will noted, the mirror image of Ben's, as Will had often teased them. He felt suddenly shy, hoped she couldn't see his face reddening, and turned his attention to rowing the boat further upstream.

The river was deeper now, dark green, the shadows under the willows black, before it curved tightly around a corner. It was millpond-smooth on the surface, but currents swirled underneath, where the rock was softer and the water's flow had cut deep pools. It was here, three summers previously, on a day even hotter than this, when Will had been swimming behind the boat – he'd fallen in while play-fighting with Ben – and nearly drowned. If Beaumon hadn't whined so that Hanna and Ben went back to see where Will was…

She wondered about telling him now about the book of spells she'd borrowed from Granda, but she was nervous. Will had been lucky not to be caught and punished with Ben during their last 'experiment'.

Will remained intent on his rowing, his sun-tanned face grimacing with the effort. His shoulders had broadened over the past year. Still slight, he was wiry and stronger than he looked. Hanna tried not to mind that he could row the boat faster than her – at least it meant they'd be done quicker. Their silvery haul squirmed in the basket. Smoking fish was just one of Ma's projects. Even when Da was at home, she earned more than him and Granda together. Da and Granda might be skilled physicians, their services relied on by rich and poor, Christian and Jew alike, but Da hated to profit from the misfortunes of others while Granda, in truth, was happier with his books about how to cure the sick than with their flesh and blood reality.

Will and Hanna made their way in silence, not entirely companionable, from one trap to the next. The air hummed with insects. Beaumon dozed.

At last they had only full baskets in the boat, and rested briefly. A pair of ducks trod water against the current, their open beaks half-submerged under the water as they fed on whatever the river washed into them.

'Will you come to study with Granda tomorrow, Will?' Hanna asked. He'd joined them each week for a couple of years now, having already learnt as much as the monks at St Mary's were willing to teach the city's Christian children, enough to follow quicker than his father the Acaster estate accounts. With Hanna and Ben, reading and writing also included stories written in books by men their grandfather knew.

Yet Will hesitated. 'I dunno as I'll have time – the Beast is back.' He paused. 'I'd like to.' In fact he wasn't sure that he wanted to be with Hanna again without Ben.

'He's back?' Hanna said, dismayed. While its lord was away, the children had the run of the estate. She and Ben had learned to ride there with Will and helped him care for the hounds. But once the Beast was back…

'How long is he staying?'

'For a while, my ma thinks. She reckons he can't bear to be at Wheldrake since his wife died. Emma's with him.'

'Is she?' Hanna looked at Will. It was because of Emma that Will had received his whipping. She'd accused him of scaring her horse so that it reared and threw her, rather than admit to her father her lack of horsemanship.

'What's she–ow!' Hanna put her hand to the back of her head, as if to shield it.

'What's the matter?' asked Will, all talk of the Beast and Emma forgotten.

'I'm not sure,' she replied. 'It feels as if I've been hit.' Her fingers explored a bump newly risen under her hair. She felt a hot rush of fear – but of what? Her heart was pounding and she was suddenly out of breath.

'There's something wrong, Will – let's go back. Anyway, Ma will be waiting. Here, let me row.'

A feeling of unease stayed with Hanna all the way down stream to the city. 'Something to do with Ben?' was the question neither Hanna nor Will felt able to utter.

They moored the boat and dragged the dripping baskets up the bank to the door in the stone wall of Hanna's family home. Its front faced onto Coney Street and the city, but at the back there was nothing between it and the wharf which served all the houses along that stretch of the river. Hanna pushed the door open and entered the courtyard. Ma, making ready for the fish, turned to greet them.

'At last,' she said, but smiling. 'Come in, come in. Jessie's gone to fetch more wood. But let's get the traps in and we can make a start.'

Tall and strong, Ma was dressed for serious labour. The sleeves of her worn and grubby grey dress were rolled up to reveal muscular brown forearms covered in fine dark hairs and she wore a red scarf on her head instead of her usual cap. She easily swung one of the traps up onto her hip and carried it across the yard to put it down next to the trestle table under the apple and pear trees. Alongside the table stood two weathered wooden half-barrels, and three stools. Together, Ma, Hanna and Will placed by the table the rest of the traps, their contents still twitching. The smoke kiln's fire glowed red at its base.

'Have some bread, Will,' said Ma, 'you too, Hanna.'

'If I could just have a drink of water, Mistress Abigail, then I'll be off. Malbisse is back – my ma is expecting me.'

'Help yourself, Will.' Ma gestured to the earthenware pot that stood in the kitchen next to the house, the water drawn from the courtyard well by Jessie each morning.

'So he's back, is he? I wondered – there were a couple of men in his colours drunk in the marketplace when I was out. He brings nothing but trouble, that man. Do you remember the big fight last time his household was here?'

Will nodded, slopping water into a bowl for Beaumon, then passing a cupful to Hanna. She avoided meeting his eyes. She badly wanted him to leave, her whole being focused on the pain in her head and the fear she could not shift that something was wrong with Ben.

'Thank you,' she mumbled, then drank deeply.

Will put his cup back next to the pot.

'I'll be off then,' he said. 'I'll maybe see you tomorrow, Hanna. I hope you feel better. Goodbye Mistress Abigail,' and then he and Beaumon were out through the door at the back of the courtyard and down to the river and Will's boat.

Ma looked sharply at Hanna. Previously she'd been concentrating too hard on getting ready for smoking the fish to give her full attention to her daughter.

'Are you not well, my love?'

'It's just a bit of a headache, Ma – too much sun, I expect.' There was no point in sharing her fears about Ben with their mother; she'd been anxious enough about letting him go with Da, convinced only by Granda and Da's insistence that he would be in more danger if he remained.

Hanna disappeared into the kitchen, re-emerging with a dirty linen sheet whose ends she tied around her neck, tugging it down and around to cover her tunic.

'We should get started, Ma. The fishes' guts will be rotting in their bellies. I promised Granda I'd help him, too, before sun down.'

They were just emptying the glistening contents of the first trap onto the trestle table, Hanna picking up any fish that slid to the floor when Jessie returned, hot and sweaty, broad back stooped under the firewood strapped to her back, thick strands of brown hair plastered to her forehead. Ma helped her lower the wood to the ground while Hanna fetched her a cup of water.

'Thank you, Miss Hanna,' she said, sitting down heavily on one of the stools. 'Look, I've brought these, too,' she said, detaching a handkerchief-bound bundle from her belt. 'Oak chips – I was passing Levi's workshop and he was working on a big oak door. Young Abe collected them for me. They allus give the fish a lovely flavour, they do.'

Hanna didn't feel well enough to do more than smile and nod as Jessie told them who the door was for, what it was like and how much it was costing and then who and what else she'd seen, including her sister and children, as she'd called in at home as she was passing. Luckily, she didn't need much response to help her tell her stories – like the fish slithering to the floor, halting their flow was the tricky bit.

So Hanna concentrated on preparing the day's catch for Ma to smoke. She wielded the knife like an extension of her hand, shaving off the fish's pearly scales, and then nimbly slicing its belly from the vent to the lower jaw and pulling out its innards in one neat movement. Next, a quick rinse of each fishy body in the half barrel of water alongside her, before she tossed it into the neighbouring barrel full of brine and at once picked up another fish to put under her knife.

3. GRANDA

It was past dusk when she knocked on her grandfather's heavy wooden door.

'Come in, my child.'

Granda was sat at his usual place at the table, an oil lamp already lit next to him. Its pool of light illuminated the thick sheets of parchment laid out in front of him and their line upon line of elegant Arabic script. These manuscripts, as he'd so often told Hanna, were his life's work – or rather the translation of their contents into Hebrew and Latin.

Granda himself was half hidden in the shadows behind the lamp, though the luxuriant white hair on his head and chin reflected its light. Hanna could hardly make out the stark lines of his cheekbones and nose and his dark eyes under his thick, still black eyebrows. The bookshelves behind him were lost in the shadows.

'Hanna, my child, good evening. I've been waiting for you.'

He sounded cross, Hanna thought, but then he often did when she was late, and it didn't usually last. 'You have allowed yourself to be distracted by the tasks your mother has set you. Come and sit down.'

The running battle between Ma and Granda as to whether Hanna's priority was the work of the household or her grandfather's intellectual/medical pursuits had been fought ever more keenly since Ben had left with Da.

'Good evening, Granda. I'm sorry I'm late.'

Hanna sat on her stool alongside Granda's chair as she was told. There was something immediately reassuring about being with her grandfather in this room. She loved its rugs and its hangings and its books, all of which had travelled with his family from Al Andalus, and the shelves of carefully labelled jars that held the herbs, spices and extracts with which he and Da made up their medicines; and the glass flasks and pipes they used in their manufacture. The room held memories of Da, but also of all the stories Granda had told them about growing up in Cordova with its abundant sun and water, exotic fruits and bread made of white flour, its crowded Jewish quarter, synagogue, mosque and palace – where Muslim, Christian and Jew lived peacefully together and where poetry, art and science flourished.

But Granda wasn't in the mood for stories just now.

'Right then, my child,' said her grandfather, 'I'd like you to carry on from where you left off yesterday.'

He opened the casket to the side of the table and lifted out scraps of manuscript whose writing was blotted, with much crossing out and rewriting, together with another, newer manuscript, on which the writing – Hanna's writing – was word-perfect. He placed these on the table in front of her.

'Let me light another lamp,' he added, already taking it from a shelf behind him and lighting it with a taper from the flame of the one which burnt in front of him. His hands were particularly shaky this evening, Hanna noticed. Granda dosed himself with medicine to treat the condition, but to little effect.

Hanna selected her favourite pen from the stand on the desk and pulled the bottle of ink towards her. She dipped the quill in the ink, took a deep breath and began to write, carefully copying the correct Latin words from the messy manuscript onto the new one.

The messy script was Granda's, his translation from the Arabic of a medical textbook, itself painstakingly written out by who knew whose hand in Cordova, the book just one of the treasured collection that had travelled with him across Europe. Once translated into Latin, he could share their contents, in particular, with his and Da's friend, Master Thomas, who tended the sick in the infirmary at the abbey.

Hanna felt herself soothed as her quill travelled smoothly across the page and she allowed her mind to focus on the clear, solid syllables of the Latin words. She revelled in her ability to make the shapes as she required them, their meaning there for all time. Her understanding of Latin was good – from the beginning Granda had taught her and Ben to write in Latin and French as well as Hebrew. And she was curious to read the cures suggested by these Arabian physicians, even if she'd rather be reading about magic...

They worked in silence, she faithfully making good the translation Granda had already done, he working on the next.

Hanna felt calm now, but sad and, finally, exhausted. She was unable to hide her yawns and found herself with tears falling silently down her face. She wiped them away, lest one fall on the manuscript and smudge her writing, and at the same time put the quill back in its stand and pushed the manuscript away from her.

Her grandfather looked up. Tears glittered on Hanna's face in the lamplight.

'My child,' he said, 'What is it?'

'I don't know,' she said. 'It was when Will and I were coming back from collecting the fish... '

And she related the story to him from the beginning, from the bump on the head, to the persistent pain and feeling of dread which had stayed with her and the fear that something bad had happened to Ben and Da. Granda felt the bump. It was real enough ('an insect bite, perhaps,' he said). He called Jessie to bring some bread and cheese for Hanna to eat and boiling water into which he shook some powder from one of the bottles on the shelves behind his desk.

Granda sat with her while she drank and ate. 'There's no point worrying about Da and Ben either, as there's nothing you can do about them,' he said. 'Your Da is a wise man – he knows how to keep himself safe.

'It's a time of uncertainty for all of us. Uncle Joseph sent word to Uncle Baruch from Rouen yesterday – King Henry is dead. We have a new king.'

Hanna looked up from her drink, startled, remembering the thud of hooves she had heard before leaving Granda's room the previous evening. 'What? Who?'

'King Henry is dead, and his son Richard now rules Normandy, including our isle of the sea. They'd fought, made peace and then Henry fell sick and died, at his castle in Chinon. The news was with your Uncle Joseph at Rouen within a couple of days.'

She knew the names, often the subject of conversation between Da and Granda and the other adults – who was in, who was out – and always discussed with a wry laugh, especially if Da was there, but also a vague sense of threat. The names were of men far off and yet very real to Hanna, whose actions, she sensed, had consequences for her family and friends.

'Will it make any difference to us?' she asked.

'That we shall see, my child. That we shall see.'

4. MARRIAGE

'It's high time Hanna was married, you know.'

'I know, Muriel.'

Ma was sat on her haunches in the courtyard, kneading the bread dough on a wooden board placed on the ground in front of her. To one side, a pot bubbled on the fire. The bread would bake later in its embers. The late morning sun was bright, and the two women were working in the fruit trees' shadow. Granda's poppies opened mauve-pink among his herbs; the chickens were pecking for worms. Flo, Muriel's youngest grandchild, lay asleep on a rug next to her.

Ma was pummelling the dough with particular force, pausing from time to time to wipe sweat from her forehead with her forearm and to push back tendrils of long dark hair which had escaped her cap. It wasn't the first time that she had had this conversation with her neighbour and business partner. She was very fond of Muriel, but her conviction that she could solve everyone else's problems could get a bit wearing.

'I was betrothed at ten and married at twelve, and married happily to my Abraham for twenty-four years, G–d rest his soul.'

Muriel, sat beside Ma on a low stool, blew her nose noisily into her apron and wiped a tear from her eye.

The ledger containing the records of the two women's current enterprise lay at her feet. It listed the quantities and prices paid for the goods that Manasser, Muriel's son, had packed into the hold of their boat some eight months ago, bound for the continent – bolts of York cloth, bales of wool, vast baskets of grain, weapons and agricultural tools forged under the auspices of Yorkshire's Cistercian monks from the iron and lead dug from their ever-deepening mines. The pages that followed remained blank in anticipation of the amount and value of the goods with which Manasser would return – Flemish cloth, herrings, furs, and amber from the north, Italian silk, oil, figs and raisins, spices and precious jewels from the south. The women's business discussions – and speculation about what difference a new king would make to them – were done for today. Unable to predict the arrival of the ship carrying their cargo, they could only wait.

Piled high to Muriel's right were branches of the summer's rosemary which she returned to cutting and tying into bunches for drying. The air was sharp with its scent. Her eyebrows arched high and grey over glittering dark eyes which missed nothing. But the laughter lines at their sides and around her mouth were deep.

'With your Moshe still away and his father lost in his books, you must take responsibility, Abigail. Ten children I've borne, seven I raised to adulthood and all seven I've seen married, twenty-six grandchildren I have now, Abigail – it's a life's work.'

Ma didn't look up from pummelling the dough.

'I know, Muriel. But you know that's why Moshe went across the sea in the first place – to talk with his sisters and make marriage plans for Hanna and Ben – and we must wait for his return. G–d willing, he'll be back by New Year. Besides, Hanna's still little more than a child, straight up and down – still often mistaken for Ben.'

'That's as maybe, Abigail, but you must be prepared – the pomegranate will be full of seeds soon enough. I don't know why you dismiss the options closer to home – there's my grandson, Elchanan, in Rouen – I'm hoping Manasser might bring him back with him – and of course there's Baruch's nephew, Deulesault, in Lincoln – now that would be a fine alliance – your half-nephew, let's not forget.'

'All possibilities I agree, Muriel –'

'And what about young Simeon, here in York, Rabbi Yom Tov's nephew? He's a lovely boy, a good family –'

'And ugly, Auntie Muriel, not to mention stupid and dull,' said Hanna. The two women hadn't noticed her coming out of the house behind them. 'And what if I don't want to get married?'

She grinned and curtseyed respectfully towards Ma and Muriel, but this wasn't the discussion she wanted to have.

'Of course you want to get married, child,' said Muriel. Hanna put an arm around Ma's shoulders while deftly pinching some dough to eat with her other hand.

Now Flo was awake and crying and Muriel lifted the child onto her lap. Flo's face was pink and sweaty. Muriel removed her granddaughter's cap and gave her water from a cup, but still intent on Hanna.

'So how do you plan to live?' she asked, 'when your Ma and I are dead and gone?'

Hanna glanced across at Ma and thought better of joking.

'Maybe I will be a canny business woman like you, Auntie Muriel, buying and selling, travelling to distant markets, having who knows what adventures.'

'What? And leave your family behind?' asked Ma, only half laughing.

'I could stay here and cure the sick like Granda and Da.' At once Hanna wished she could take the words back. Muriel had already made known – at great length and on several occasions – her views on the unfitness of girls to work with the sick.

But this time she let it pass. 'I didn't build up this business on my own, you know.'

'I know – you've Ma to help you.'

'Your mother, of course. But before her it was my Abraham, may his soul rest in paradise, who devoted his life to it while I was busy with our babies. It was he who travelled to distant markets – oh the worry and fright when he was away on his journeys – but he provided for us and never turned away any neighbour who needed help – as well you'll remember, Abigail.'

Ma nodded, covering the dough with a cloth and moving it into the warmth of the sun.

'And he took advice from me and no one else. When the rabbi asked him on his deathbed if he had any last

wishes he replied, "None. My wife knows everything."
And we loved each other, Hanna.' Muriel wiped another
tear from her eye with her apron. 'My only regret is that he
died before I could embrace him one last time. "Dearest
heart, shall I embrace you?" I asked. "I am unclean." "G–d
forbid, my love," he said, "it will not be long before you
take your ritual bath." But he died later that day.'

Hanna hadn't heard that part of the story before.
'Couldn't you have embraced him anyway – you know,
without telling him?'

'Hanna!' Ma exclaimed.

'It's all right, Abigail. I've wondered that myself,
Hanna. But if it's G–d's will. You'll know, my child, when
you have your own husband who you love and care for as
much as he does you.'

There was a loud knocking on the front door. Hanna,
grateful to escape the conversation, went in answer. It was
Aelred, one of the constable's men from the castle. A pale,
spindly youth, with blonde hair, he cut a conspicuous
figure in the town in the constable's red and grey.
Everyone knew him. He knew Hanna, but didn't greet her
beyond a brisk nod.

'Is Master Samuel here?' he said. 'One of the
constable's men is injured – his head cracked right open.
Master Thomas is asking for Samuel.'

Granda had come out of his room and was standing
behind Hanna, slightly stooped, and barely taller than his
granddaughter. His white hair was tousled, as if he had
been running his hands through it while he worked.

'I am here,' he said. 'Let me collect my things. Hanna
– you must come with me. Go and tell Ma and I'll wait for
you outside.'

Hanna could tell that Ma was angry when she heard
Granda's orders – her face darkened and she frowned –
but she said nothing. She clearly didn't want an argument
in front of Muriel.

'You shouldn't let him use the young girl like this,'
said Muriel. 'It's not right, her running about town, going
into people's houses…'

Hanna quickly pulled on her cloak and kissed Ma goodbye.

'I have to go, Ma. Granda is waiting for me. I'll see you later. Goodbye Muriel,' she called as she ran through the house to the front door, not stopping for a reply.

5. MEDICINE

It was a direct walk along Coney Street, past the stone houses belonging to the wine merchant, the monks of Fountains Abbey, and Uncle Joseph and Anna – theirs with synagogue and miqveh adjoining; then past other houses of wood, both grand and humble, down the hill to the northern gate of the castle where the constable, Gospatric Fitzhorn, lived. The square keeps of both the city's castles were visible, dominating the skyline to the south as the crane and growing towers of St Peter's – and those of the abbey, already complete – dominated it to the north ('just in case we should forget who's in charge,' Da would joke).

As well as keeping the local population in line, the two castles were well placed to keep out the Scots, should they ever think of invading again. The constable's castle stood next to the royal fishponds of the River Foss; the second castle, on the other side of the River Ouse, close to where the rivers joined, was used by the county sheriff, Ranulf de Glanville, when he was in York. Ben and Hanna had as small children accompanied Granda there for him to debate and play games of chess with the educated, much-travelled sheriff, leader of the army which had defeated the Scots.

They passed a group of merchants joking noisily and gutturally together. 'From Flanders,' said Granda. 'The world is on the move, Hanna.' He smiled. The town was busy in preparation for St Peter's Fair. Hanna could see the juggler surrounded by a small crowd on the corner, but there wasn't time to stop.

Granda had taken her on several home visits now. He didn't like to go alone. His powers of diagnosis were acute, but his hands were shaky and his manner of talking to patients awkward. Da had done almost all such visits before he went away, only occasionally accompanied by Granda, more often by Ben.

But Hanna had never accompanied Granda to attend to the constable, had never had reason to venture inside the castle walls. Not long before Da took Ben away, he, Hanna and Will had been told off by a couple of the guards for taking Will's boat right up to the sluice gate which controlled the flow of river water into the moat, but that was as close as Hanna had come.

As they approached the castle, to enter through the main gate facing the town, its keep towered above Aelred, Hanna and Granda, the dark shadow it cast feeling all the cooler in contrast to the bright sun. There was a strong smell of yeast.

Aelred led Hanna and Granda through the gatehouse into the lower bailey. To left and right there were more buildings close up against the bailey wall. Hanna glimpsed the horses in the stables as she passed and heard the ring of hammer on metal from the blacksmith's workshop above which soft grey smoke spiralled into the warm afternoon air. Huge pots bubbled on the cooking fires outside the brew house. The keep now rose behind them; the hall, where they were headed, stood straight ahead.

'Careful, Granda!'

Hanna pulled at her grandfather's sleeve to prevent him tripping over three brown chickens pecking in the dirt. There were geese and several goats, too, but the rope which tethered the goats outside the constable's quarters was short enough to keep them from butting their head inside the visitors' pockets in search of food. The billy goat 'maa-ed' at them in frustration.

Outside the hall a couple of lads with tearstained faces were comforting a woman holding a baby in her arms and with a toddler at her skirts. Hanna tried not to stare. Aelred opened the door to the hall and Granda and Hanna stepped inside.

The injured man lay on the huge table in the centre of the room, Master Thomas bending over him. The window shutters had been opened wide to give sufficient light. Above the table, a haze of dust and smoke particles danced in the soaring arc of the roof's oak beams. Granda and Hanna drew closer.

The man – from his red and grey tunic one of the castle's garrison – was unconscious and Hanna could see the break in his skull, smashed in one portion like the shell on a hardboiled egg. There was blood in his hair, but his chest was rising and falling with steady breaths. Hanna held Granda's leather bag, pleased that she didn't feel squeamish – Ben had been known to faint. She had never seen an injury to the head before, wondered what lay inside, underneath its covering of hair, skin and bone.

'He weren't that far up the ladder when he fell,' said Gospatric, 'but he struck his head on the corner of a masonry block as he landed. Unwin, his name is. One of my best workers, and father to six – two of his lads were working with him.'

The boys they'd passed in the yard on the way in, perhaps, Hanna thought.

It was the first time Hanna had ever seen the elderly constable not on a horse and without a helmet on his head of white hair, which kept the shape of the helmet even now it was removed. He had the red face and shiny nose of a man who likes a drink. Maybe he'd already had one – his eyes looked glassy. He'd looked at Hanna askance when she'd arrived with Granda, but had made no comment. Granda's status as an older man and an outsider known for his ability to save lives meant that he was allowed to break the social rules, as now, by insisting that his granddaughter accompany him when he worked.

Granda and Master Thomas, a small, neat man in a black cowl, were conferring as they examined the patient. Hanna could hear in her head the words of the healing spell in Granda's book of magic – they came near the beginning and she'd memorised them the previous night:

> *Arise in the first or second hour of the night and*
> *take with you myrrh and frankincense. Put this*
> *on burning coals while saying the name of the*
> *angel who rules over the first encampment, who is*
> *called Tzaphqiel, and say there, seven times, the*
> *names of the seventy-two angels who serve before*

But none of that was any use now (even if she could
remember the seventy-two angels' names), with the injured
man, Unwin, stretched out on the table in front of them
and the hole in his head in need of immediate physical
repair.

Thomas stood upright, turned and spoke to the
constable. 'The skull is damaged, but the outer membrane
of the brain is unbroken. Samuel has read of such cases.'

'Praise be to G–d. I don't like to lose any man, but
particularly not one with so many children.'

'We'll need your help, Gospatric. Have one of your
men bring us water which has been boiled,' said Granda,
'and a clean jug.'

Thomas caught Hanna's eye and smiled. The monks
from St Mary's were a friendly bunch. They allowed both
Jews and women to wander freely around their abbey –
though Granda and Da had little respect for most of them,
known as much for their love of wine as of G–d.

But Thomas was a friend, to Da in particular, who
was the closest to him in age, and a frequent visitor to their
house. He and Da had delighted in discussing long into the
night, arguing points of medicine and religion; each joked
that the other was destined for hell unless he recognised
the error of his religious ways. Ma, when she overheard
them, was scandalised; the men laughed uproariously.

While they waited for the water, Granda prepared the
tools for the operation. He took his physician's box from
his bag and checked the selection of small silver knives,
hooks, needles and probes held in its compartments. He
also brought out lengths of silk cloth, moss from the well
at home, a small sponge and a bottle of poppy juice which
Hanna and Ben had helped to collect last summer from
the unripe seedpods of the poppies in the courtyard
garden. Now he shook some drops from the bottle on to
the sponge, put the cap back into the bottle and handed
both it and the sponge to Hanna. The box of silverware he
placed on the table, to the side of the sick man, together
with the cloth and moss.

The bowls of water were brought in and the jug and Granda and Thomas took turns to pour water over each other's hands, splashing it onto the hall's earth floor. Granda took the sponge from Hanna and held it under the patient's nose – his grip was steady enough for that – though the trembling was apparent in his other hand as he handed Thomas a knife, its blade flashing as it caught the sunlight.

The two men held each other's gaze briefly, a look which expressed the trust each had in the other's ability and their mutual reliance one upon the other. Then Thomas began, cutting out the broken bone before enlarging the opening in the skull to some three finger widths. Hanna could see the grey of the brain inside. Thomas swapped the knife for the pair of tweezers Granda passed to him and removed one by one the splinters of bone that might yet pierce the brain, dropping each 'plink' into the bowl Granda held out for him. This was more like the deftness required of carpentry or silver-smithing than magic – though if the man recovered to embrace his wife again and teach his boys his masonry skills, it would seem a sort of magic, Hanna thought.

Granda removed the sponge from under the man's nose as Thomas cleaned the wound right down to the outer membrane. Then Thomas took the moss, filled the wound with it and together he and Granda bound the man's head with the strips of silk. The patient was already regaining consciousness. He groaned, half raised himself from the table and vomited copiously – on himself, the table and Master Thomas who was still stood at his side.

There were cries of disgust and dismay from Thomas and the constable and further groans from the man.

'It's quite normal, quite normal,' said Granda.

Hanna handed one of the bowls of water to Thomas, taking the other herself to clean their patient, as her mother had done for her and Ben when they were small – though could feel her body revolting as she did so. She turned her face away, swallowing hard to stop herself retching.

'No, no,' said the constable, still with a look of disgust upon his face. 'Fetch his wife, Mary, this is her job. She's outside.' Then, changing his mind, 'I'll fetch her.'

Hanna wasn't sure if he'd made it clear in the yard whether it was a living body or a corpse the woman was being asked to tend to. She looked terrified. She scarcely glanced at Thomas and Granda, but gave a great sob as she looked at her husband, with his bandaged head, eyes closed.

When finally Hanna, Granda and Master Thomas emerged into the late afternoon sun of the bailey, Hanna was feeling faint with hunger, wondering if any of the broth that had been bubbling on the fire at home still remained.

All of a sudden, there was uproar outside the castle – horses' hooves, shouting, and banging on the gates. They were flung open and two riders entered. The men's faces were smeared with sweat and dust, and the horses' flanks were dark with both.

Granda, Master Thomas and Hanna slipped through the gates before they shut again.

'What news are they bringing, I wonder,' said Thomas.

'That we have a new king,' said Granda quietly.

'What? How do you know?'

'We received word yesterday. Joseph sent word to Baruch from Rouen. I was about to tell you.'

'And the new king is?'

'Long live King Richard.'

Thomas crossed himself. 'Long live King Richard.'

'And may he protect his Jews as well as his father did,' Granda added wryly.

'Better!' said Thomas, and both men laughed.

As the three of them entered Coney Street, up the hill a crowd was dispersing outside Uncle Joseph's house and the synagogue. It was the end of prayers.

'I'll leave you here. I've an errand to run,' said Thomas. 'Thank you again for your help – both of you.'

'It was a pleasure,' said Granda.

Thomas waved and was gone.

The only woman Hanna could see was Aunt Comtessa. She was clad in scarlet trimmed in rabbit fur, and holding Cresselin in her arms, heavily asleep, his head lolling over her shoulder onto her back. And there, next to his young wife, was Uncle Baruch, a head taller than anyone else in the crowd, fine-featured, like Ma, but dark-bearded. He too was dressed in scarlet, and in lively conversation with the rabbi. The bulky figure of Serlo stood just behind them, Cresselin's shawl incongruously wrapped over one of his muscular arms. There was no sign of Comtessa's maid, nor Uncle Baruch's secretary, who usually made up their party.

Uncles Baruch and Joseph had always been part of Hanna's life, though Uncle Baruch, her mother's half-brother, was the only one to whom she was related by blood. The families had all moved to York at the same time. Joseph and Baruch worked together lending money to nobles and monks throughout the north of England and beyond. It was this money, Granda said, that enabled the nobles to build their castles and the monks their abbeys. And, Ma said, it was the profit that her half-brother and Uncle Joseph made on their deals that enabled them to build their grand houses, grander even than those of the local nobles.

Uncle Baruch kept hunting birds and horses, and threw fine parties, with music and storytellers. But he also began each day with prayer and showered with coins the beggars who gathered outside his gate on holy days. Together with Uncle Joseph, he helped pay for the building of the community's synagogue and miqveh. Joseph was a respected elder by virtue of his years and piety; Uncle Baruch, though much younger, was leader by force of personality.

But Baruch's life in York had not been easy. His first wife, Leah, and their three boys, Hanna and Ben's cousins and playmates, had fallen ill and died. Baruch, distraught, had taken to his bed for a full year. The house was kept in sombre darkness. Finally he had travelled to Rouen, town of his birth, where he married Comtessa, a sleek, fair-skinned seventeen year old, herself recently widowed, but childless. Baruch brought his bride home to York with all his old vigour and love of life restored – doing business, holding parties, hunting with birds and even riding to hounds – and, soon, the doting father of Cresselin.

Hanna caught Uncle Baruch's eye and waved. He grinned his boyish grin, pointed her and Granda out to Comtessa and Rabbi Yom Tov. Granda and Hanna joined them.

'We were just discussing my search for a new clerk,' said Baruch. 'Meir has gone to Rouen and it seems there's no one here in York to match his skills.' He tugged gently at the neat beard which accentuated the squareness of his chin, smiling with the confidence of one who enjoyed finding a swift solution to whatever problem he was presented with. His eyes, grey like Ma's, disappeared momentarily into the creases of his laughter lines.

'He definitely isn't coming back?' asked Granda.

'It doesn't look like it. With his older brother dying so soon after their father...   I was trying to persuade the rabbi that his nephew Simeon might like to help me out –'

'But he is too much engaged in his studies,' said Rabbi Yom Tov. The rabbi was a slight figure next to Baruch, but very upright, resolute. His black moustache and long beard curled silkily, his features were sharp and his eyes bright. In his dark tunic, Hanna thought, he resembled nothing so much as a blackbird, especially with his head cocked on one side listening to Baruch. His voice, too, was melodious, delighting his congregation when he led them in worship. But there was a sadness, too, about him.

'It's a pity that your Ben isn't here,' said Baruch to Granda. 'And that my favourite niece is not also a nephew. With you as their teacher, I am sure their skills in writing and numbers are exemplary.'

Rabbi Yom Tov frowned. He disapproved of girls studying, though the boys in his charge were fine scholars, well versed in the Torah. Cresselin was stirring in Comtessa's arms and beginning to cry.

'*Mon cheri*,' she said, 'Our son needs his tea.'

Baruch was all solicitousness. He handed his prayer book to Serlo and took Cresselin from Comtessa, prompting the child to bawl. The problem of his father's lack of a clerk would have to wait after all.

6. JERUSALEM

Hanna stepped out of the way of a woman with a live chicken firmly clamped under each arm, and turned to make her way up the street, towards Will's aunt's bakery. The town was abuzz with the fair and Hanna felt properly happy for the first time since Ben and Da had left. She'd woken early that morning, found Ma gone, and taken her 'borrowed' book out from its hiding place to fill her head with its spells, leaving no room for anxiety about Ben and Da. Then, the day's patients were few and Granda let her go early – unknown to Ma, who was therefore unable to occupy her with other tasks. Now Hanna was hoping to find Will. She knew she hadn't been very nice to him both during their fishing trip and afterwards, and wanted to say sorry – and she badly wanted to enlist his help in experimenting with one of the spells.

It was Will's ma's sister who ran the bakery, with her husband. Will often stayed with them after his lessons with Granda, Hanna and Ben, rather than go straight home to Acaster. And he was there, Hanna could tell, as she could see Beaumon waiting patiently outside the shop. The dog recognised her as she approached, standing up, ears twitching and tail wagging. Then Will himself came out of the shop, with Jack, his jackdaw, perched on his shoulder. Will caught sight of Hanna just as he took a huge bite out of a hunk of bread. She laughed as he spluttered crumbs at her in greeting.

'Hello Will, Jack,' she said. The jackdaw turned his head towards her, his eyes with their almost-white irises making him look disconcertingly human. Will had trained him to fly with messages between Acaster and the town, so the bird was well used to Ben and Hanna. He cocked his head to one side. 'Cy-aw.' This time Will laughed with Hanna.

They walked together up the street, stopping at the back of the crowd gathered round the jugglers. The same troupe came every year.

'We really should have kept practising,' said Hanna, 'it wasn't that difficult.'

She, Ben and Will had spent some time when they were younger learning to juggle, but had never quite got the hang of it. Now Hanna mimed throwing balls up in the air, hopping from one foot to the other as she did so, sending her cap wonky and allowing dark curls of hair to escape. 'See? And you, Will, could take your hood round and collect money from the punters.'

She pulled his hood off his head to demonstrate, leaving his light brown hair sticking up and out in all directions. Jack cy-awed in protest. Hanna grinned, and dimpled.

'Hey – give me that!' Will made a grab for the hood but Hanna was too quick for him as she spun round, only to bump into Muriel as she came up behind them, accompanied by Gentill, her buxom daughter-in-law, and Gentill's three children.

'What are you two up to?' Muriel asked Hanna, looking suspiciously at her and Will and then nervously at Jack. 'That bird – it gives me the shudders.'

But there was no need to answer her, all words now lost in the loud clanging of the bells of the church in the square. A group of men on horseback entered from the far side. The red-and-grey dressed crier walked up the church steps, with a priest on one side and a prosperously clothed older man on the other. Hanna, Will, Jack and Beaumon were swept up in the crowd surging forward to find out what was going on.

The fork-bearded, older man kitted out in dark blue velvet and silk Hanna recognised as Ranulf de Glanville, the sheriff. As well as Scotland, he'd fought for the king in more distant lands. The days of his friendship with Granda – when he'd pit his tales of Syracuse and Porto against Granda's of Cordova and they'd shared a vision for the city they could build in York, a centre of learning and trade – were long gone. There'd been some sort of scandal –

something to do with confiscated goods being put to his own use – and he'd been sent to Wales to drum up support for the Christian struggle to wrest control of Jerusalem from Saladin and the Muslims, Granda said – 'no longer a friend of ours'. He had a Christian cross sewn upon his back, as did each of the men newly arrived on horseback around the square.

The crowd seemed little inclined to listen at first, until the impact of the first words hit those standing closest, who then 'shushed' those behind them.

'The king is dead, long live the king. King Henry is dead, long live King Richard.'

Muriel and Gentill were trying to escape the crowd as baby Flo was crying and Gentill's two boys, Leo and Hakelin, were squabbling and about to land punches on each other.

Hanna concentrated on the crier. Henry, he said, had died in Anjou some six weeks previously and his son, Richard, would be crowned king in a couple of months' time, in London. After that, he proclaimed, King Richard would proceed to the Holy Land with his cousin, King Philip of France, to reclaim Jerusalem from 'the infidel'.

Next it was the priest's turn to speak. Any who had not yet taken up the sign of the cross, he urged to do so. And those who had not yet paid their tithe to the church to fund the expedition, were reminded that it was due. Ranulf de Glanville then stepped forward, his chest puffed up. Hanna and Will looked at each other.

'Let's go,' said Will.

They slipped out of the square and pooled their pennies to buy a white doughy bun from a street seller, which they ate as they walked. Hanna fed small pieces to Jack on Will's shoulder and Beaumon snaffled up any crumbs that dropped.

'I hope there won't be any fighting,' said Will.

'What do you mean?' said Hanna.

'Richard becoming king and all that. Don't you remember?'

Hanna shook her head.

'My ma's da used to tell us stories about the fighting before King Henry. My grandad had two brothers killed in some big battle with the Scots just north of the city, but he was too young to fight.'

'Granda's family wasn't here then,' Hanna said. 'But he was talking to me about Richard a bit – Uncle Baruch told him the news yesterday. He seemed to think it would be all right except that –'

She hesitated.

'What?'

'Oh, I dunno – I just felt there was stuff he wasn't saying.'

Will nodded. He remembered how his aunt and uncle had sniffed at talk of the infidel in foreign lands, muttering about 'dealing with those at home first' and Joseph and Baruch in their fine houses. Will's ma would have none of it. 'You just remember who saved my life and yours, Will,' she told him. Will had never talked about it with his friends. He and Hanna walked on in silence for a while.

'The Beast wants to go to Jerusalem,' said Will.

'He would,' said Hanna. 'Riding and killing – just his sort of thing.'

'He was talking about it with my da – how Da'd be running the estate while he's gone. But Da reckons he's not going to while he's rebuilding the manor at Acaster – he's not got the money to do both. Though he may not be happy about it.'

'What about you, Will?' asked Hanna. 'Would you like to go?'

'Me? No, this is my home – why would I want to go chasing off so far away? What's Jerusalem to me? And who would look after my ma and da if I went?' He paused. 'But what do you think – about Jerusalem an' that?'

'That it's a long way away,' said Hanna, laughing. 'Come with me – I've got something to show you before it's time for our lesson with Granda.'

7. MAGIC

A week later, Hanna's eyes glittered with excitement in the candle light as she peered at the book's pages. The sun had not yet set, but little of its remaining light penetrated through the dense canopy of leaves. It was the beginning of the lunar month and there'd be no moon. The air was still. Small animals rustled in the undergrowth – or at least Hanna hoped they were small animals. An owl hooted in the distance.

She'd memorised most of their chosen spell and written its incantation on a separate scrap of parchment, but she just wanted to make absolutely sure that she knew what was required. If only Ben were here – but at least Will had joined her in the trio's usual hiding place among the trees between abbey and river.

He was crouched down next to Beaumon by the ring of flickering candles Hanna had set into the ground.

'Come on then, Hanna, tell us what to do,' he said.

'Wait – just a minute.'

Will kept one hand resting on the back of the dog's head, lest the woodland scents prove too tempting for her – but she was as well trained as she was loyal. It was a ring of fire he had saved her from when she was a puppy – a burning circle of straw. Ordered by the Beast to cull the litter so they raised only those needed for the hunt, Will's da had placed the five puppies inside the circle. 'The mother will take the strongest first,' he told Will, 'then the next strongest…' The puppies whimpered at the sparks and crackling straw. Will had watched as the mother took one and then a second, but before she could return for another Will's da had plunged two of those remaining into a pail of water. Instinctively, Will seized the last puppy and ran. He took her to the river and hid in the small boat, holding her tight to his chest. When Will's da found him he gave him such a beating. But de Malbisse was already packing up to leave. Will's da relented and from that day Will and Beaumon had been inseparable.

Will focused on this ring of fire, Hanna's candles. The plan, they had agreed, was to make Will invisible. Ben had been so convinced they could do it that last time… 'It'll be no fun on my own,' Will had said this time. 'Let's just see if it works first,' said Hanna.

Something had been bothering Will since Ben's ill-fated experiment. 'If it does work, how do you stop it, return to normal, I mean, so that you can be seen again?'

'That's easy, the book tells us that. You just have to say the charm in reverse, that's all. You'll see – it's not difficult.'

'You're sounding just like Ben,' he said. 'So sure everything will work out all right in the end.'

Hanna made a face. 'Well, why shouldn't it? Come on, the candles will have burnt out. Right then, first, you need to step inside the circle of candles and kneel down so that you can focus on just one of them.'

Will gave Beaumon a last reassuring pat and did as Hanna told him. Hanna handed him the scrap of parchment.

'These are the words that we're going to chant together, when I tell you.' Will looked down at the list of words Hanna had given him.

'It's the list of the angels' names who have power over light and dark, and of names for G–d, like I showed you this morning,' she said. 'It's best if you can memorise them, so that you're not struggling to read while you should be concentrating on becoming invisible.'

The last of the daylight had gone and the glade outside the candles' circle was deep-dark. Hanna could see nothing but blackness when she glanced into the shadows between the trees, attempting to quash all thoughts of what demons and ghouls might lurk there. (There's no such thing.') The owl hooted again, nearer this time. Inside the circle Will's skin glowed yellow in the candles' light and the shadows on his face made it look more death's head than living boy. Beaumon, her eyes fixed on Will in the circle, whimpered gently. Hanna reached down to stroke the dog's ears, reassured by their animal warmth.

'How do we know that we're not summoning up demons?' asked Will and immediately wished he hadn't voiced such a thought.

'Sshh,' said Hanna fiercely, 'don't be so stupid – we're not summoning up demons because that's not the spell we're using.'

'But what if I get the words wrong?'

'You won't. And anyway, it's completely different for demons – no candles or anything. And Granda says that they don't exist. We should start,' she said impatiently.

She read from the book. '*If you wish to render yourself invisible and at one with the shadows, wait until evening on a moonless night and then make yourself a circle of candles.* All right, we've done that bit. Next, *place yourself at the centre of the circle and fix your gaze on the candle opposite you*' – Hanna paused to check that Will was doing as she said – 'And say, *Angels of the sixth firmament, I adjure you to cloak me so that I may not be seen by any human eye* – and then you need to repeat the names I've given you seven times. And I need to chant with you. All right?'

Will nodded. He stared into the inner blue light of the flame of the candle in front of him. '*Angels of the sixth firmament, I adjure you to cloak me so that I may not be seen by any human eye...*'

And then his voice rose and blended with Hanna's as they repeated the names of the angels. '*Raphael, Raziel, Adriel, Qaphsiel...*'

Once, then twice and then a third time the boy and the girl were repeating the names when suddenly Hanna shivered as she chanted, her arms all at once covered in chilly goose pimples. Next to her Beaumon was making low growling noises at the back of her throat and Hanna could sense that the dog was holding herself ready to leap or to run.

A fifth time Hanna and Will began the names and then the candles blew out and they found themselves in total darkness.

From behind them came a sudden crashing and thrashing of branches. They froze in fear. Hanna held tightly onto Beaumon's collar as the dog began to bark wildly, at the same time turning to try to see by what they were about to be attacked.

'Let Beaumon go,' Will urged Hanna but she couldn't hear him over the barking.

It came with a light, two large shapes, one of which, thought Hanna, had horns on its head... Despite themselves, Will and Hanna squealed in fright and clung on to each other.

'What in G–d's name are you doing?' The voice hissed rather than shouted. 'And get that dog under control.'

It was no demon, but Granda, and behind him a much taller figure – Uncle Baruch, who burst together into the small clearing. There were no horns, just Baruch's jauntily worn scarlet cap. He was holding a burning torch. Granda looked scared, Hanna thought, as well as very, very angry. He kept his voice low.

'Give me that!' he demanded, holding out his hand to Hanna to take the book which she was failing to conceal in the folds of her cloak. 'So, you are not just fools, but thieves as well, I see. I thought we had put an end to this nonsense when we sent Ben away.'

He kicked at the candles lying on the ground in front of them. Hanna was shocked.

Uncle Baruch made as if to speak. 'If this is what I think it is' – but Granda silenced him – 'No, please, Baruch, let me handle this. You and I will talk later, please.'

Uncle Baruch looked taken aback, but did as the older man requested.

Granda looked at Will. 'If ever I catch you involved in this sort of activity again, Will, you will be banned from my house, receive no further lessons, and never again be allowed to see Hanna – or Ben, when he returns. Do you understand?'

Will, trembling, nodded.

'Where are you staying tonight – at your aunt's?'

Will nodded again.

'Then go, boy, go – and if you know what's good for you say nothing to her of what you've been up to.'

Hanna looked at Will, but he wouldn't meet her eyes, just clicked his fingers at Beaumon and left, the dog at his side.

Granda was hiding the book in the folds of his own garments.

Hanna began, 'It was just a bit of fun, Granda, to see if it would work – a scientific experiment –'

He held up a hand to silence her and turned abruptly. 'Come, let's go home.'

Hanna followed as Granda and Uncle Baruch pushed through the trees to rejoin the path by the river, alongside the abbey walls. Hanna felt wretched for causing Granda so much distress. And, she thought, it could only make things worse that Uncle Baruch must surely now learn what both she and Ben had been up to before he had left with Da. Ma had insisted her half-brother shouldn't know that Ben was in trouble.

Granda made Hanna stand and listen as he told Ma where he had found her, who she was with and what she'd been doing. Each time Hanna tried to speak, he silenced her with a look, his dark eyes fierce under his black eyebrows.

'Fun! An experiment! Do you know what trouble you could bring upon us – not just you, not just our family, but our whole community? Do you want to undermine the work that I and your father do as doctors? Have us accused of sorcery? Take away our means of earning a living?'

Granda put his head in his hands and Hanna thought for one awful moment that he might cry. Ma, she could tell, was furious, but held her anger in check because of Granda. Hanna would rather Ma had been able to shout and storm at her as she would have done if Granda had not been there – at least then it would have been over and done with.

Granda looked up, took a deep breath. 'There are two things you should know, Hanna, which I should perhaps have told you more explicitly before.

'First — and I think I have tried to tell you this — just because something is written in a book, doesn't make it true. Fools have composed thousands of books of nothingness and emptiness — and you're wasting your time if you imagine that the follies in the book you took from my shelves are science. But that's not what makes it dangerous. Which brings me on to the second thing' — he paused, took another deep breath — 'this is something I have never told you' — he looked across at Ma — 'nor even your Ma and Da, not properly. And it's this.

'When I was much younger, not long after your Da was born, we were living in Narbonne, very happily — your grandma, Miriam, may her memory be blessed, myself and our children. Miriam had grown up there, had all her family around her, and my family had settled there, finally, after being driven from Cordova. I was working as a physician with my father, and studying and writing — life was good. Then, one day, one of my patients died — a Christian, a young man, the much-loved son of a rich and powerful merchant who, though suspicious of Jews in general — and, possibly, also jealous — had been persuaded by his friends to bring his son to me, on the strength of my growing reputation as a doctor.

'When his son died the father was, naturally, beside himself with grief — and turned on me, blamed me for his son's death, said that it was because I used magic, sorcery — and he began stirring up ill-feeling against all the Jews in the town... That was it, my life in the town was over, my father's life, too, since we worked together — and for the good of the community we had to leave. Thank G–d my sisters were already settled elsewhere with their own families. Once more we were exiled. We headed north and kept going, made another life for ourselves here. I was all right — but those I loved... My father died not long after, and Miriam never truly settled, missed her parents and her brothers and sisters — I don't think she was every properly happy again, not until she died...' Granda's voice trailed off. There was a long silence.

'Your granda is right,' said Ma, finally. 'I knew it wasn't healthy, you spending so much time with old books.

And you and Will in the woods together, at night, alone! You are no longer a child, you know. How could you do this, Hanna? First Ben, now you – and now Uncle Baruch is involved…'

'I'm, I'm sorry, Ma. Granda, I'm sorry, I never meant to cause you trouble and I'm so sorry for what happened to you and Grandma Miriam. But I really don't see that it's the same as what I was doing – I'm not a doctor, after all. But the last thing I want to do is bring harm on anyone else, I promise –'

Granda cut her off. 'It's too late for apologies, Hanna. If you can't see what is wrong with what you have done – go to bed. I need to talk with your mother, and then I am going to see Uncle Baruch, to discuss the matter with him.'

Lying on her bed, Hanna could hear Granda and Ma talking, but not what they said. Ma sounded angry, Granda's replies were brief. Hanna had never felt so alone. Ben would have understood what she had done, but she knew that Da would share Ma and Granda's anger and disappointment. And Will – what would he be thinking? She hadn't meant any harm, it was only a bit of fun. York was a world away from Narbonne. Why did everyone have to take everything so seriously?

8. BARUCH

Hanna stood with Ma and Granda at the massive gatehouse of Uncle Baruch's house. Its pale grey stone – like that of York's new church, from the quarries owned by the monks to whom Baruch lent money – gleamed white in the afternoon sun. Repeatedly rebuilt and extended, it wasn't beautiful, but exuded strength and solidity. It occupied almost all of one side of the lane in which it stood, named Spen for the aspen trees which grew in numbers nearby. The door knocker on the side gate, a recent addition, was cast in the shape of a falcon's head and it was with this that Granda announced their arrival.

The gate was opened at once, by Serlo, who greeted them with his familiar grunt and a warm smile across his broad face. The paved courtyard was full of warm afternoon quiet, the only noises those of the stables. Two horses, a mighty dark bay and a chestnut, were tethered in the yard, munching on a pile of hay. A stable hand was whistling and another horse whinnied gently from inside one of the stalls. The dark bay Hanna recognised as belonging to Prior William and she guessed that it was also his bird which sat on the block in the yard, hooded. A game bag, smeared with fresh blood, was tied to the chestnut's saddle. The door to the mews where Baruch kept his own pair of peregrine falcons was open and Hanna could dimly see the birds on their perch inside, also hooded. 'My superior birds from the north', he called them. Not content with sparrow hawks caught and trained locally, he had bought the pair six months ago, travelled specially to the port of Lynn to fetch them, after their journey across the sea from Norway. He'd had the shoemaker sew their hoods in leather dyed the bright scarlet he favoured for his own and his household's clothes. Da used to tease him – 'You'd make such a fine knight, Baruch' – and Baruch always laughed.

But now there was a commotion on the first-floor balcony as a doors was flung open. It was William, the prior of St Mary's, his blonde hair as usual all askew, and a younger monk Hanna didn't recognise, followed by Uncle Baruch and Aunt Comtessa, Cresselin clinging to her tunic and her belly round against her gold-embroidered girdle. The couple's matching silk caught the sun in a flash of kingfisher blue (no scarlet today). There was an excited shouting of greetings on seeing the new arrivals.

Prior William was the first into the courtyard. 'Samuel, Mistress Abigail – how good to see you! And Master Ben!'

He winked cheerily at Hanna who was half hidden from him by Ma and Granda – and then realised his mistake. 'Miss Hanna – I do beg your pardon. You do look so like your twin!' He was apparently not in the least embarrassed.

'I'm just off – a fine morning's hunting we've had, but now the chapel bells are calling me – Baruch will tell you all about it – and you can probably smell the rabbit stew that's cooking. I'll pass your greetings to Master Thomas, Samuel – no doubt we'll see you soon! Baruch, Mistress Comtessa – thank you once again for your hospitality – Cresselin, Hanna, goodbye.'

And, scarcely waiting for their replies, he swung his considerable weight up on to the dark bay and with a clattering of hooves he and his fellow monk, hunting bird upon his wrist, passed through the gate Serlo held open for them.

It was pleasantly cool inside; all the shutters to the windows looking out over the orchards were open. From where she sat with the adults at the large oak table Hanna could just see the tops of the fruit trees and the leaves of the aspens shimmering beyond. A blackbird was singing. Many hours Hanna and Ben had spent playing here, in games of chase among the trees and across the meadow which lay between the house and the River Fosse, or hide and seek among the beds hung with rich curtains and deep chests full of fine clothes and furs, while the adults feasted and talked.

But now, she, Ma and Granda were stiffly upright in the high-backed chairs, yet somehow Uncle Baruch contrived to loll elegantly back in his, relaxed, while still the dignified host. He smiled genially at them, as if this were simply another opportunity for him to welcome them into his home. With his richly coloured clothes and neatly trimmed beard, he looked as if he had just stepped out of the elegant gathering depicted in the finely worked tapestry which hung on the wall behind him.

Hanna could hear the sounds of children playing outside, but made herself concentrate on what Uncle Baruch, Granda and Ma were saying. Aunt Comtessa had left, taking Cresselin with her, once the initial social pleasantries of the visit were over. Hanna could sense Ma's tension. She never willingly involved her half-brother in her life.

But Hanna's mind kept drifting back to the scene in the woods, to the power she had felt as she chanted, to what might have happened if Granda and Uncle Baruch had not arrived when they did. If Will had made himself invisible, what would they be doing now? Perhaps it would have been an error for Will to be invisible on his own. Next time, whenever that night be… For now, he was away with his father to help an uncle who was sick, he'd sent word with Jack.

'It's quite obvious to me what the solution to this problem is,' Uncle Baruch was saying. His tone was bright, his eyes twinkling. 'Hanna must be married. It is not easy while Moses is away, I know, but I am happy to help you, to act on your behalf to find the right boy in the right family… '

None of them so much as glanced at Hanna. Married?! She wanted to interrupt to check that she had heard correctly. Surely Ma would say something.

But it was Granda who answered. 'That is most kind of you, Baruch – we appreciate the offer, of course. But as you know, that was one of the reasons that Moses had for travelling across the sea to visit his sisters, to find a suitable husband for Hanna.' He sounded polite, but decided. He and Uncle Joseph were the only men Hanna had never heard defer to Baruch; even Da had on occasion sounded diffident with him, for all Da's joking.

'How long is it now, since you last heard from him?' Baruch asked.

'Not yet six months,' said Granda. 'If something had happened, we would surely have received a letter from another member of the family, or from someone known to the family. It is improper for us to act in my son's absence, after so short a time. I must ask you to respect that.'

Baruch, frowning, tugged thoughtfully at his beard. 'All right, yes, I can,' he said. 'But that still leaves us with a problem to solve here and now: what are we to do with Hanna meanwhile, to ensure that she does not get herself – and all of us – into trouble? I'm sure you don't need reminding that this is a dangerous time, what with the king's death and more talk of the infidel and the so-called reconquest of Jerusalem. We all know families whose relatives were killed last time our Christian compatriots sent their soldiers to march to Palestine. And who knows what the new king has in mind for us – don't forget it's his young cousin, Philip, who's expelled all the Jews from Paris, given our houses to his friends, turned the synagogue into a church and is using our money to build the city anew… I'm summoned to London, by the way, by Joseph, for the coronation… So this is not the time to get ourselves branded magicians and sorcerers. I don't need to remind you, of all people, Samuel, where that can lead. And I know you deny the existence of demons, but I don't. As Rabbi Yom Tov says, start meddling, invoking angels' names, and who knows what might happen – with his own eyes he's seen Jews burned at the stake for less.'

Granda opened his mouth to speak but Baruch held his hand up. 'No, Samuel. I haven't finished. Forget the spiritual realm – there is also the question of Hanna's friendship with the Christian boy, the one who was with her in the woods – what was his name? Walter, Will.'

'Will. His father is Lord Malbisse's steward at Acaster,' said Granda.

'Will, that's it. I know they have been friends a long time, but it is hardly suitable, especially with Ben now gone. They are no longer children.'

'I understand your concern, Baruch, but Will is my pupil and like a brother to Ben and to Hanna. They have known each other since birth. The feeling is strong between the two families – I'm sure you remember that both the boy and his mother would have died if Moses and I had not been there at the time of his birth.'

Baruch spoke curtly. 'I ask you to put an end to it, Samuel. The relationship is improper.'

Then he took a deep breath and began again, more gently. 'The fact that you kept your problems with Ben from all of us – I am not going to talk about it as deceit – it shows that you understand how the rest of the community would view the matter. I too have no desire to involve the rabbi in this current problem – I feel I owe you and your son that. I have no wish for you and your family to be viewed as any stranger by the community than you are already.

'So let's look for a further solution… There was one other that I have been considering, that would enable Hanna to be safely away from York, like her brother and, like him, under close, family supervision.

'I am, as you know, looking for a new clerk and Hanna, you've often told me, is just as adept at writing and numbers as Ben – reading and writing in Latin, French and Hebrew. While I have often doubted your wisdom in investing so much time and effort in her education, it does make her extremely well suited to act as my clerk – and then, of course, she can come safely away with me to London, away from both the boy and the spells. What do you think?'

He smiled, triumphantly. Hanna wasn't sure she had heard him right.

'But as a girl,' Granda began. 'I know she comes with me when I visit patients and that some look askance even at that, but for her to travel with you to London, without a female companion… Perhaps Abigail could accompany you?'

They all looked at Ma, whose face was red and her knuckles white where she gripped each side of the seat of her chair.

'I must be here when Moshe returns. I cannot leave my home, my business. My daughter's place is here in York, with me. I can keep her safe and out of trouble. '

Baruch ignored her.

'What I was thinking was this,' he said, 'though this is the bit you may have more difficulty with. We can disguise Hanna, dress her up, change her identity – don't you see – she *becomes* Ben! And comes with me as my nephew and clerk. She'll have plenty of work to do, I can assure you.'

Ma and Granda looked at Baruch as if he'd taken leave of his senses. Hanna could not believe what she was hearing.

'But everyone knows that Ben has gone with his father, that we haven't heard from him,' said Granda.

'But one of my nephews is due to arrive any day now from France – we had word. If not today, then tomorrow. Ben could have returned with them – sent back by Moses, – because he was ill, or had become an encumbrance, or had urgent family news for your ears alone that could not be entrusted to anyone else – and Moses has continued on his journey alone. And then we dress Hanna as Ben – and she *is* Ben! They are so very much alike, in figure as well as in face. Why, didn't you hear Prior William mistake her for Ben just now?'

Granda stayed silent, thinking. It was Ma that expostulated.

'And then what do we say has happened to Hanna? How do we account for her sudden disappearance? How do you think this improves her marriage prospects?'

'You say she is ill…'

'But for how long? How long will you be gone in London? And then what, when you return, does she remain Ben then?'

'No, better still – we've already said that Joseph's son is returning tomorrow to Rouen with his wife. We could say that Hanna has gone with them, to stay with her aunt.'

'Baruch, please, you cannot take my daughter away from me,' said Ma. 'I already have no idea where my son and husband are, you cannot take my daughter from me as well. Let Hanna stay with me, Baruch, and I will keep her out of trouble, and teach her to look after herself and her family. And what of those travelling with you, who already know Ben – how do you think Hanna is going to pretend to be her twin with them? And what will Joseph say?'

Baruch thought for a moment, again pulling his beard, before answering more slowly. 'We will meet with Joseph in London. I am sure he will respect my decision. As for those travelling with us, I trust implicitly all those in my household who will need to know.'

Hanna felt hot tears of outrage prickling at her eyes and wiped them angrily away. She did not know what to say, beyond, 'How can you do this to me?' and that if she did speak she would cry, which would do nothing to persuade her uncle to change his mind.

They were all silent for a few moments, then Granda spoke. He sounded thoughtful. 'It could be made to work,' he said, 'and it is a great opportunity for her to learn about the world beyond York – but I still don't see how I can manage without Hanna in the long term.'

'Perhaps you should be looking beyond the family to recruit an apprentice, Samuel,' said Baruch, standing up from the table. 'I think your interest in medicine is clouding your judgement as to the best course of action for your granddaughter.'

Ma was also on her feet – 'I cannot let you take my daughter away from me like this' – half-crying, half-shouting. 'Samuel, you can't allow this! I can keep her safe, but you can't, Baruch. You've always delighted in making my life difficult. Men like you, Baruch, even good men, they are murdered with impunity by their lawless Christian debtors. Our father's cousin in Norwich—'

Uncle Baruch cut across her, unsmiling, his tone even and cold. 'Hanna is a child, my niece, who has behaved badly, and, with respect, I don't think the decision is any longer yours to make, Abigail, when your daughter's behaviour and attitude put all of us at risk and when Moses is not here. I'm making your life easier – and my business dealings are none of your concern. Hanna comes with me, as Ben, as my clerk, and you will leave her here with me now. I will send Serlo with you to collect Ben's clothes from your house – I will furnish her, or rather him, with others as necessary. If he is to be my clerk, then he must look the part.'

And with that he left the room.

9. THE BEAST

'Our Lord Malbisse is in trouble, you see' Baruch was saying. He sounded amused. It was through the knight's forest that they rode – or rather the king's forest, at whose behest Malebisse protected the trees and maintained a stable population of deer and boar. Deep leaf mould muffled the sound of their horses' hooves and Hanna was listening intently to her uncle. This time, she was actually interested in hearing his explanation to his new clerk.

She knew of the Beast's cruelty and capricious temper, caught sight of him during his occasional visits to Acaster and even, with Ben and Will, formed part of his hunting party, on foot with Beaumon and the other dogs – but, when the knight was away, had regarded his estate as belonging to her and Ben and Will, climbing its trees, messing about on the river, riding the horses bareback and caring for the dogs.

'What kind of trouble?'

'He borrowed substantial funds from Aaron, of Lincoln – are you old enough to remember him? He came to York most years. When Aaron died, some four years ago now, the king – King Henry – took control of all Aaron's assets – which meant that Malbisse now owed money to him. To pay it off, Malbisse borrowed from me – and now he's behind on those payments. We just need to give him a *gentle* reminder.'

He smiled, his eyes crinkling up with their laughter lines – he appeared to find it all genuinely entertaining. 'He has lands to the north and south which are security for his loan – and he's not going to want to lose those, they yield him a good income. He can afford to pay – there's many that pay rent to him and he doesn't let them fall behind. And he's greedy, with a chip on his shoulder, a dangerous combination – he knows he'd be richer if only his grandmother had been wife, not mistress, to his grandfather. He hates not being as rich as his Percy cousins, and is a reluctant host today.' He half-turned in his saddle to look at the two riders behind. 'So carefully does it, eh, boys?'

Serlo smiled in response and his fellow, Elias Quatrebouches, raised his hand to acknowledge Baruch's words. Elias was taller than Serlo, but similarly square-shouldered and powerfully built. Serlo, as a Christian, had a sword in the scabbard at his side; Elias, as a Jew, was forbidden to carry a weapon. But everyone knew that Elias had been fined for striking a knight while on business in London for his brother, the sharp-tongued, talkative Ursell Quatrebouches. As for Serlo, he'd been found in the street as a young boy, bleeding copiously from his mouth, his tongue stuffed into his jacket pocket. What or whom he'd seen for his silence to be guaranteed in this way he never revealed, even when he resumed a slurred speech – though it was said that for some years after he broke into a fit of trembling at the name of Richard de Malbisse. Da had staunched the boy's bleeding and made him well and Baruch had taken him into his household. There he had remained, devoted both to Da and his patron, growing up into a young man nearly as wide as he was tall and famed throughout York and beyond for head-butting a horse whose rider was late in paying his debts, sending both horse and rider sprawling; Baruch got his money.

The four rode on without talking, their scarlet tunics alternately bright and dark as they passed between sunlight and shadow among the trees. Their horses, too – a neat black and white gelding, Lief, for Hanna; a matching pair of bays for Serlo and Elias; a lightly dappled, pale grey stallion, Turstin, for Baruch – were all done out in their best, their coats and tack polished to a shine by Baruch's stable boys that morning. Serlo (not trembling) carried a smoked pike that Baruch was to present to their host.

'Impressions matter,' Baruch had told Hanna, 'especially when dealing with a man like Malbisse.'

It was odd how being disguised as Ben made her feel – as if none of it was actually happening to her; which, in a way, it wasn't. She found herself pleased with how easily she became Ben – and with the finer material things in life that had come her way since becoming a member of Baruch's household. Lief, she loved already. She kept her notes of the spells in the pocket of her leather breeches and relished the freedom of movement that her new, boys' clothes gave her and the feeling of the wind in her hair. Aunt Comtessa had cut it short, like Ben's. Ma had wept when she saw it.

Suddenly, 'Stop!' Baruch ordered. There was the sound of men's voices and the thwack of axe striking wood.

'What the –'

There was a tearing and groaning some way ahead of them as they saw the crown of an oak falter and then begin to fall, but not cleanly, its descent impeded by the branches of its neighbours, which cracked as they too broke and fell under the impact.

Baruch glanced briefly at Hanna, and Serlo and Elias behind, before urging his horse on.

A short distance ahead they entered a large clearing, recently made, and the work of men, not nature.

On the far side lay the tree they had just seen fall, the branches and leaves of its crown still twitching and quivering, like a sheep whose throat is just cut. A team of men was already hacking off its branches, stripping off the leaves and dragging the wood to join the existing pile.

Baruch greeted the men, who of necessity had to look up at him to reply, as he remained mounted on his fine stallion, which danced and chafed at its bit as Baruch spoke. His English had an accent different from the men's – it wasn't often that Hanna heard him speak it. They exchanged pleasantries about the weather and then Baruch asked about the trees. The men were nervous.

''Tis Lord Malbisse that's ordered the trees down,' one was telling Baruch. 'He's for rebuilding his manor at Acaster – you'll see when you pass.'

'He's enough here to build his own palace,' said Baruch. 'They're all for his own use, then – he's not selling any?'

'Are you interested in buying, sir?'

'Not me, no.'

Baruch sounded affronted at the suggestion that he might be interested in a good deal in raw oak.

'Well, well,' Baruch said to Hanna once they had left the clearing. 'So Lord de Malbisse is taking trees from the king's forest for his own use – I wonder what our new King Richard would make of that, eh, Hanna? And what it's worth to de Malbisse for us to keep quiet about it…'

Baruch grinned at her, for all the world like Ben when he'd thought of a joke to play.

The sun was still high when they emerged from the forest and the manor of Acaster came into view, surrounded by ramshackle outbuildings, among them Will's family home – though Will was still away at his uncle's, Hanna knew from his aunt at the bakery (how would she ever have pretended to Will to be Ben?) The manor itself was well proportioned, but plain. Smoke rose from its central chimneys and as they drew nearer Hanna could see scaffolding had been erected at one side, where there lay more piles of recently hewn oak.

But they weren't the only ones approaching. For coming down the hill behind the house was a hunting party, some ten strong, men and women on horseback, at least two with birds on their arms, Hanna thought. More of the party followed on foot accompanied by the dogs. Two men carried a pole between them on their shoulders, on which were strung the bodies of a dozen or so small birds and a couple of ducks.

As they came closer Hanna could see one of the party was a young girl, swathed in folds of soft green fabric and sat side-saddle on a dainty chestnut pony. Her light brown hair had come loose from its covering and her cheeks were flushed pink: Emma – though she was scarcely recognisable as the girl who'd dismissed Will and his companions as 'too rough' when invited to join their games.

Lord Malbisse led the way, astride a huge white horse, accompanied by two other riders. His hair was blonde, almost white in contrast with the rich blue of his tunic. His smile, as he rode to greet them, was crooked, as was his nose. A scar rose jaggedly from the corner of his mouth towards his right ear. His eyes were pale blue and the smile did not reach them. He pulled harshly on the horse's reins to bring him to a halt.

'Baruch, my friend, welcome.' His greeting was loud, hearty. 'As you see, we are just returning from the hunt. I think you are already familiar with my hunting companions?'

He turned in his saddle to gesture to the two men just behind him, who brought their horses forward as de Malbisse spoke.

'Marmaduke Darrell and John Marshall.'

Hanna recognised the second man, quite the smallest she'd seen, but not the first. The only other business meeting that she had accompanied Baruch to so far was in York with Marshall, who had sought to renegotiate the terms of his debt in order to meet the new king's demands for money to fund his trip to the Holy Land. Marshall had a house in the city, though nowhere near as fine as Baruch's. As Baruch was under pressure to pay the king an even more substantial tithe than Marshall for the royal campaign to restore Christian rule in Jerusalem, the meeting had not been easy.

It seemed Baruch was already acquainted with Darrell, too. He was younger and, from his red hair and accent, Hanna judged he was Scottish. For now, the two men greeted her uncle warmly enough and Hanna did her best to smile confidently as Baruch introduced her to Malbisse and his friends as, 'my nephew and clerk.' Elias and Serlo remained a solid presence in the background.

'And this,' said Malbisse, holding out his arm towards the young girl on her pony and waving her forward, 'is my daughter, Emma.'

She inclined her head and smiled as Baruch and Hanna both said how honoured they were to meet her. Her face was pretty, but her smile was cold. She gave no sign of recognising 'Ben'.

'Those are fine sparrow hawks you have there, my friend, and quite a haul that you've brought back with you' said Baruch. 'Are they locally raised and trained?'

'They are indeed – in part by my own daughter here. She has quite a skill for it.'

Baruch nodded his head and smiled at Emma. Hanna didn't.

'And how are your two foreign birds?' asked de Malbisse.

'They are hunting very well, thank you. I was out with them just the other morning.'

'And that's a beautiful beast you're riding,' Malbisse jerked his head admiringly towards Baruch's stallion.

'As is yours, my lord.'

'He'd make a fine hunter – you should come with us again this year, Baruch. You're an excellent horseman, I remember – if not so enthusiastic about the feast afterwards.' That crooked smile again. 'Next week, we're riding to hounds – in pursuit of the stag, not the boar. Join us.'

It was a challenge as much as an invitation.

'It would be my pleasure.'

'And your nephew, of course. We should blood him.'

'Thank you, my lord.'

Hanna looked at Baruch in disbelief. Ma and Granda would never agree. But maybe it wasn't a decision that Uncle Baruch was going to allow them to take.

Boys came from the stables to help the riders dismount. Hanna avoided meeting anyone's gaze. Baruch was busy presenting the pike 'king of fish' to their host so that it could be taken with the freshly killed birds to the kitchen. Emma had already disappeared inside the house.

De Malbisse put an arm around Baruch's shoulder.

'Come, Baruch, let me show you round the place – we've been busy since you were last here, made some improvements.' He turned to the others. 'Marmaduke, John – you go on ahead. We'll join you in a short while.

'You will take food with us, Baruch, won't you?' Again, it sounded as much a challenge as an invitation.

'Thank you, my lord, we will.'

Hanna walked just behind the two men as Malbisse led Baruch around the outside of the manor house, explaining his plans to dig fishponds, to build on a chapel to one side and extend the main hall, as well as renovate the stables, mews and kennels. Hanna was hungry.

'I'm glad you're doing well at the moment then, my lord,' Baruch said. 'It's always good to be able to accept repayments on a loan knowing that it's not causing any difficulty to the debtor.'

Malbisse said nothing and met Baruch's gaze with the cold stare of his pale blue eyes, though Hanna noticed a reddening in his face, against which his scar showed shiny white. Baruch continued in the same conversational tone:

'But if it's not a convenient time, then I can wait. I don't want to put pressure on you – and I'm sure you'll get a good price for the oak you are felling in the forest. Our new king is already most generous.'

'I will give you the money, Baruch, please be assured' – Malbisse paused – 'when I am ready.'

'I am sure you will meet all the terms of our agreement, even if a little late – and incurring more interest,' said Baruch, 'Though of course, if you prefer, the monks of Fountains Abbey would be happy to purchase your land at Wheldrake, and pay me the balance – they're looking for more land for their sheep.'

Hanna thought Malbisse would now surely lose his temper, but instead he turned to Baruch and said coolly, 'I'm sure they are, my friend. Come – and you, Ben – let's eat.'

There was just one more exchange between the two men that Hanna wished she could tell her twin about.

De Malbisse and the others took large quantities of wine with the meal, though Uncle Baruch did not. De Malbisse's daughter and her attendant sat slightly apart from the men, though Hanna was aware that several times as they ate Emma was looking at her curiously.

De Malbisse became even more expansive after he had drunk, and even fuller of bonhomie. He drew close to Baruch and gestured to Emma and then Hanna – or, as he thought, Ben – sat next to him.

'Now that would solve both our problems,' he said, 'for these two to marry. Then I could have your money and you, my dear Baruch, could belong.'

De Malbisse laughed heartily, apparently oblivious to the shadow that darkened Baruch's face and the whites of his knuckles as he clenched and unclenched his fists.

10. THE HUNT

The second-relay hounds, all quivering noses and taut sinew, tails held aloft, straining at their leashes, were leaving to take up their position in the forest. On previous occasions, Hanna had been one of their handlers, together with Ben and Will. She could see their two pairs – Brifault, who was Beaumon's brother, and Richer, and their offspring, Blonde and Belle. Ben, Hanna and Will had known them all since they were tiny puppies. They took great pride in the dogs' hunting skills: their role was to join the chase once the first running dogs began to tire. The end of the hunt was always horribly anxious, when they surrounded the stag at bay, and one well-aimed kick of the hoof or a jab of the antlers could kill.

Hanna felt sick and gripped Lief tightly with her knees. She wasn't sure that either she or Lief were up to the rigours of the hunt; Baruch had allowed Serlo and Elias to excuse themselves. When she'd taken part on foot, Hanna had longed to be one of the riders, but now she wasn't sure which she feared most – her real identity being discovered, or falling off and making a fool of herself.

The discussion with Uncle Baruch about whether she should take part or not had been brief.

'Haven't you always wanted to take part? Properly, I mean, on horseback, not with the servants on foot?' he asked.

'Well, yes, but Ma and Granda –'

'Ma and Granda nothing. It's business. If Malbisse has invited us, we must go. Next to no one there knows either you or Ben and you'll simply have to keep your head down and stay out of their way.'

Later, he'd added: 'You're a good horsewoman, Hanna – I know the hours you've spent with Will and Ben at Acaster when my sister thought you were at your studies. This is your chance – enjoy it.'

Now, as they waited for the call of the huntsman's horn, Baruch was chatting with Prior William, who she hoped would not want to have a conversation with Ben.

'I just love the irony of it, Baruch,' Prior William was saying, 'you enjoying our Lord de Malbisse's hospitality – at your own expense.' The prior roared with laughter. Baruch smiled wryly.

Most of the party were mounted by now. The horse and cart, in which the results of their hunt would be carried back to the manor house, stood ready, as did the litters which were to transport the spectators. Lady Emma, riding the same pretty pony and wearing the soft green riding clothes that had so flattered her the last time Hanna had seen her, laughed ostentatiously as she talked to the young man the Beast had introduced as his squire, de Cuckney, and Marmaduke Darrell, the red-headed young Scot Hanna had met on her previous visit. Emma, de Cuckney and Darrell each carried a bow and a quiver of arrows. The squire's face was smooth and girlish, his hair dark blond and curling. Emma appeared equally bored by him and Darrell. She looked over in Hanna's direction every time she laughed – could it be that she was trying to flirt with Ben? Hanna had caught her eyes once by mistake and was now making a conscious effort not to look at her.

Malbisse, again riding his huge white stallion, which snorted and stamped his impatience, beckoned de Cuckney and Darrell over to him. The three talked for a few minutes, the young men glancing briefly at Baruch, before shaking Malbisse's hand just as the chief huntsman approached to talk to him. They turned their horses and trotted back to join the Lady Emma.

Finally, the chief huntsman blew three notes on his horn, and the hounds at once began to bay. It was time!

The hunting party cantered in the full heat of the sun up the hill behind the manor house to the woods, the hounds and the other hunters streaming ahead, the hounds still leashed in their couples. The archers, including Emma, de Cuckney and Marmaduke Darrell, then turned east –

'Watch out for my arrows, father,' Emma called behind her as she went. They were heading towards the river, as were the litters and the cart. There, arrows notched and bows half-tightened, the archers would await the arrival of the quarry which de Malbisse's hounds and hunters – Baruch, the Prior and Hanna among them – would drive towards them.

Entering the green cool of the woods with the rest of the hunters, Hanna shivered, as much with nervous excitement as with the change in temperature. There was sweat on Lief's neck as Hanna patted it. 'Good boy,' she said, 'good boy.' She could feel the horse's heart pounding as well as her own, but she was the one out of breath. Baruch and Prior William and the monks were just ahead of her, together with de Malbisse and Marshall, as well as others whom Hanna didn't know. Hanna hoped that Baruch would find a way of separating from the Prior, who was the only one there who could recognise her.

Lief trotted on through the trees. The ancient oaks and birches stood further apart here; the undergrowth had been cut back by those harvesting wood for cooking and fencing. They reached the clearing where the huntsmen were waiting with the running dogs, whining and straining to be set free. Malbisse raised his hand in the air to indicate that his party should halt. Lief cocked his ears forward and listened. Hanna waved away the flies buzzing around his head and tail. Her heart was thumping hard. The air was peppery with the scent of wild garlic crushed under the horses' hooves.

All was quiet, except for the occasional whining of one of the dogs, soothed by its keeper, the soft snorting of the horses and teeth champing on metal bits, the gentle call of the wood pigeons. Baruch, who had manoeuvred his stallion round so that he stood next to Hanna, turned to her and grinned.

'Are you ready, boy?' he asked, but gently. Hanna nodded, feeling anything but.

The bugles sounded again, in a different sequence, immediately answered by the baying of the hounds. Unleashed by the huntsmen, they pelted off through the trees, followed at once by the horses and their riders. Hanna lurched forward in her saddle as Lief and everyone around her set off at a gallop. Lief took control and Hanna was swept along with them. She had no time to feel fear.

A doe and two fawns ran out in front of them, the youngsters still delicately spotted. The hunters ignored them, drawn on by the cry of the hounds in pursuit of the stags. The woods resounded with the voices of dogs and huntsmen and the pounding of the horses' hooves. Hanna found that she too was shouting with the others, 'halloa, halloa, halloa'.

Immediately in front of them the forest became denser, the way obscured by a mess of fallen branches and brambles. By now the hounds were out of sight of the riders, outrunning the horses over the uneven ground and under low-hanging branches. Malbisse, Marshall and the rest rode to the left, while just Baruch and William rode to the right, closely followed by Hanna.

Ahead of them, the antlered head of a stag burst out of the bushes. All three horses pulled up short and Hanna almost fell out of her saddle. Breathless, she clung on, Baruch holding Lief steady for her until she had regained her seat.

The stag paused for a moment, looking at them, his antlers soft with velvet, then broke cover and stretched away from them between the trees, his bounding trot easing swiftly into a long, steady gallop. Hanna, Baruch and William gave chase. The crying of the hounds ahead told them that at least some had the scent. Hanna concentrated on keeping up with Baruch and William.

And then, suddenly, they were out of the woods, and a bend of the river was in sight. The stag was running towards it, drawing further away from the dogs with every second – they were tired. Hanna found herself willing the stag to escape – though the river was wide and deep here and it would be a long swim. Now out of the trees, Lief was able to draw level with Baruch and William's horses.

'Which way are our archers?' William asked, 'upstream or downstream?' Hanna and Baruch were unsure. At once they were overtaken by four dogs in full cry – it was Brifault, Richer, Blonde and Belle, their handler hallooing behind. The dogs blurred into a grey streak across the bright green of the meadow, overtaking their fellow hounds, and gaining on the stag with every bound. Hanna's sympathy switched back from pursued to pursuer and she spurred Lief on. The ground was soft here and it was easier for Lief and Hanna to go fast than Baruch and the Prior, though she could feel every muscle in her body stiff with the effort of staying with the black and white gelding.

Now she could see the archers – away up to the left, closer to the woods and further away from the river than she had imagined they would be. Momentarily she thought she could see Emma among them and alongside her Cuckney and Darrell, their bows taut and ready to shoot. Had they and their fellows even noticed the stag that Hanna, Baruch and the Prior were pursuing? It was just within range of a skilled archer, but there were several other deer being driven at the same time towards the archers from the opposite side of the wood to that from which Baruch, the Prior and Hanna had emerged.

Hanna was desperate to reach the river before Blonde and Belle and their parents – she knew from the hours she'd spent messing about in boats there with Will and Ben how treacherous the currents could be. The boys who had been looking after the dogs, following on foot, were still some way behind. Hanna tried to whistle as she'd heard Will do, but it was impossible while galloping into the wind. Arrows flickered through the air ahead of her but all fell short of their target and, thankfully, the hounds.

'Blonde, Belle,' Hanna yelled, but her voice didn't carry. The stag was splashing out into the water, surrounded by a halo of droplets glittering in the afternoon sun. Blonde and Belle, shortly followed by Richer and Brifault, leapt in after him. At least the river was too deep for the deer to stand, so he had no chance of kicking any of the dogs with a sharp hoof, or piercing them with the prongs of his antlers.

'Richer, Brifault,' she shouted again, in despair and frustration.

Then, behind her, Hanna heard another cry. Turning, she saw that both Baruch and Prior William had stopped. Baruch was slumped in his saddle and the Prior was dismounting. Hanna looked back towards the river. She could still see the antlers of the stag above the water, just over half way across. She could make out three bobbing heads swimming behind, but couldn't see a fourth.

'Ben, come here!' Prior William was shouting at her. Hanna turned Lief back the way they had come, sliding inelegantly off the horse's back in her hurry to help the Prior lower Baruch from his horse on to the ground.

'I – will – not – die!' Baruch spat the words out in fury. An arrow protruded from just below his right collar bone, its feathers quivering with each of Baruch's stuttering breaths.

'You're not going to die, my friend,' said William.

Blood was seeping through Baruch's tunic, darkening its fine red wool. Hanna was cold with fear. Surely none among Malbisse's party was a bad enough shot to have hit Baruch while aiming for the stag running some 50 feet in front of him? And if none was...

'Water, we need the boiled water, Hanna,' said Granda.

He turned impatiently to Hanna just as Serlo, his broad face pale with worry, came into the room, carrying two steaming jugs of water, followed by Ma, who held a tray on which were balanced bottles, small pots, another, smaller jug, a bowl, a pair of pliers, wool and scraps of fabric; lengths of linen were draped over her arm. She put that and the tray down and turned to Granda.

'Don't say I didn't warn you both.' She almost spat the words. 'And there'll be none punished for this, you'll see.'

Before the door closed, Hanna could hear the sound of Comtessa sobbing. Granda had banished her and the child from the room as soon as he'd arrived. 'I need quiet to work,' he'd said, 'He will be yours to look after as soon as I'm done.' He spoke sharply and Hanna had flinched from the hurt and fear in Comtessa's face as Baruch too had feebly waved his wife and son away.

Now he lay in a poppy-induced sleep on the table around which only a week or so previously he had met with Ma, Granda and Hanna to discuss her future. The blackbird was singing in the garden again, but an arrow was sticking out of the folds of tunic on Baruch's chest. The bleeding seemed to have stopped; the dark halo of blood around the arrow was no bigger now than when Prior William had helped Serlo place Baruch's body onto the table, before hurrying to services at the abbey at which he had to officiate.

Granda leaned over his patient's sleeping body, poised to cut the fabric away from the wound, the knife in his elderly, elegant hand – shaking. Light flashed in Hanna's eyes as the quivering blade caught a ray of sun and sprayed it around the room. Granda tutted and stood up straight.

'If only Thomas were not busy saying his prayers… I'm as likely to wound our patient again as I am to safely cut away his tunic. Hanna, here, you take over.'

'Me? But I – couldn't Ma?'

'No, Hanna. It must be you. You've seen it done. Ma hasn't.'

Hanna took the knife and looked at the body on the table. She focused all her being on the knife, as she had the other night on Will's candle flame in the woods. Would it be so different from removing the intestines from a fish?

She deftly held up the fabric of the patient's tunic with one hand and cut it away with the other, the knife once more a familiar extension of her hand. The fabric had been pinioned in several folds by the arrow. She pulled the cloth away from the arrow, to reveal a linen undershirt. This, too, she pulled away from Baruch's chest to be able to insert the knife and cut first around the arrow and wound, and across to the arms and neck.

Then she pulled the shirt away from the body, taking care not to tug where the blood had congealed and stuck the linen to the hairs of the chest. She felt skilful, powerful. She saw in her mind's eye not herself, but her Da, leaning over a body to be treated, made better.

'Now, we need to remove the arrow,' said Granda. 'Galen may have left arrow heads in his gladiators' bodies but it's my experience that the object is better removed, and the wound cleaned – the trick is to do it without tearing more of the flesh with the arrow's barbs on the way out.'

Baruch stirred and Granda once more held the poppy-juice soaked sponge under his nose.

Granda turned and took from his box of implements the pair of pliers which Hanna had seen him use several times before. He and Da had had them specially made by the silversmith – a copy of an older pair which Granda's father had originally brought with him from Cordova. The pliers' gripping parts at the base were rounded like spoons, snapping tight shut at the end, so that they would curve around whatever it was that they were removing, shielding the body from the object as it came out.

'First, though, we need to clean around the wound so that we can see what we are doing,' Granda was saying. He poured water from the jug into the bowl, dunked some of the sheep's wool into it, squeezed out the excess moisture then handed it to Hanna. She cleaned around the arrow, rinsing the blood from the wool at regular intervals in the water in the bowl.

Next, she took the pliers. She positioned the spoon heads on either side of the arrow shaft and and pushed them down, all the time feeling for the head of the arrow. It hadn't penetrated far into the chest, its impact lessened by the tunic's woollen folds.

'Got it,' she said. She squeezed the two sides of the pliers together, gripped and gently pulled. Fresh blood overflowed the edges of the wound and onto the chest and shoulder. It felt too much like pulling the hook from a fish's mouth, when it had swallowed the line. She twisted the pliers slightly, pulled and then the head was out, still attached to the shaft with its feathers.

'Well done, my child,' said Granda, taking the arrow and pliers from her. He emptied the bowl of bloody water out of the window, refilled the bowl from the jug and gave it to her with more wool. The wound was bleeding again, and fast. Hanna looked up anxiously.

'It will stop once you've dressed it. Here,' Granda said, handing her a pot of ointment. 'Rosemary and beeswax – they will aid healing.'

Hanna dabbed the ointment onto a clean wad of wool and pressed it down into the wound. After that, she took the first of the long strips of linen (old undershirts, washed and stored by Ma) with which to secure the dressing tightly enough to stop the bleeding. Granda raised Baruch's upper body from the table sufficiently to enable Hanna to pass the bandage round. Baruch was wan, his eyes closed. She wiped away the silver string of saliva drooling into his beard. It was the first time that she had looked at his face since she had begun to treat him, and was suddenly aware of him again as her uncle.

'Shall I fetch Comtessa and Cresselin?' asked Hanna.

Granda nodded.

'Wait – Hanna?'

'Yes, Granda?'

'You have a gift for this, my child.'

11. JOURNEY

Six days later, Hanna left York for London with Baruch. Granda protested, but Baruch insisted that his wound was well enough healed for him to travel. Hanna was excited – they would meet other travellers who might have news of Da and Ben; she was to be in London for the coronation of the new king; and she was taking with her the notes of her magic spells.

She continued with her clerical duties while they were getting ready to leave. Baruch met with three monks from the Cistercian abbey of Fountains in the abbey's York residence, just down the lane from her own home – and Hanna nervously clerked the content of their meeting.

She instinctively distrusted the monk who did most of the talking – tall and broad, imposing in his light grey habit, obviously very clever, but slightly snooty in the way in which he addressed them. Hanna carefully wrote down the grades and quantities of wool and wheat and prices paid, in business dealings which she did not fully understand and her uncle did not explain. The wool Baruch intended to sell for export at Lincoln – a collection of bales that had been overlooked in the monks' dealings with their usual middleman.

Baruch praised his niece for the speed and accuracy of her note-taking and the neatness of her handwriting.

'It seems I've acquired a very fine clerk,' he said.

Ma was still raging, Hanna knew. She had said nothing to Baruch and Granda when they announced that Hanna was to leave, but was short with everyone, even Jessie.

'Ma, it's not my fault that I'm going,' Hanna said. 'Uncle Baruch has taken charge of everything.'

Hanna pressed her to talk about the uncle with whose family they would be staying in Lincoln – Sampson,

Baruch's youngest brother, Ma's second half-brother; and the third brother, Jacob, the middle one, from Northampton, whom Uncle Baruch hoped they would meet with in London – but Ma remained tight-lipped. She also refused to say more about the cousin in Norwich whose murder at the hands of his Christian debtor had gone unpunished.

Hanna shut her mind to the question of how she would maintain the pretence she was Ben. Deulesault, Sampson's son, Baruch's nephew and Hanna's half-cousin – one of Muriel's suggestions as a suitable husband for Hanna, in fact – was only a couple of years older than Hanna and Ben. They'd played together at Uncle Baruch and Aunt Comtessa's wedding, but she and Ben hadn't taken to him. Too thin, too pale, they both thought. He couldn't keep up with outdoor games, but whined when he wasn't included. They suspected that he was insulting them when he spoke to them in Flemish, which he'd learned from the merchants with whom his father traded in wool. They'd mocked him – sometimes even to his face, for which they had been roundly rebuked by Granda. Was Deulesault really not going to realise that Baruch's clerk and nephew, Ben, was in fact his niece, Hanna? And then what about Uncle Joseph, when they reached London? There was nothing for it: she was simply going to have to brazen it out, and trust Uncle Baruch to do any explaining that was needed.

For the first part of their journey, they were travelling with Master Thomas, who had a longstanding invitation to share his medical knowledge with the monks of Lincoln's Benedictine monastery, and two Scottish monks, also Benedictines – Roger, the aging Abbot of Dunfermline, and his young chaplain, Lambinus. They had arrived in York after everyone else bound for the coronation had already left, so were seeking security in numbers for their trip; though Baruch was initially uneasy about travelling with them, he was reassured by Master Thomas. Like him, they both wore their order's black cowls, Abbot Roger stooped and thin, with a flowing grey moustache and beard, and Lambinus, short and stocky, his red-brown hair precisely tonsured. After the coronation, they were intending to make pilgrimage to Canterbury: having opposed an English king and been murdered by his men, Saint Thomas à Becket was beloved by many Scots.

Granda had told Master Thomas what had happened with Hanna, or an approximation of the story, so he knew that it was her, not Ben, who was acting as Baruch's clerk. The two Scots, however, knew nothing – knowing neither Ben nor Hanna, it was assumed they would accept her as Ben without question.

The rest of their party was made up of Serlo and Elias and four guards from the castle garrison – a useful extension of the king's protection, given that Baruch and Elias were prevented by the same king's law from bearing arms.

They took with them a cart, whose main cargo was the bales of wool Baruch had bought from the Cistercians, as well as food and drink for their journey and a couple of large chests containing their clothes. Concealed within, however, was the contribution of York's Jewish families to the treasures it was intended to present to their new king on behalf of all 'his' Jews of the Isles of the Sea and Normandy – a token of their continuing loyalty to the Anglo-Norman crown, given in hope of the new king maintaining his predecessor's promise to protect them. Precious stones were sewn into the seams of clothes packed into the chests. Baruch had also shown Hanna a hidden compartment in which lay three small bags stuffed full with gold and silver coins.

'You need to know where they are, in case anything happens to me.'

'What do you mean?' she asked. 'Do you mean that the Beast will try to kill you again?'

'What do you mean, 'again'?' Uncle Baruch laughed. 'He wouldn't dare – and didn't dare, my nephew and clerk' (this was what her uncle had taken to calling her – the roundabout formulation seemed to come more easily than the straightforward lie of 'Ben'). 'We have no proof that I was not wounded by poor marksmanship – an arrow shot inaccurately at a deer by one of the squires, distracted by the presence of the Lady Emma, perhaps.'

The cart also contained a chess set, lute and wooden bathtub. 'Who does he think he is? Royalty?' sniffed Ma when Hanna told her, but Hanna saw no reason to complain about travelling with someone who insisted on pleasure and comfort.

And she carried her own hidden treasure: a full set of notes that she'd made from Granda's book. She'd spent several nights at home before she left, while Baruch was recovering from his injury. So, on each of the nights that she was there, Hanna had crept into Granda's study while he and Ma were sleeping, removed the book of magic once more from its shelf, and copied out more spells onto scraps of vellum. She'd made a leather pouch to hold them and a girdle with which to secure it against her waist under her tunic – Ben's tunic, that is, for she was, of course, to remain Ben for the duration of the trip.

She'd even had time to try one of the spells concerning travelling – to find out if the journey to Lincoln and London would be lucky or not. As instructed, she'd taken a field lettuce with open leaves and, standing before the sun, had recited a long list of angels' names while watching the lettuce. *If the leaves close and shut, then do not go; but if they remain in their natural state, proceed, and you will prosper.* The leaves on Hanna's lettuce had remained open; in what ways will I prosper, she wondered, and wished that Ben and Will were with her to share the excitement.

Hanna helped Jessie and Ma prepare for Shabbat, the last before she went away. She swept the courtyard and savoured the scent of the bread baking. Ma's eyes glistened with tears as she lit the candles and prayed. 'My G–d, bring my Moshe, Ben and Hanna safely back to us,' she added.

Granda was determinedly upbeat. 'I do envy you, my dear,' he said, as they were eating. 'You must make the most of this opportunity to see more of the world. Such sights you'll see.' He tried to tell her some of them, but Hanna found it hard to concentrate on his stories of destruction by earthquake, riches lost at sea and a Christian bishop and a swan, though she did take note of what Granda said about ports teeming with boats and people from other lands – who might, she thought, be the ones who could give her news of Da and Ben.

'You be careful, my love,' Ma said three days later, as she gave Hanna a last hug goodbye. They clung to each other for a moment, then Ma pushed Hanna away. 'Off you go,' she said. 'Come back soon.'

'Learn everything you can, Hanna, everything. Don't worry – we'll manage without you,' said Granda, his tone just a little too bright.' Leo, one of Muriel's grandchildren, was going to come every day while Hanna was away, to help with the practical, day-to-day tasks. 'The manuscripts can wait until your return… Send us letters when you can, won't you, my dear?'

Hanna had already written one letter – to Will. He remained away helping the family of his sick uncle, though Hugh, his da, was by now back at Acaster, Will's aunt had told Ma. The letter was just a brief note, saying goodbye, and telling him that she'd been sent in disgrace to Rouen. She didn't dare risk telling him the truth. But this way he'd at least know she'd thought of him. They still hadn't spoken since that night in the woods. Ma had promised that she would make sure the letter reached him.

Baruch's wasn't the only party to leave York bound for London and the coronation. Another was made up of Prior William – who, as acting abbot of St Mary's, was to take part in the coronation ceremony – various other monks and the sheriff, Ranulf de Glanville. Then, of course, there was the Beast himself with his daughter, Emma, his squire, de Cuckney, and the young Scot, Marmaduke Darrell – each party further accompanied by its own entourage of companions, servants and guards. But they followed different routes – Prior William and his monks had business with the abbey at Selby and then St Alban's, while Malbisse had family and lands to see at Nottingham.

So, while Prior William's and the Beast's parties had left the city a week or so earlier travelling by boat on the River Ouse to the south (that was how Da and Ben had left), Hanna's party followed the paved Roman road to the east.

They passed through the city's eastern gate just as dawn was breaking. A blanket of cloud lay heavy and damp over the landscape and Hanna pulled her cloak tight around her and her hood well up over her ears and head. She felt tired, but the morning chill ensured that Lief's rolling walk did not lull her to sleep. All the party rode on horseback, save one of the guards, who took the reins of the cart. Serlo and Elias led the way, followed by Baruch, Master Thomas and Hanna, then the covered cart pulled by two horses with one of the guards on either side, with Abbot Roger, Lambinus and the fourth guard riding behind it. The three guards on horseback each carried a crossbow and wore short swords at their belts.

Riding in silence, they left the pasture and peat fields of St Leonard's leper hospital behind them, then made their way for several hours through woods and uncultivated land.

It was still early morning when they reached the next settlement – no more than a few houses and a small church. The sun was bright, though the air remained cool. A higgledy-piggledy patchwork of oats and wheat was almost ripe for harvesting, scattered through with scarlet poppies and blue cornflowers. The road crossed the River Derwent here, by ferry. They followed the road through the village – a motley collection of timber-framed wattle and daub houses – causing chickens to squawk and some of the children to give chase, shouting and laughing, then down through the water meadows to the ferry crossing. The meadows shimmered in a dew-pearled gauze of spider webs. The river, though too deep to ford, was not wide and the ferry was small, able only to carry a couple of horses and men at a time. The young ferryman, Alan, his hair a startlingly bright red, seemed pleased to see them, familiar with Baruch and his men from earlier journeys. It was a profitable morning's work for him.

Remounted, and in the same formation as before, the party rode on as swiftly as the terrain permitted. The land

through which they were travelling was flat, but the road's
Roman paving stones were often badly cracked, so there
was a constant possibility of the cart getting one of its
wheels trapped and overturning to left or right into the
steep ditch at either side.

Hanna had never been so far from York before. Now
properly awake, she felt herself fizzing with nerves and
excitement. If only Ben and Will could be there with her.
But perhaps she would hear news of Ben, and Da, at the
port in Lincoln.

Among the magic spells hidden within her tunic were
those against highwaymen and wolves. She concentrated
on trying to remember both without becoming confused
about which angel to invoke for each. But the landscape
here was still cultivated farmland – it didn't seem possible
that they could be attacked by either thieves or wild
animals in this tame and sunny place. Skylarks flew high up
in the sky above, singing and singing and singing.

Uncle Baruch was talking.

'It's Percy land we're passing though – our friend
Malbisse's rich cousins. The wheat looks healthy, don't you
think? It'll fetch a good price for them – no wonder our
friend and debtor is so bitter that his mother could not
share in the Percy fortune – he's forever playing catch up.'

'He's a mill downriver at Wheldrake though, hasn't
he?' said Master Thomas. 'That must earn him a fair bit?'

'But not enough to pay me what he owes,' said
Baruch. 'I'd say he was reckoning on my early death – what
do you think, my nephew and clerk?' Baruch laughed.
Hanna and Master Thomas smiled politely but said
nothing, unsure how to respond.

The farmland was soon behind them and again they
made their way through rough woodland. The road
narrowed, with room for only two riders abreast. Hanna
had to follow behind Uncle Baruch and Master Thomas,
no longer able to hear the peculiar banter of Serlo and
Elias in front of her (they appeared to be competing to see
who could produce the most convincing wolf's howl) or to
talk with Baruch and Master Thomas. Abbot Roger and his

chaplain were keeping themselves to themselves and the guards were also maintaining an aloof silence. She was bored.

By mid-afternoon they had reached a further settlement, next to another river. Hanna – and everyone else – was hot and tired, but, having briefly fed and watered their horses again, their party set off on the final leg of their journey for that first day, to the River Humber.

Surely it couldn't be far now, thought Hanna, as the landscape changed again and she found herself riding through a vast expanse of marshland, criss-crossed by silvery becks. She was sore and even tireder now, as was Lief, to judge by his slowing pace. The cries of the birds were ones she had never heard before, mournful calls rather than trilling songs and she no longer knew the names of the flowers, purple, pink and yellow, which grew among the low grasses.

And then ahead of her she could see reed beds and a vast expanse of brown mud streaked with silver. Birds waded in the patches of water, feeling for food in the mud with long, curved beaks.

'What is that?' she said.

'That,' said Baruch, 'is the River Humber.'

'A river? But it's five, six times as wide as the Ouse.'

'We're near its mouth,' said Baruch, 'where it meets the sea. It'll take us most of tomorrow to load up the boats and cross it. That's Lincolnshire on the other side. Tonight we stay there.' He pointed to a collection of buildings just visible in the distance. He spurred Turstin on, calling to the others as they went, his words lost on the wind. Hanna urged Lief into a canter. She wasn't going to get left behind.

It was mid-day the next day before the river was high enough for them to cross to Lincolnshire. While they waited, Baruch dictated to Hanna a letter to Comtessa and Cresselin and insisted she also write herself to Ma and Granda. The next travellers passing through on their way to York would take the letters with them – or if none appeared in the next couple of days, the inn keeper would send one of his own men to deliver them (Baruch had paid him generously).

Their horses and cart were loaded onto the boats Baruch and Elias had secured the previous evening – three flat-bottomed keels with square sails, the same type that brought cargo up the Ouse to York. Hanna helped Serlo and Elias entice the horses safely aboard, using generous amounts of oats and vetch. Thomas, Roger and Lambinus watched from the shore until the water was lifting the boats off the mud banks; the tide, still coming in, would help them in their crossing. Each boat had a crew of three – one to take the helm, two to manoeuvre the sail. The monks and Baruch, plus their horses, went on one boat; the four guards and their horses on the second; Hanna was to cross with Elias and Serlo, their horses and the cart. After the long ride the previous day, it was good for the horses to be able to rest, but they were not at ease, she could tell.

'You'll be all right, my beauty, you'll be all right,' she comforted Lief, rubbing his muzzle. His mane fell softly across his eyes. If there was a spell to ensure a safe journey over water, she could not remember it, and she concentrated instead on the horses in order to forget her own fears.

For the Humber, now recognisable as a river, was the widest expanse of water Hanna had ever seen. The day was warm and the river calm, but it was a muddy brown and its surface was patterned with whorls of currents as the water passed over the sandbanks underneath. Lincolnshire was a thin line on the far horizon. Hanna could tell just how shallow the river was in parts, as they sailed past a line of gulls apparently standing on the water, in fact with their feet in the mud just below the surface. There was enough wind blowing from the east to fill the sail and to make Hanna shiver. She was used to boats, but this wasn't like the Ouse at home, not at all. Yet, despite her fear, she felt exhilarated to be experiencing the new, the unfamiliar – all manner of good things might lie beyond that horizon. She fixed her eyes on the river's southern bank, willing the boat to reach it soon.

At the bank a creek led up through marshes, but Hanna could see no sign of human habitation. The two boats lowered their sails and the crew-turned-oarsmen propelled them round the bends of the creek until finally they reached the collection of houses containing the inn in which they were to lodge for the night. Again there was the time-consuming business of moving horses, cart and luggage between boats and dry land. It was hard work, but Hanna enjoyed being part of it.

Once they were all installed in the inn, Hanna, under the pretext of settling the horses, made herself comfortable with them in the stable so that she could spend some time studying her spells. It was not long, however, until Elias came to call her for prayers and their evening meal.

Afterwards, while the guards, Serlo and Elias busied themselves with beer and backgammon, Baruch challenged Master Thomas to a game of chess. Lambinus and Abbot Roger looked on with Hanna, though the elderly abbot's head was already nodding on his chest by the time Baruch had lost his second pawn. Baruch threw himself into the game in the same way Hanna had often seen him lose to Da and Granda – playing on instinct and sparring piece for piece. Soon checkmated by his wilier, more cautious opponent, he roared with laughter.

'You've out-thought me, truly, Master Thomas! I congratulate you. Come, Elias Quatrebouches, give us a song before sleep, something to cheer us on our way.'

So Elias took up the lute and began to play. Baruch sang with him, his voice rich and strong. Abbot Roger and Lambinus made their excuses and went to bed, which left Hanna and Master Thomas free to embark on a slower, more thoughtful game of chess of their own. Hanna matched the monk, move for move, for quite a while but once she began to yawn Thomas soon called checkmate.

From the inn, soon after dawn, it was back onto the paved Roman road. It climbed steeply out of the village, and then followed the gently undulating ridge whose width it occupied. They had to negotiate the occasional outcrops of sharp grey rock among the gorse bushes and the bracken.

There were no trees and the travellers were buffeted by the wind. The land fell away steeply to both left and right, but wheat and oats grew on its lower slopes. There were also vast numbers of sheep, their maa-ing and baa-ing just audible above the wind.

'One good thing about the sheep,' said Baruch. 'There's no wolves hereabouts – all hunted down, on the king's orders, to protect the precious wool.

'This land, it's almost all owned by Bishop Hugh, in Lincoln, or one of the abbeys,' he went on. He was riding close to Hanna, so that his words wouldn't just be blown away, and there was some distance between them and their fellow travellers. Hanna could hear snatches of Elias and the Scots teasing Serlo about his snoring, alternately snorting and guffawing with laughter. Master Thomas rode up ahead, alone. Their guards were concentrating on guarding. Hanna made an effort to focus on what her uncle was telling her.

'When I first travelled this route,' he said, 'there were more people living here, on the lower slopes. But the church has moved them to make room for crops and sheep. These sheep, the grain you can see growing in the fields, they're what pays for their fine buildings and fancy robes.'

Hanna nodded.

'But they can't always get the silver for it when they need it – Bishop Hugh may need to give the master builder silver so that he can pay the workmen on the cathedral – and that's when he needs us. We can advance the silver even while the wool is still on the sheep's backs and the grain is growing in the fields. They may not like us, but they cannot do without us, these Christian priests.' He grinned.

The day's journey was peaceful, their guards required to do no more than ride alongside them until they reached their ridge-top destination for that night.

The next day, they continued once more upon the straight, paved, ridge-top road. There was a brief shower of rain, but they soon dried out again in the warm summer air.

As they rode, Hanna fell to thinking about how to be Ben in Lincoln. Being Ben with her current companions was straightforward: those who knew her true identity were complicit in the effort to hide it; the others took no interest in her at all. She enjoyed the expectation that she would play her part in tending the horses and helping load and unload the cart, while as Hanna she would have been expected to watch and wait. Even all the business of washing and dressing had been without problem, with Uncle Baruch showing great tact and sensitivity.

But in Lincoln and in the house of Baruch's brother, her uncle Sampson and his wife, Margaret, it would be different: everyone there knew of Granda and Da and their family; they would have expectations of Ben – which didn't necessarily tally with his role as clerk to Baruch. The thought of Deulesault, in particular, troubled her – would have troubled her even if she were arriving openly as herself. Was he really not going to realise that Baruch's clerk was Hanna, not her twin?

12. LINCOLN

The soft, showery morning had turned into a hot, sunny afternoon. They were travelling due south, with the sun high up above them. Their progress now was slow – the horses were tired, after more than twenty miles on the road. Wherever they passed strips of ripened grain, there were men and women wielding scythes and carrying the cut stalks to tie into shocks. As the day wore on, more were sat or lying down in whatever shade was available, empty flagons at their sides. Then Hanna saw in the distance ahead of them, stretched out against the horizon, the line of a city wall. Gate towers rose up at the point where it met their road. As they rode nearer, Hanna could see the soldiers guarding it and, beyond the wall, to the left, a building, dark against the clear blue sky, half-built – or half-ruined – surrounded by scaffolding and with a crane on either side. She turned to Serlo. 'Lincoln?' she asked. He nodded. At last! Hanna felt the same mixture of excitement and nerves as on the day of the hunt...

But first there was an inn and a few houses, with chickens scratching in the dirt outside and children playing, who waved at Hanna and Serlo and their fellow travellers as they passed. They were in time to enter the city before curfew and had no need to stop. There was some banter with the guards on the gate, as Master Thomas and Abbot Roger and Lambinus paid their tolls to enter, and Baruch produced his letter with the seal of the king to allow him free passage. Hanna had a clear view of the massive castle keep to the west, bigger than either of those in York.

Then they entered the city with a clatter of hooves on the cobbled street and heads turned to appraise the new arrivals. To their left, market stallholders were packing up their wares for the day. Beyond them, rose the ruins of the church.

'They've even more to build here than you have in York,' said Abbot Roger.

'Not us, exactly,' said Elias.

'Oh, aye – Master Thomas though,' said Abbot Roger.

'It looks a mess, doesn't it?' said Baruch, with some delight. 'It was finished when I was Hanna's age, and then one day the earth shook... Our synagogue, on the other hand, was undamaged. Now, what does that tell us?' He laughed.

'That the shaking of the earth was the devil's work, obviously,' said Thomas. 'Bishop Hugh's palace, too, came tumbling down.' He pointed to the ruined building they were now passing on their left. 'But the castle, the damage done to that they repaired straightaway – King Henry made sure of that. Now what does that tell us?'

The three monks, Elias and Uncle Baruch laughed.

But their guards were impatient to leave – the castle here in Lincoln was the end of their commission.

Baruch gently pressed Turstin's flanks with his spurs. 'Come on, let's find my little brother. His house is just down the hill. We'll be in time for evening prayers.'

The narrow street descended sharply – not easy for their tired horses. On either side there were close-built houses, most of wood, but a few of stone. Hanna caught glimpses of the port, its water shining white in the sun, and a mass of masts and sails. Her heart leapt up – perhaps there she would hear news of Da and Ben.

'Well, this is where I leave you, for now,' said Thomas. 'My fellow monks are waiting for me down there, I hope' – he pointed to the road to the east. 'Anon,' he said, with a flourish, then turned and cantered away.

Baruch, Serlo, Elias and Hanna took the road to the west, with golden hills rising up far ahead of them on the other side of the city. Almost at once they arrived at Sampson and Margaret's house and were overwhelmed by a welter of greetings, exclamations ('Ben, how you've grown!') and offers of food and drink.

Deulesault, too, had grown and he, though still thin and pale, was now young man rather than boy, his voice a couple of octaves deeper than when they last met, and bumps of stubble on his chin. And quite good-looking, Hanna couldn't help noticing. As soon as he looked at her, she was absolutely sure he recognised her, even if no one else appeared to. She could feel him staring at her, while she tried to stand close to Baruch, in the way she remembered his former clerk doing, and took Ben's place in the men's section of the synagogue to pray. She concentrated on avoiding Deulesault's gaze. Neither he nor his father were coming with them to London – the Lincolnshire community's representative had already left. She was relieved when the men – including Deulesault – gathered together after the evening meal and Baruch asked her to make a note of their discussions – of the implications for their community of the accession of Richard to the throne. With pen and parchment in hand, at least she had a clear role to play.

Afterwards, however, it was only natural that the older men should talk together and Hanna found herself unavoidably next to Deulesault.

'Why are you dressed up as your brother, Hanna?' he challenged her straightaway, but quietly.

'What do you mean?' she asked, knowing that she was looking pink and panicked as she answered, but unable to prevent herself blushing.

'You know perfectly well what I mean,' he said. His tone was teasing, though, not threatening.

'You're being ridiculous, Deulesault. Just because my voice hasn't broken and I've no hairs on my chin –'

'It's you that's being ridiculous, Hanna. I remember, your dimple is on the left, and Ben's is on the right.'

He remembered that… She met his gaze. He was smiling at her, gently. She looked away again, embarrassed.

'Of course you're right,' she said, angry that there was no way that she could prove him wrong.

'Don't worry, I won't tell anyone.'

She looked in his eyes again. He seemed to mean it. 'Thank you,' she said.

'But I want you to tell me what you and Uncle Baruch are up to,' he said. 'What on earth is going on?'

'You're really not going to tell?' she said. 'Not even after Ben and I were so horrible to you when you came to York?'

He laughed. 'You were pretty vile, weren't you? Don't worry – I've forgiven you. Your grandfather was very nice to me at the time, I remember, told me to ignore his two ruffian grandchildren – that he thought you could benefit from being a bit more like me…'

'How dare he!' said Hanna.

'I don't suppose he really meant it. But come on, I promise I won't tell anyone that you're Hanna, as long as you tell me what is going on,' he said.

'It's complicated,' Hanna began. 'Well, maybe not that not complicated. I was caught – I was in trouble. It's to protect me.'

Deulesault looked embarrassed and shocked by her story in turns.

'No wonder they thought they had to do something with you,' he said, when she'd finished. 'Alone, in the dark, in the woods, with a Christian boy – trying out magic. I guess my parents were right to be worried about me playing with you,' he said, and laughed.

Hanna judged it best not to tell him that she carried a comprehensive collection of spells within her tunic, and was still fully intending to carry more of them out when she had the chance. But there was something he could do to help her.

After prayers the next morning, Hanna accompanied Uncle Baruch on foot to Lincoln's port, together with Deulesault and Sampson; Elias and Serlo drove the cart containing the consignment of wool. It was another sunny, cloudless day.

The mass of masts and sails which Hanna had glimpsed the previous day now appeared as serried rows of boats tied up in the harbour pool. Uncle Baruch pointed out to her the Flemish wool ships, recognisable from the lion flag at their masts. There was no wind, so the flags drooped rather than flew. The wool house, where the business of trading went on, was close by, a tall, windowless stone building, next to the merchants' dwellings which overlooked the pool. Beyond the merchants' houses were several taverns, already noisy with shouts and laughter. On one of the ships, a lone boy was energetically scrubbing the deck; the others were apparently deserted. These were the ships whose traders came each year to buy the high-quality wool from the long-haired sheep of Lincolnshire and Yorkshire – among the traders Sampson's business partner, Segar.

There were also a few larger boats from Norway and Germany. Smaller, fishing vessels were moored on the far side of the dock, where Hanna could make out several fishermen sitting amid a tangle of nets, apparently mending them. A large flock of swans – some twenty or thirty birds – crowded the dark, smooth water of the dock at its far left corner, where the river flowed in.

Hanna dutifully wrote down the details of the deal her uncles struck with Sampson's partner, Segar, for the sale of the wool, but once Elias and Serlo had started helping the trader's men unload the heavy bales and transfer them to the wool house for weighing and taxing and Baruch and Sampson had gone to share a cup of wine with Segar to seal their deal, she turned to Deulesault.

'Now,' she said, 'Please help me. I need you to speak Flemish for me and ask if any of these traders and seamen have seen or heard anything of my da and Ben in the different markets and ports they've been to.'

'But everyone's in the taverns.'

'So?' said Hanna. 'We just need to make sure we keep out of sight of your father and Uncle Baruch.'

Deulesault made a face. 'Hanna –' he began to protest.

'Come *on*,' she insisted. 'We haven't got long. We can start with that boy, if you like. He's not in a tavern.' She pointed at the boy now standing up and stretching, his deck-scrubbing done.

But despite Deulesault's best efforts – and he really did try, politely interrupting as many traders' and seamen's conversations as he could, each time giving a brief description of the missing father and son, and in such a way that he mostly elicited equally polite replies – no one was able to say for certain that they'd seen or heard anything about Da or Ben.

'I'm sorry, Hanna,' he said. She looked so miserable.

'It's not your fault,' she said. 'Thank you for trying.'

She was determined not to cry.

Elias and Serlo had finished moving the bales and Baruch and Sampson had said goodbye to Segar. They walked back up the steep hill to Sampson's house. There was another meeting that afternoon they had to prepare for, with Bishop Hugh, which Hanna's clerical expertise was required for.

She could feel her spirits rising even before the end of their walk. After Shabbat, they would be leaving, heading south towards London. And in London, there was an even bigger port, Granda had said, with boats from lands to the south as well as the north. Their traders were far more likely to have news of Ben and Da, Hanna thought – she wasn't giving up, not yet.

13. AMBUSH

Two days later, they were – apparently – in the middle of nowhere. Hanna was travel-sore and all of them, horses and humans, were tired. Their day had started late, as Master Thomas's horse had a loose shoe, so they'd had first to go to the blacksmith's forge. Hanna had watched for a while and then hidden herself among the nearby trees, where she read her magic notes, finally succeeding in committing to memory the spell to dispel a group of enemies. Baruch was not best pleased at the delay, though it was scarcely Master Thomas's fault, and he had remained grimly silent for most of the day. Hanna briefly wondered if perhaps his not-quite-healed wound was troubling him, for of course he'd never say…

Fresh guards had set out with them from Lincoln, four men from the castle there taking over from those from York, who kept firmly to themselves. Abbot Roger and Lambinus had finally exhausted their stock of stories and songs, while Serlo and Elias had stopped their joking around at least an hour or so ago, when they'd begun the steep climb up a ridge of hills, on the other side of which, they told Hanna, lay the town of St Albans, with their evening meal and some sort of bed for the night. Baruch, Hanna, Elias and Serlo were going to stay with one of Elias's cousins, their guards at an inn and the three monks at the abbey.

The land they were passing through was mostly grazed by sheep, though the road had also taken them past some mean-looking peasant hovels. Dusk was falling, and they had one more stretch of woodland to go through. It was a couple of hours since they'd seen anyone else travelling in either direction. The trees grew right up against the road, forming a dark tunnel through which they had to pass. Hanna and Master Thomas were riding just behind the two guards at the front of their small convoy, some way ahead of Baruch and Serlo. Then came the cart, driven by one of the guards, followed by Abbot Roger and Lambinus and then Elias and the fourth guard bringing up the rear.

'Uh, uh, uh, ooh.' Elias tried his wolf howl once again, but Serlo and Hanna scarcely laughed; Baruch scowled.

There was a scuffling in the undergrowth to Hanna's right, and suddenly their way was blocked by a gaggle of men – or men and boys, Hanna came to realise later.

She saw the gleam of a dagger brandished by one, others were armed with sturdy looking staffs and several held a bow ready to fire. Serlo at once drew his sword.

'Give us all you have.' The man spoke in English though in an accent new to Hanna.

She swivelled in her saddle to see that they were surrounded and outnumbered and that at least a couple more of their assailants also held bows taut to fire their arrows, while others had rocks ready to fire from small catapults.

'Not just your money and what's in the cart,' the man was saying. 'Your horses, your clothes – we want the lot.'

In the growing dark, their attackers looked as much animal as human – their dirty, raggedy clothes hung off them, their hair tangled and filthy. For a moment Hanna locked eyes with one of the boys – and saw there a look of desperation mixed with hatred.

The three guards on horseback had their crossbows drawn, and Roger and Lambinus their swords, but against so many Hanna did not reckon their chances. With her hand resting on the parchment hidden beneath her tunic, she began to recite under her breath in Hebrew the spell she'd learnt that morning:

> '*Harbonah who dwells in the east, Shamdon who dwells in the north, Kasbiel who dwells in the west, Kesef who dwells in the south, angels of anger and wrath, break our adversaries' bones, crush all their limbs and shatter their power, like pottery vessels…*'

Master Thomas looked at her askance, but Hanna ignored him and continued to murmur.

Hanna, still murmuring, at the same time was waiting for the guards to loose their arrows, or for Baruch to take command, to reply – but now the man yelled, 'Quick!'

His voice was drowned out, however, by a snarling and growling and then a screaming, as out of the trees leapt one, two, three, four, five, six wolves, their eyes bright in the night.

Hanna continued to murmur:

'Harbonah who dwells in the east, Shamdon who dwells in the north, Kasbiel who dwells in the west, Kesef who dwells in the south, angels of anger and wrath, break our adversaries' bones, crush all their limbs and shatter their power.'

The men armed with staffs fought off the wolves as they lunged at them, but the one who had spoken, who was holding a bow and arrow, was unable to defend himself.

The largest of the wolves jumped at his throat, knocking him to the ground. Blood spurted out. The other wolves seized the man's body, seemingly oblivious to the blows rained down on them by the remaining men and the boys.

'Pa! Pa!' Hanna was aware of a desperate voice shouting.

As if in a parallel world – *Harbonah, Shamdon, Kasbiel, Kesef* – Hanna completed her spell. The wolves, it seemed, were uninterested in the riders and their horses. Next to her, Elias's horse was rearing up and neighing in fear and panic at the smell and sight of wolf and blood. The guards lowered their cross bows – why shoot at the wolves when they were attacking thieves?

'Let's go,' Elias was yelling. His horse needed no encouragement to bolt from the scene. Lief, too, surged forward, followed by Baruch, Master Thomas and the Scots. Serlo and the guards fell in behind the cart to ensure that it and its cargo remained safe from both thieves and wolves.

Hanna galloped only briefly, however, mindful of the risk of Lief stumbling on the uneven ground in the dark. They left the woods behind them, and the thieves to their fate.

The others were full of it. 'Did you see...?' 'I thought we were dead...' Baruch said nothing.

Hanna rode in a sweaty and stunned silence. All her strength had drained from her and it took all her effort to remain upright in the saddle and ride the rest of the journey to St Albans.

Soon they were at the walls of the town. Once Baruch mentioned Elias's cousin's name and proffered a couple of coins to the gatekeeper they were allowed through. They were all made welcome at their various destinations, fed, and provided with space to sleep, their respective hosts well recompensed by the travellers' account of their journey and the dangers they had just survived.

'You're quiet, Hanna. Are you all right?' asked Elias as she went to find her bed for the night.

'Yes, I'm fine.'

'Who'd have thought that we'd owe our safety to a pack of wolves?'

Hanna hesitated. 'The man the wolves attacked,' she asked, 'do you think the others rescued him? That he could have survived?' (that voice: 'Pa! Pa!')

Elias sounded surprised. 'I doubt it – that much blood...'

And it was her words, Hanna thought, that had summoned them.

The next day they rose late and continued peacefully on their way to London. The road was busier than it had been at any other time in their long journey, both with pilgrims on their way to or from St Thomas's shrine in Canterbury and those conducting business in London. Hanna was still trying to take in what had happened to her during their journey the previous evening: her magic had worked – not just a tiny spell with a lettuce, but one invoking powerful angels, which had enabled them to escape both highwaymen and wolves… She shut her mind to images of wolves at a man's throat and the cry of a boy, 'Pa!'

Having again started late, they did not make it inside London's city walls and Uncle Joseph's house before curfew. They stopped just north of the city, in a busy settlement near a river. It was a warm evening, and young people were gathered outside. There was a large priory behind high walls with two more churches in the process of being built, but also several inns, one where Uncle Baruch was on good terms with the landlord and where all of them – guards, the three monks, as well as Baruch, Serlo, Elias and Hanna – chose to spend their last night on the road together.

While they were eating, Abbot Roger raised his cup of wine and proposed a toast: 'To a successful stay in London and a safe journey home!' he said. 'To a successful stay and safe journey home,' they echoed.

Next day, they made their way south, past the market already busy with horses being put through their paces by their sellers, and entered the city of London by Alders Gate.

14. LONDON

London, Av 4949 / August 1189

London, thought Hanna, was scary, but exciting. It was huge, confusing, intoxicating: churches and houses going up, hovels falling down; a stone bridge inching across the vast River Thames pillar by pillar, next to another of wood; everywhere, scaffolding and cranes. In each neighbourhood, it seemed, a half-built abbey reared up above high walls that firmly excluded outsiders. There were newly finished markets, grand palaces and, on the river's north bank, two solidly complete castles. The synagogue and miqveh, a short walk from Uncle Joseph's house where she and Uncle Baruch were staying, were larger and finer than those of either York or Lincoln. And around and through the city whirled and eddied merchants and masons, tailors, sailors and troubadours, knights, nuns and priests, beggars and pilgrims, and the Jewish traders, travellers and scholars of her uncles' acquaintance.

Hanna exulted in the freedom that her disguise gave her to wander, unnoticed. She just wished again that Ben and Will could be with her to share in the experience and, now, in the knowledge that she – they – could work magic, vanquish wolves and highwaymen. She kept her notes of the spells with her at all times, though her opportunities to study them seriously were few. And soon she would see the king!

Uncle Joseph's disapproval of her disguise scarcely touched her. Uncle Baruch took the first opportunity he could after they arrived to explain why his niece was dressed as her brother and performing the duties of Baruch's clerk. He insisted on Hanna being with him for the explanation, but dismissed from the room Joseph's ancient, stooped factotum, Mordecai. Hanna raged inwardly as Uncle Baruch then described how he and Granda had found her together with Will in the woods 'experimenting with magic'. He put it all very matter-of-factly, yet somehow managed to make their activities sound both childish and sordid. Hanna dug her nails into her palms, fixed her eyes on the floor and said nothing.

But at the same time there was something in Uncle Baruch's tone that defied the older man to criticise. Uncle Joseph, smaller, paler, rounder than Uncle Baruch, listened without interrupting, his hands resting on the book of prayers he had been reading before they arrived. His beard, like the hair which curled from under his dark blue cap, was a beautiful silvery white. His face bore few wrinkles, just large, fleshy bags under his eyes. Like giant blisters, Hanna thought.

He looked sorrowfully at her. 'If you were my niece,' he began, then sighed.

He started again. 'It is a madcap, hare-brained scheme, Baruch, the likes of which I am too old for. Let me be clear: this child is your responsibility –'

'I would never have suggested otherwise,' said Baruch. 'Hanna is my niece and has proved an excellent clerk. I will look after her as if she were my own daughter.'

Joseph continued as if Baruch hadn't spoken. 'And nothing, nothing, is to get in the way of our main purpose – to gain the goodwill of our new king. Our livelihoods – our lives – depend on it. And I, for one, am too old, too tired, to think of uprooting myself and my family, have not long had them settled, and my wife is not well. But for the good of our whole community...'

After that, though they were staying in Uncle Joseph's house and saw him every day, he barely acknowledged Hanna. He responded to her polite greetings, but that was all. His house, close to the market of West Cheap, was known as the House of the Franks, as it was home to several families who had not long left France, including one of Joseph's daughters, Elise, who was married to the poet and rabbi, Jacob of Orléans. She was glad to hear news of her mother and sisters in York, as well as their husbands and children.

This London house, too, was built of stone, on a lane which ran along the west bank of a river, the Walbrook, on its way south to join the Thames. There was a charcoal market at the top of the lane, several noisy, smoky, blacksmiths' workshops, and a recently built church. Their neighbours were both Christians and Jews. The synagogue was just down the lane towards the Thames, at the back of Rabbi Abraham's house. It was Abraham's father, not long dead, who had founded the synagogue some twenty years previously, and organised their community to build it, together with a study room and miqveh. It was too small now to accommodate everyone, full to overflowing on Saturdays and at festivals; discussions were underway about how to fund an extension.

Since arriving in London, Hanna, Uncle Baruch and Serlo had spent much of their time at the rabbi's house, eating with his family most days. (Elias was with his Quatrebouches relatives who lived not far away, among fields where Lief, Turstin and their other horses were resting.) Hanna felt at home with Rabbi Abraham and Sarah, his wife, and their five girls and one boy, Reuben. All of the children were younger than her. The girls, to Hanna's relief, were shy and reluctant to talk to her; Reuben, who was five, a lovely looking boy with big, brown, trusting eyes and smooth, pale skin, reminded her of Hakelin, Muriel's younger grandson in York. Usually out playing with the other children in the lane, Reuben took a strong liking to Hanna – or rather Ben – in that way that small boys often do to their elders; there was no reason for him to doubt that Hanna was a boy. Sarah, strong and capable, often baking, frequently laughing, reminded Hanna of Ma – or at least Ma before Da went away.

And, throughout the week, more visitors arrived, representatives from each of the Isle of the Sea's communities of Jews – Jurnet of Norwich; from Lynn, Isaac le Docteur (Hanna thought he looked worryingly infirm, given his profession) and Deulebene; Benedict le Puncteur from Oxford, with his son, David; Deulecresse from Winchester; Crispin from Northampton (not Uncle

Jacob – but Hanna pushed aside her disappointment); Isaac le Gros from Canterbury (who was, indeed, *gros*). Lincoln's representative, Haim, son of Aaron, was also there, having arrived the previous week.

For all of them, Hanna played the role of studious clerk, Ben, in the service of Baruch, remaining at his side, parchment and quill in hand. She wished she could talk with le Puncteur, the author of the stories about a fox that she, Will and Ben had so much enjoyed reading with Granda – but wished to avoid David, as the most likely to see through her disguise. Fortunately, the father and son were staying with their relatives, not Joseph or Rabbi Abraham's family, so it was not hard for Hanna to keep out of David's way. The two of them had been nominated, it transpired, to carry one of the caskets containing their collective gifts to present to the king on the day of his coronation, but Hanna pushed this thought, too, to one side: she'd worry about it when the time came.

Uncle Baruch's business meetings were few, in fact, and, once she'd written letters to Comtessa for Baruch and another to Ma and Granda, Hanna's time was largely her own. If she were there as Hanna, she'd have been expected to spend it with Sarah and her children; as Ben she was left to her own devices. Baruch insisted only that she be accompanied by Serlo, and Serlo was happy simply to follow her lead. Though more nervous than Hanna of being somewhere new, he had the brawn to protect her if a problem arose. Hanna wasn't sure this was quite how her uncle would treat his own daughter, but was nonetheless grateful for her freedom.

It was the Thames and its traffic which drew her most powerfully, the daily ebb and flow of the river's tides navigated by so many vessels. Could Da's and Ben's be among them? The weather was sunny and warm, Hanna was happy, excited, the failure of her efforts in Lincoln forgotten. Each morning she and Serlo made their way south along the bank of the River Walbrook down to the docks and their stone warehouses. Here, as in Lincoln, there were Flemish merchants who emptied their boats of wine and reloaded them with bales of wool to take across the sea to the weavers of Flanders – they had their warehouses on the west bank of the Walbrook. Then opposite them, across the river's large, wedge-shaped basin, just before it flowed into the Thames, stood the vast hall and warehouse of the Easterlings, the merchants of Kőln.

Hanna watched the ships arriving, after who knew what adventures on the sea, then moored by their crews, sails furled, cargoes muscled ashore. She listened to the sailors and merchants shouting to one another in foreign tongues, and tried to read their meaning in their weather-beaten, different faces. Tongue-less, Serlo was unable to help. She needed Deulesault or Granda…

She allowed Serlo to make sure they were out of the docks before the day grew late, however, for crowds gathered to drink the wine that was sold from ships and wine-cellars, and where there was wine, later there was sure to be trouble – but not before Serlo had tried the delicacies roasted, boiled and fried in the public cook-shop. They would find a spot near the river away from the wine-drinkers where they were able to hunker down and, while Serlo ate, Hanna pulled out her sheaf of notes and read.

It was Friday, their last opportunity to visit the docks before the coronation on Sunday. Serlo was eating, Hanna was reading: this time she really would master the spell for invisibility. A shadow fell over her.

'Ben?'

It was as much question as greeting, in an accent she didn't recognise. Above her towered a smiling, dark-skinned, dark-haired man with a gold ring in his ear and a leather cloak over his arm. The hand he held out to her was missing its forefinger. Hanna grasped the hand and shook it, standing up as she did so. Serlo stood, too, casting a chicken leg to the ground, wiping the grease from his mouth, and bristling.

'I'm not Ben,' she said, 'I'm his twin – his twin brother. Do you know where Ben is? And our Da? Who are you?'

She didn't know which question to ask first and they all came tumbling out at once in rapid French. Serlo shifted his ground slightly so that he was standing half between Hanna and the dark stranger.

The man looked confused. He replied in slow and careful French; it clearly wasn't his native tongue.

'You are Ben's brother?'

'Yes. Do you know where he is? Is he alive?'

The man's reply was agonisingly slow. 'I, Todros, was with him in Sicily –'

Just then a shout went up from the nearest wine shop – 'There he is!' – and two men, thick-set, burly, came hurtling towards them. Hanna looked around to see who it was they were after and in that one half-moment the man took off and Serlo picked Hanna up, swinging her over his shoulder.

'Put me down! Todros, stop!' she yelled alternately, arms and legs flailing, as the man who had seen Ben in Sicily disappeared among the wine sellers and drinkers, half-knocking several over as he pushed his way through, pursued by the two men.

'Todros, stop,' she sobbed, beating her fists on Serlo's broad back.

As soon as they got back, Hanna, still furious, found Uncle Baruch and told him everything that had happened.

'You can't blame Serlo,' he said. 'He was doing his job – looking after you, and he's really upset that you're so cross with him. We've no idea who this man, this Todros was, what his intentions were – Serlo did the right thing.'

'But I must find the man, Uncle. He was with Ben' – to her annoyance, she was becoming tearful – 'please help me.'

It was late in the afternoon by now, only a couple of hours or so before the Sabbath. Uncle Baruch sighed.

'We can take a walk,' he said. 'Though we've no way of knowing where this man might be… But there was something I wanted to show you anyway. And we'll send Serlo and Elias to the docks, to make a thorough search of the wine shops there and to see what they can find out about this Todros.'

It turned out that the 'thing' Baruch wanted to show her was the half-built stone bridge – though it was busy there, a counter-flow of people, animals, carts and wagons surging north and south on the old wooden bridge, and Hanna supposed it was conceivable that Todros might want to cross the river. She looked closely at the crowds, but there was a marked lack of gold earrings and, as far as she could see, everyone had a full eight fingers and two thumbs on their hands. Many were pilgrims on their way to or from St Thomas's Canterbury shrine – and Todros didn't really seem to be the pilgrim type.

Uncle Baruch insisted on Hanna taking a look at the workmen and their machines on barges in the river, while they were there. He had watched the building work each time he'd been in London since 'just before you were born', he told Hanna. Some seven piers had now been sunk into the riverbed from the north bank, not yet reaching even half way. The afternoon sun was hot and sweat was dripping off the workmen on the barges as they heaved on a rope to raise a block of stone on a chain which they then dropped onto a timber support to drive it into the riverbed. But Hanna couldn't believe that her uncle really expected her to take an interest in this when, somewhere in this city, was a man who had definite information about Da and Ben.

A sudden gust of wind had both Baruch and Hanna pulling their cloaks up over their mouths and noses, to avoid breathing in the sickening stench of urine, faeces and decaying flesh blown from the tanneries further down on the south bank. Finally, Baruch conceded defeat. They turned out of the wind and began to walk back to Joseph's house.

'Perhaps Elias and Serlo will have found out more,' he said, 'and I promise we'll look again once the coronation is over.'

But Elias and Serlo returned with no more information. It was the Sabbath and there was nothing more she could do for the moment. Hanna willed herself to forget about it, as her uncle advised, until after the coronation.

On the Saturday night, after the Havdalah prayers, the elders seated themselves on benches taken from the synagogue into the courtyard between it and Rabbi Abraham's house and arranged in a square so they could all see each other as they talked. The evening was warm and muggy. Hanna sat between Uncles Baruch and Joseph, her clerk's pen at the ready, keeping her head covered despite the heat. Rabbi Abraham sat opposite, with Reuben, wide-eyed, curious.

The discussion, in Hebrew, was taking some time to get to the point. Instead of it being simply about how best to present their gifts to the new king, it had turned into an argument about whether that was the best course of action at all – whether they should avoid the Christian ritual of the coronation, and present themselves at some other time – or whether it was a waste of their money and assets to be giving the new king such generous gifts in the first place.

Deulebene of Lynn was talking. 'We are just a sponge for the royal treasury. We soak up all the floating money of the country, to be squeezed from time to time into the king's treasure chest.'

'And then lost at sea,' said Haim. His father was Aaron, whose coins and jewels were taken on his death by Henry II to pay for his wars against his sons, only for the ship in which the treasure was being transported to him in Rouen to sink shortly after setting sail from England.

'But what we don't want is for him to copy his cousin and banish every last Jew from his kingdom – which, let me remind you, includes Rouen as well – there's no nearby refuge for us,' said Jacob of Orléans.

'There's always Scotland…' said Uncle Baruch, to general laughter. 'No, no, I'm serious –'

Uncle Joseph spoke for the first time, cutting across him. 'It won Philip of France the support of his noblemen, expelling the Jews – reason enough for Richard to do the same.'

'I'm not saying we shouldn't be generous in our gifts to the new king – above all, we need his protection,' said

Crispin of Northampton, slowly. One of the oldest present, he twisted the tip of his long grey beard meditatively he spoke. 'But why would we want to be anywhere near the coronation, in their place of idolatry? Particularly when rumours have been rife all week that we are not wanted there.'

'And there's all the prisoners he's released… A fine way to celebrate becoming king, granting them amnesty!' said the doctor, Isaac.

'If our new king, as you call him, didn't want us there, he would have sent us letters to inform us, I'm sure of it,' said Jurnet.

Baruch nodded. 'We have heard nothing since we received official notice of the coronation. As for the prisoners – a bunch of petty thugs and thieves – what are they to us? We have our guards, do we not?

'With respect, Crispin,' he continued, 'we have no intention of going into the Christians' Minster.' His deference to the older man was token, his tone impatient. 'The king will expect to receive our gifts along with all the others at the start of the banquet. Trust me, I know these people – have Joseph, Jurnet and I not dealt with them, together with Haim's father, our late departed Aaron of Lincoln, for the past twenty years or more?

'Presenting our gifts is a necessary token of respect, which all his nobles, foreign princes and anyone wanting the king's favour will be making. We must publicly demonstrate our loyalty, our generosity. Are you ashamed to take your place along with the rest? The value of our gifts will far exceed theirs. The mistake would be not to take part, to risk offending King Richard.'

Reuben, nestling in the crook of his father's arm, was taking it all in, his large brown eyes looking from one to the other as they spoke.

Jurnet spoke again. 'Bishop Hugh was adamant when we spoke to him in Lincoln that we should present ourselves and our gifts at the coronation – and Aaron said Hugh was the one we should rely on as a friend of the Jews – and now he has the new king's ear.'

'Aaron said this, Aaron said that – but Aaron's four years dead,' Crispin replied, his voice rising. 'And what happened to all that he acquired over his long life? King Henry took it – and then lost half of it at sea, as Haim has reminded us. Richard may accept our gifts graciously now, but soon enough he'll be bleeding us dry – Deulebene is right.

'You know these people, you say, Baruch – do you not think that I have come to know them as well? And it's not just Richard we should be worrying about – but his other loyal subjects… We need to flatter the new king, but not to risk our own safety tomorrow.'

Uncle Baruch was angry now, Hanna could tell from the way his face had darkened, just like Ma's did. He wasn't used to his will being thwarted. He leaned towards Crispin. 'We cannot let your cowardice hold us back.' He spoke quietly, but everyone could sense the threat. Crispin, despite his years, made as if to stand up and Rabbi Abraham put his arm out to motion him down again. Uncle Joseph placed a restraining hand on Uncle Baruch's arm.

Abraham spoke slowly, his voice deep, and with the authority befitting a rabbi. 'Gentlemen, gentlemen, this is an argument we have already been through – several times. I suggest that we put the issue to the vote. Those in favour of presenting our gifts at the same time as all those others who wish to show their loyalty to our new king, Richard – raise your hands.'

Eight raised their hands to signify their agreement.

'Those against.' Four raised their hands.

Hanna didn't vote. But if her uncles Baruch and Joseph thought it was the right thing to present their gifts to the king, Hanna was happy with that. Besides, when else would she get the chance to see a newly crowned king?

15. RIOT

Next morning, they sailed down the River Walbrook and up the vast silver-grey Thames to the Minster under a hazy sun, just two boats among many, propelled up the river by the incoming tide and an east wind. The journey gave Hanna her first sight of London west of the City's walls, beyond Fitzwilliam's castle, past the Knights Templar water mill on the River Fleet and the island prison, and then the grand houses of various Christian nobles, with their gardens sloping down towards the river – until the towers of the Minster and the bulk of the king's palace came into view.

They moored their wherries one alongside the other on the south side of the island on which the great West Minster stood.

It had been decided they would stay there until the bells announced that the new king was leaving the church to go to the Hall – no point in courting trouble by being among the crowd any longer than necessary. And so they waited.

The river was high now, but the wherries lay low in the water, weighed down by the chests containing the party's gifts for the new king. In addition to the jewels and gold coins from York, there was intricate jewellery wrought by the goldsmiths of Norwich to include the new king's initial R and a roaring leopard, while the other towns had sent rich cloth and furs and more gold coins.

They were a delegation of twelve, in the end, including Reuben – Deulebene of Lynn, Ursell Quatrebouches, Uncles Baruch and Joseph, Hanna (or Ben, rather), Isaac le Docteur and David, le Puncteur's son (though his father had remained in West Cheap), Rabbi Abraham and Reuben and Haim of Lincoln; plus Serlo and

Elias and two of Ursell's guards. The latter were to carry the heavier of the two chests, on a litter. Serlo was the only one of them armed, wearing a short sword at his hip with some swagger.

Hanna wanted to be out among the crowd. She was bored, would have studied her spells if she were not sitting too close to others who might glance over her shoulder at what she was reading. David was sitting just behind her, with the frail figure of le Docteur. Fortunately for Hanna's disguise, her fellow cask-carrier seemed loath to have anything to do with Ben, almost to the point of her feeling indignant about it on Ben's behalf.

It was uncomfortably hot and sticky in the boats now they were moored. They both belonged to the Quatrebouches – on an ordinary day they earned a good income for Ursell's family as river taxis. The one Hanna was in had a cormorant's head carved at its prow. She could feel the sweat trickling down her armpits and back. She tried to test herself on the names of the angels required for the invisibility spell, and failed. Reuben sat next to her, leaning into her, making her even hotter. Serlo sat on the other side, his huge forehead beaded with perspiration and his face a sick white; he was unused to travelling by boat.

From their mooring Hanna could see the Hall, the grey towers of the Minster behind it and the other buildings of the monastery and palace, as the still rising tide knocked their boat rhythmically against the wharf. The land was marshy, the shore shingle. Hanna started, as all of a sudden a heron flew up out of the reeds, its vast wings a monstrous flapping.

The elders were rehashing their arguments of the previous evening. They looked distinguished, Hanna thought, each with his particular style of beard, sitting in parallel rows in the boats, in their fine, brightly coloured tunics and caps. Uncle Baruch was particularly resplendent in his trademark scarlet. The sound of the Minster's bell brought the argument to an abrupt end. She could see the bell swinging in its tower next to the church and the black-robed monk who pulled the rope at its foot.

'That's just to announce the arrival of the king's procession,' said Ursell.

'Well, I'm going to see what's going on,' said Uncle Baruch. 'Ben, come with me.'

He was already climbing out of the boat and onto the wharf. Hanna at once scrambled after him. Finally, thought Hanna, she could be a part of what was happening. If anyone in the rest of the party protested, she and Baruch were gone before they could hear.

Away from the river the air was stifling. Hanna had never seen such a crowd. It seemed that visitors from all corners of Richard's kingdom were here to greet the arrival of the new king. Those with money were keeping themselves amused while waiting, while those without were taking the opportunity to earn some. Uncle Baruch and Hanna ignored the sellers of coronation trinkets, but Baruch bought them each a seed cake from a boy sitting on the ground with a whole basketful in front of him. Hanna made sure her coins were deep inside her tunic pocket, beyond the skilful fingers of any would-be thief, remembering le Docteur's warnings about the prisoners released by the new king. She also pressed her hand against her hidden pouch; it was quite safe, her notes were still secure inside.

She and her uncle dodged and ducked their way through the hordes, then scrambled to the top of a grass bank so they'd have a good view.

Just below them a cockfight was underway, surrounded by a shouting, jeering crowd, who shouted all the louder when one of the birds was wounded and spurted blood. The beer seller stood nearby was selling out fast, it seemed, tipping the barrel to get the last of the liquid. He was being urged on by two loud and impatient customers, one with a head of blazing red hair and the other – Hanna knew them! – Marmaduke Darrell and de Cuckney, Malbisse's squire.

Instinctively, she pulled her hood up over her head. She felt sick. Of course they were here. After all, that was why the Beast had left York for London. She scanned the other faces, but of the Beast himself there was no sign.

She was about to speak to Uncle Baruch, but the royal procession was now approaching, the crowds cheering. Hanna had a good view of all the Christian high-ups as they made their way into the Minster in their fancy dress – bishops, abbots and what-have-you in white robes and richly coloured, heavily brocaded shawls, and so many priests, their heads deep in their silken hoods, following behind a huge great wooden cross in front, which required two men built like oxen to carry it, with boys of an age with Hanna carrying lights, swinging incense burners and water buckets immediately behind. Her nostrils filled with the intense, heady aroma.

Next came the nobles, very grand in their robes and carrying all manner of ceremonial gold – candlesticks and spurs, two rods – one topped with a dove, the other with a cross, swords in fancy scabbards. A team of some twelve men bore the chequer, upon which were placed the royal arms and robes; and then came the crown itself, glittering with precious stones. Soon-to-be king Richard Hanna could scarcely see. He had a tall-hatted bishop on either side of him. They walked under a scarlet and gold silk canopy held up at each corner on a lance carried by a swanky baron.

'I thought he'd be taller,' said a man standing next to Hanna, 'he doesn't look like much of a warrior to me.'

The procession passed and Hanna and her uncle returned to the boat at the wharf. There, they waited until, finally, the bell rang out once more, then joined by the bells from churches across London, to announce the crowning of the new king.

'Friends, it is time,' Baruch said.

Together with Ursell's men, Serlo and Elias hauled and pushed the caskets out of the wherries. Whereas before Hanna and Uncle Baruch had passed unremarked, now with the caskets and so many older, bearded men all in their finest tunics, blue and green and red, they constituted a conspicuous procession of their own. Rabbi Abraham led, with Reuben at his side, Baruch and Joseph following next, then Hanna and David with their casket (David still avoiding eye contact), the Quatrebouches men carrying the chest on the litter, and the others behind that, including, Hanna assumed, Serlo and Elias, as she couldn't see them anywhere.

Their party was carried inexorably along by the mass of people intent on entering the Hall. Hanna and David walked awkwardly together, the casket between them pulling painfully on their arms. Hanna began to feel quite faint in the heat. She doubted she could make it into the hall and to the king's table without first putting the casket down and resting.

She became aware of murmurings in the crowd, and then as they were about to pass through the great doors, a voice shouted, 'Here come the Jews, come to cast their enchantments on our new king!'

She started. What did they know? 'Enchantments?' They must be talking about her, but she wished no ill upon the king. Her notes might be concealed within her tunic, but she had no plans for 'enchantments'.

There was no time for further thought. Hanna felt a sharp blow to the head. A general outcry arose against their party. Hanna and David both stumbled, not quite dropping the casket, and the fists of others in the crowd were bearing down upon them.

Through the mounting cries of 'Expel the Jews, on the king's orders!' 'Seize the Christ-killing Jews!' Hanna heard Uncle Baruch shouting, 'Leave the chest, boys, and go – make your way back to the boat.'

He and Uncle Joseph were swallowed up by the crowd ahead, Rabbi Abraham and Reuben had vanished. She looked across at David and saw in his face the terror that she too felt. They both let go the chest. The man who had struck Hanna on the head now fell instead upon the coins and it was this that saved her. David ran in one direction and Hanna in another. Those nearest them in the crowd were more interested in fighting each other to seize what treasure they could than in beating either of them to a pulp. Hanna heard someone cry out in pain but didn't know who it was. She ducked out of the scrum around the casket. She needed to get out of the way – people were falling, being trampled in the crush. She had no idea where David had gone, or the others of their party. She squeezed her way through, alone, but anonymous. Her head hurt. Those around her were shouting, baying for Jewish blood, unaware of the young Jew pushing past them and away from the Hall.

Wildly, Hanna elbowed her way through the crowd and up the same bank from where previously she had watched the coronation procession arrive. She jostled against the seed cake seller, who clutched the basket holding his remaining cakes to his chest. Ahead of them a young man tripped and nearly fell. He was carrying a small boy on his shoulders, and dragging another, slightly larger, wailing boy by the hand and out of the way of danger – unless they were to fall and be crushed under the feet of all the others who were pushing behind them.

Realising that she was not being chased, Hanna made herself slow down, despite her pounding heart, to merge with the crowd and so disappear quite naturally, without any need for tricks – if indeed she could remember any, which she couldn't. Terror had driven every last word from her brain. She felt her head where she'd been hit – there was a bump and it was painful, but no blood – her thick curls and hood had protected her. Outside the Minster, below, all she could see was a seething mass of humanity. All around her the air rang with the chants of 'Kill the Jews! The king's orders!' This was the sport that the crowd had been waiting for – forget the mere ceremony of a coronation and the glimpsed view of wealth in which they had no hope of sharing. Now was their opportunity for a punch-up on a far grander scale than any paltry cockfight. Drunk on beer and bloodlust, the crowd was united – for now – in the heat of a violent hatred of a common enemy – the Christ-denying, Christ-killing Jews – and enjoying the fight.

A young man Hanna recognised not just from the cockfight burst out of the crowd – de Cuckney. Looking frantically around him, he shouted, his words somewhat slurry, 'There's no more Jews here – let's to West Cheap – to find the gold in their houses and burn them down!' Hanna watched as young men and boys, their faces ugly with hate, surged behind their new leader, as they ran east towards the City.

Yet the fighting in front of Hanna continued. The man who'd been selling pewter coronation souvenirs, now all scattered on the ground, was throwing punches at another – perhaps the one who'd sent the trinkets flying – while his boy bobbed between their legs, trying to gather up the merchandise before it was all trodden into the dust and ruined – and then it seemed that others joined in, just for the fun of it, while those among whom Hanna was concealed stood laughing.

'Kill the Jew! Kill! Kill!'

Hanna turned in terror to the sound of renewed shouting, but it wasn't her they shouted for. A group of men was dragging a body along between them. His head was all bloody and his scarlet robes torn. It was Uncle Baruch. At his head rode a Christian priest on a fine dark bay, the priest's sword drawn and held aloft in front of him. His boyish face, substantial form and untidy blonde hair were familiar… Prior William. He was accompanied by several soldiers, their swords also drawn and keeping at bay those of the crowd who still howled for Baruch's blood like dogs.

As the crowd pressed closer once more Prior William rounded on them and shouted in a mixture of English and French, but his accent clearly that of York. 'I know this man,' he said, 'and he is dying. Better we should save his soul for Jesus than send him unbaptised into eternal perdition. Call yourself Christians – you should be ashamed of yourselves in your lust for blood. Come with me rather, to pray for this Jew's soul.'

Prior William was saving his friend's life, it seemed, but claiming his soul. He had already turned his horse away and was continuing to clear a path through the crowd for those carrying Uncle Baruch's body.

Should Hanna follow? What could she do – plead with the prior? Seize Baruch's body – on her own? Where were Serlo and Elias and the others? 'Go back to the boat,' Uncle Baruch had said. Hanna looked around – but knew no one. William and her uncle were already almost out of sight. She turned and ran back towards the river, now heedless of the crowds around her, desperate for the sanctuary of the wherry and to know she wasn't alone.

The boat was still there, the cormorant's head at its prow. Hanna hurled herself in, landing heavily, and lay, a sweaty heap of sore limbs, her face pressed against the musty-smelling floor. The sounds of the crowd had all but faded; a curlew cried mournfully overhead. Her panting subsided and she felt her heartbeat slow. She was safe.

Then the pile of rags next to which she had landed stirred, grunted and sat up. It was Reuben, his face pale and streaked with blood, snot and tears. By the look of him, his clothes torn, bloody and muddy, his escape had been narrower than Hanna's.

'I thought you were dead,' he said. 'I thought they got you. I thought we were all dead.'

'No, I – I got away.' Hanna felt suddenly ashamed to have escaped so completely unscathed. 'Are we the only ones here? Where are the others?' She raised herself up to check the second boat. It was still there, but empty.

'It's just us. I don't know where my dad and the others are.' Reuben was gabbling. 'I – I thought I was dead, Ben. I ran, but they caught me, the crowd, I kept running and my clothes tore and then I fell and they were kicking me and kicking me and then others came and pulled them off, said to let me go, I was only a boy. They had swords and threatened the crowd with them, held them off while I turned and ran again, ran out into the marsh, and stayed there until there was no sight of anyone, then came here – but I don't know where my dad is, or any of the others.'

Hanna said nothing, just handed him the flask of water they'd brought with them on the boat. He took a swig and handed it back. They sat in silence. A mosquito whined past Hanna's ear. She swiped at it and missed. They waited, but no one came.

16. FIRE

Then, finally, the tide turned, the current ready to take them back the way they had come that morning. The sun, still hazy behind the clouds, was now midway towards the horizon in the west and the wind had dropped. 'We should go,' Hanna said. 'No, we should wait,' said Reuben. 'My dad… What if the others come back to the boat, and find it gone? They won't all fit in the other boat.'

'There's no time,' Hanna said. 'We have to get back to your home and mother, your sisters. To the others at Uncle Joseph's…'

She left her sentence unfinished.

'But what about my dad?' Reuben was close to tears.

'They've probably found a safe way to walk back,' said Hanna. 'There's people that'll help them – like the people that helped you.' Hanna didn't sound certain enough to reassure the small boy.

'Come on, let's go, Reuben,' said Hanna. She reached across, untied the wherry from its moorings and pushed off. She took the oars and began to row. It was bigger and heavier than the boat in York, but the tide was with them. There were plenty of other craft around, but nowhere near as many as in the morning; no reason why any should give Hanna and Reuben's boat a second glance.

She welcomed the familiar feeling of strength and physical wellbeing as her rowing settled into a steady rhythm. It stopped her heart thumping and eased her feelings of panic. She made herself smile at Reuben, who was keenly scanning the river ahead.

'You're doing a grand job, lad,' Hanna told him.

She knew she needed to keep Reuben distracted so that he wouldn't start crying for his dad. Reuben was young enough and Hanna (Ben) near enough to adulthood for Reuben to trust his older companion to know what to do. But Hanna found comfort too in the notion that the two of them were somehow working together to reach their destination and face whatever they found there, that she wasn't alone.

Yet even as she rowed she saw again Uncle Baruch's body borne away by the crowd, bloody and broken, and the heap of bodies on the ground – trampled, misshapen, crushed – where they had fallen in the sudden rush as the crowd turned mob. Which of her companions had lain among them? Her last glimpse of Uncle Joseph and Rabbi Abraham was just before Uncle Baruch told her to 'go back to the boat'. If only she'd fully mastered the powers in Granda's book, if only she could have magically beaten off the mob, dismissed them with a spell – but the voices also kept repeating in her head, 'Here come the Jews with their enchantments'. Was the attack her fault? Had she somehow put them all at risk?

She forced herself to focus once more on the rhythm of her rowing and keeping the boat close to the north shore, afraid of what currents might take hold of them midstream. Swallows swooped to catch the midges massed above the river's surface. The boat was again passing the grand houses and gardens which faced south towards the water. This morning, she'd been so happy... It was still stickily hot; the sky was growing dark with storm clouds.

'Ben, what's that?' Reuben was talking to her. 'In the sky – look – what is it?'

Hanna didn't want to stop, but rested the oars in their rowlocks, and turned round. Even against the dark clouds, the columns of smoke climbing up into the sky in the east were unmistakable.

Hanna snatched up the oars again. They couldn't afford to rest. The outward tide and Hanna's rowing had carried them rapidly down the river and they had passed the west wall of the city, but it wasn't fast enough.

'Can you see the bridge, Reuben?' she asked.

Reuben nodded, 'And the ships moored in the middle of the river. And there's lots of small boats, Ben – lots of people, too.'

Hanna brought her oars into the boat and turned round to look. Reuben was right – quite a crowd of small boats, this side of the bridge, and apparently full with people. A little ahead on the left, Hanna could see the towers of the church they called St Paul's and, just coming into view further downstream, the White Tower of the castle at the city's easternmost point. Between them, the storm clouds were now half hidden by smoke, billowing as it rose, and every so often glittering with orange stars. Hanna saw again the snarl on the face of the man she'd watched at the cockfight and heard again de Cuckney's words: 'Let's to West Cheap and burn them alive.' She saw too the raggle-taggle regiment which had assembled behind him, armed with sticks and swords and whatever weapon came to hand. 'Here comes the Jew with her enchantments' – was that what they had said? (but of course not – to the crowd there was no girl…).

She felt sick. Dimly, she was aware of a great ringing of church bells, all of them peeling at once, on and on and on – surely not because of the coronation now? They had to get there, to find out what was happening, what had happened. How far would the fire reach?

But then the boat was beginning to turn, spinning round. Transfixed by the smoke and its meaning, Hanna had failed to notice that they had reached the point where the Thames was joined from the north by the waters of the Fleet joining it. The currents created by the meeting of the two rivers swirled in a corkscrew, taking the boat with them, dragging it as if by an underwater rope towards the prison island and the large hewn rocks placed on its shore to ruin any boat which tried to land there.

Hanna pulled hard on the oars, fighting the pull of the rivers' whirlpools, directing the boat towards the moored ships and the flotilla of small boats which surrounded them, and away from the treacherous eddies where the waters of the Fleet and Thames disputed and mixed. Her shoulders ached with the effort, the first time on their journey that she'd been working against the river, rather than with it. Her face was dripping with sweat. She could see the concentration in Reuben's face as the small boy willed them on. And then, as suddenly as it had begun, they were free, shot from the sparring rivers' grip like a stopper from a bottle, back once more in the steady flow of the Thames' mainstream.

'We've done it, Ben, we've done it!' Reuben cried in triumph.

Hanna knew there was no time either for triumph or even relief. They needed to land, but Hanna wasn't sure where. That morning they had all embarked from the tiny wharf on the Walbrook, close to Uncle Joseph's and Rabbi Abraham's houses. But now it seemed as if all in that direction was ablaze. Up the hill from the river Hanna and Reuben could see orange and yellow flames surging into the sky. White smoke and grey smoke streaked through the black; and white, grey and black flakes of ash wafted down upon Hanna and Reuben and the passengers of the other small boats among which they now found themselves, and floated around them like petals of death on the dark water.

These boats weren't on a journey. Their passengers were refugees from the fire, inhabitants of the houses ablaze onshore, carrying whatever possessions they had been able to seize as they fled. The orange glow of the flames was reflected in the river and lit up the features of those Hanna and Reuben rowed past with a queer, flickering light.

'Could my ma and sisters be here, Ben, do you think, in one of these boats? Or my dad?' Reuben asked.

Hanna rested the oars momentarily as they passed a boat in which were crowded a mother, holding a baby, the dad, grandma and grandad, a huddle of soot-blackened children, a stool, a sack of wheat, cooking pot, chickens and a baby pig. For it wasn't just the houses of the Jews that were in flames – fire, once lit, being unable to discriminate between the thatched roofs of Jewish homes and those of their Christian neighbours.

'I don't know, Reuben. Maybe.'

Hanna was torn. Should they search among the passengers of the boats? But what if Sarah and the other children were trapped in the fire…

She made the decision. 'If they are in one of the boats, then they're safe, Reuben, and we'll be able to find them later. We must go to your house.'

She pulled harder on the oars as the boat moved towards the shore and was engulfed in a cloud of dark, acrid smoke gusting across the water.

Hanna's voice was hoarse and the smoke was making her cough. Reuben continued to cry.

But they were close now to the small wooden jetties between the stone warehouses which lined the docks and again beyond the Walbrook. Each jetty marked the end of a lane which led up to the markets of West and East Cheap. That morning the wharves had been busy with farmers noisily unloading their produce to take up to the markets and they were noisy still. Now, however, they were lined with people lowering buckets into the river and hauling them out again to be passed from one person to the next away and up the lane. Hanna and Reuben were close enough to see the sweat and smoke on the bucket-owners' faces. They were too caught up in what they were doing to bother about two children. Hanna selected the pier she thought would lead most directly to Reuben's house and rowed towards it. It would be quicker to go on foot, she thought, than to row up the Walbrook; she was exhausted.

Hanna brought the boat up alongside the ladder up to the jetty around the corner from the bucket people and grasped hold of one of the rungs. She handed Reuben the rope.

'Tie it round the post at the top,' she said.

He did so and she climbed up the ladder behind him.

The sound of the fire was louder now, and they could also feel its heat, though as far as Hanna could tell it had not yet spread south of Thames Street which ran parallel to the river. But the soft rain of ash which had fallen on them in the river was falling here too, and the smoke made it difficult to breathe.

Hanna bent down to Reuben to pull his hood up and round to cover his mouth and nose before doing likewise with her own.

'I'm scared, Ben. I want my ma,' said Reuben.

'I know, lad. I'm scared too. But we'll find her together, eh?'

Just then lightning flickered in the sky ahead of them, barely visible through the smoke and the flames, but followed some five or six seconds later by an immense clap of thunder. The two children clung to each other in terror.

'It's the storm coming, Reuben – it'll put out the fire,' Hanna said. 'We don't need to be scared of that.'

Keeping close to the warehouse wall, they made their way from the wooden pier and into the lane. Men and women stood at intervals all the way up it, passing the buckets of water north towards the fire, but periodically also dousing the warehouses next to which they stood. There was slippery mud underfoot, and several times she and Reuben nearly fell as they ran. Hanna was near tears with frustration: how were they ever going to reach Reuben's home?

Ahead of them and to their right the fire was burning fiercely, its underlying roar punctuated with sudden cracks followed by a glittering shower of sparks. The heat was intense upon their faces, turning them a feverish red. The members of the human chain passing their buckets along the lane glowed orange, oblivious to Hanna and Reuben.

At West Cheap they were face to face with the fire itself. The market place was alive with flames. The roofs and walls of the buildings were gone, only their beams and posts remaining, their angles haphazard, ablaze.

'Ma!' Hanna could scarcely hear Reuben's cries above the roar of the blaze. Hanna held tight to his hand. The fire extended as far as she could see, to west and east. She could see no way through to reach their lane, or any of the other streets where she knew that Reuben's family and friends lived.

Lightning flickered again and the clap of the thunder followed almost immediately.

Then with a terrible 'crack' a beam snapped and fell towards where Hanna and Reuben were standing. Hanna had to pull them both hard back out of its way and into the shadow of the alley away from the fire, just as the heavens opened and the rain began to pelt down, hissing as it hit the flames and hot ash.

'Reuben – is that you?' The man sheltering next to them shone black with sweat and soot, an empty bucket at his feet. Reuben had his face hidden in Hanna's tunic. The man, whose face appeared kind, his smile wrinkles white creases in the grime, asked Hanna instead. 'That's Reuben, isn't it, Rabbi Abraham's boy? I'm Walter the smith.'

Hanna nodded, shivering as the rain hit her skin. She'd never seen this man before, but with powerful shoulders and forearms he was every inch the smith. Friend, or foe? He seemed to sense her mistrust.

'My smithy's in the lane where Reuben's family lives. Reuben plays with my children. Rabbi Abraham' – here Walter hesitated – 'Rabbi Abraham, Sarah and their family, we're neighbours.'

The rain was falling in sheets in front of them.

'They're good people,' he added.

'Have you seen Reuben's ma and the girls? Are they safe?' Hanna asked. Reuben lifted his face from Hanna's tunic for Walter's answer.

'I don't know. The houses were ablaze when I got there, and everyone was saying it'd started with some bad feeling against the Jews to do with the coronation – but it's all our houses that's gone up, too, all our livelihoods. It was the valuables what they wanted, to thieve and plunder. Some of the king's men came, soldiers – but there weren't enough of them to stop the mob.'

Reuben broke in. 'My ma! Have you seen Ma and my sisters?'

Walter hesitated. 'No, I haven't. But many got safe away to the White Tower, went there to take refuge, seek the king's protection from the constable. You'd best go there. You'll be safe enough now, I reckon, to go on foot – the bridge is still there, over the Walbrook. That's what you should do. Your ma and sisters as likely as not got safe to the Tower, Reuben. You go there.'

The Tower. The king's protection? Hanna took Reuben's hand once more. Steam rose. The ash under their feet had turned to a filthy sludge. Water ran in rivulets down all their faces, streaking the soot on Walter's.

'Thank you,' Hanna said. 'Come on, Reuben, let's go.'

17. THE WHITE TOWER

The watchman belched loudly and smelt the beer and roast meat he'd eaten earlier repeated on the damp night air. A funny old evening it'd been, he thought. The day had been easy enough – with the constable and the castle's men away at the coronation, he'd even dozed his way through the sticky mid-day heat – then late afternoon some of the men had come roaring back, with news of fire and riot, the king's Jews under attack. From his vantage point on the walkway at the top of the Tower he could hear the church bells' alarum and had a fine view of the fire's flames, now pretty much extinguished by the storm. And what a storm.

After the soldiers on horseback had come some of the Jews themselves, on foot and by boat – a rum crowd, he thought – among them faces he knew from the markets of West and East Cheap, escorted by more of the constable's soldiers. Some – the Jews that is, not the soldiers – were in tears, looked as though they'd been through a bit. Some were carrying blankets and pots and pans, as if they expected to stay for a while. Later still had come the constable himself and a group of men, all Jews, the watchman had guessed, in fine clothes, though some of them also looked the worse for wear – maybe those who'd gone to see the king.

Anyway, he'd been given orders that the castle was on high alert – whether to give more Jews the king's protection, or to keep out those who threatened them – so no snoozing on his watch this evening. But now who was that banging on the gate below?

Holding his torch aloft, he leaned over the wall and shouted, 'Who's there?' What was the porter up to? The torch was no use, it lit him up, but not whoever it was below, in fact it put them into even deeper darkness from where he stood. A voice drifted up to him faintly, but he couldn't make out properly what it was saying. 'Who's there?' he shouted a second time and this time he heard. It sounded like a young boy's voice.

'I am Ben, one of the Jews of York, and this is Reuben, son of Rabbi Abraham of West Cheap. We seek the king's protection.'

He might have guessed that there'd be more of them. He shouted down to the porter. 'Open up down there!'

Hanna waited, too wet, cold and exhausted to be afraid, listening to the rattling of bolts and keys on the other side of the massive gate in front of her – far bigger than York's. Reuben mutely held her hand and stared dully ahead. His hair was plastered against his face, water running down it. He hadn't spoken a word since they left Walter and the fire, not even to complain that he was cold and his clothes soaked through. The storm had only finally eased off as they made their way along the field paths that led from the city to the castle. Please let Sarah and Rabbi Abraham and Reuben's sisters be inside, Hanna thought. And the others… She just wanted it all to be over, for someone else to take responsibility, to make it all right. These weren't the sights she'd expected to see…

Suddenly a door within the gate opened to their right. A man's blonde-bearded head poked out and spoke gruffly.

'Where are you then? Oh there you are – no more than boys, you're right – let's be having you then.'

Hanna and Reuben passed the porter, holding the gate, and entered within the castle walls. Ahead of them loomed the keep, silver-white in the light of the moon. To one side of the gate Hanna briefly looked through a door into a small room lit by the glow of a brazier in front of which lay the hulk of a huge wolf-hound. It half-opened one eye but shut it again, taking no further interest in the new arrivals. Hanna wondered with a pang how Beaumon was faring, and then Will… Other buildings stood indistinctly against the walls of the castle.

'Follow me,' the porter said. 'Stay close.' Hanna stayed close enough to notice that the broad top of their guide's head was shiny bald, except for a few stray blonde wisps, and like the tower gleamed white in the moonlight. He led them across to a large wooden building to the right of the keep. The guard stood to one side as the porter approached. He banged with his fist on the door.

'Open up,' he said, 'I've brought you another two, young 'uns this time. And hurry up, it's cold out here.'

The door creaked open and the porter again stood to one side to let Hanna and Reuben through, giving them a shove to hurry them on their way and shutting the door behind them, his duty done.

Hanna was hit by a wave of warmth, murmuring voices and crying. The fire was burning in the hearth at the middle of the large hall, which was lit with more torches. The smoke drifted up towards the opening in the roof, but also hung thickly in the air. Its bitter, woody smell was mixed with that of sweat, wet wool and whatever it was that was cooking on the fire. Men sat grouped around it. Away from the fire, the floor space was covered by straw and people, men to one side, and women to the other, some asleep, some talking to each other, some soothing wailing children and settling them down to sleep, others weeping or comforting those weeping – several hundred people, it seemed to Hanna: as many as those who had crowded into the synagogue the previous day? She wasn't sure. Everything to Hanna seemed a smoky blur.

She could sense Reuben next to her, anxiously scanning the room for his family. Hanna couldn't see them among all the confusion of bodies, but caught sight of Uncle Joseph's silvery beard and curls where he knelt by a youngish woman who was crying – was that his daughter, Elise? He was holding a letter, Mordecai was at his side…

Then Hanna was distracted by the figures of Isaac le Docteur and Elias bending over an unmistakable large form to one side of the fire – Serlo. He was lying down, inert… But he must be alive as Hanna could see his chest periodically shuddering and just hear the loud rasp of his snore. What on earth was he doing, asleep? His clothes were torn and wet. Isaac and Elias were together struggling to remove some of them. Elias looked up and saw Hanna and Reuben by the door.

'Reuben! Ben!' he cried, dropping Serlo's foot with its boot still half on, and making his way towards them as quickly as he could without treading on anyone.

'Elias! I am so glad to see you,' exclaimed Hanna. Elias swept Reuben up in his powerful arms. Hanna could see tears rolling down the burly bodyguard's cheeks as he turned to carry the small boy towards the men closest to the fire.

'Rabbi Abraham,' she watched him say, 'Reuben is alive.'

'My son,' Rabbi Abraham uttered the words in a guttural animal cry, lifting his head from his hands as he sat hunched over. His face, above his dark beard, glowed dark red in the firelight, his eyes swollen – from crying? Where were Sarah, and the girls? Hanna recognised some of the men who sat with him – the rotund form of Isaac le Gros, Haim, Deulebene, grizzle-bearded Crispin – so at least they were safe, but she couldn't see David or his father, le Puncteur.

Elias returned to Hanna and hugged her, speaking softly into her wet hair. 'Hanna, praise G–d, you are safe.' It was the first time that anyone had used her real name for so long and, after all that had happened that day, she burst into tears. Elias at once pulled away.

'Ben,' she heard him say, as if to remind her who she must be, 'Come, dry yourself by the fire and eat.'

He took her by the elbow and guided her, still sobbing, closer to the fire. Someone gave her a cloth to wipe her face and she managed to greet those who sat near her. Elias disappeared briefly, returning with a blanket and a cup of the soup that was simmering in the cooking pots. Hanna was by now shivering uncontrollably, but couldn't take off any of her wet clothes, not here. Elias roughly rubbed her hair dry, then wrapped the blanket around her and Hanna sipped the scalding liquid gratefully, letting the hot cup warm her hands. He squatted down beside her. Hanna wished he'd sit, settle next to her. She dimly realised that he was overwrought, his eyes too bright.

'Joseph has had a letter,' he said. 'Prior William sent a messenger. Baruch is with him, in the king's palace. He's alive but' – he hesitated.

'But what?' Hanna asked.

'The prior says he's become a Christian.'

Hanna said nothing. She'd stopped shivering, but she felt numb inside.

'Joseph and some of the others, they're going to see the king tomorrow. Serlo, he wouldn't stop crying – howling, he was, inconsolable, because he hadn't managed to protect his master, to keep Baruch safe. The Doctor dosed him with wine, till he fell asleep.'

'Your family...' She couldn't bear even to ask the question.

'Ursell and I – we got horses – we rode back. We got home before the mob came – were able to warn everyone. We got Lief and Turstin and the other horses, too.'

'And Mistress Sarah and Reuben's sisters?'

Elias couldn't meet her eyes. He was getting up to go. 'We don't know,' he said. 'The mob went first to the synagogue... My brother and his men are going now to look, with some of the constable's men. Under the king's protection. I must go with them.'

'Be careful,' she said. Elias held his hand briefly against her cheek for a moment, then left.

Hanna wanted Ma and Da, Ben and Granda so badly. She didn't want to talk anymore. She didn't want to ask about David, to find out who else was missing, to hear how any of the others escaped, or to tell anyone what had happened to her. She felt empty of all feeling, exhausted. She'd thought that when she reached the Tower it would all be over, but it wasn't.

18. NORTHAMPTON

14 Elul 3949 / 5 September 1189

Hanna reached forward to pat Lief's neck, comforted by his familiar horsey smell and regular, ambling gait. They were walking alongside the litter carrying Uncle Baruch to the house of his brother, Jacob, in Northampton (closer than Sampson in Lincoln). King Richard had released him to Uncle Joseph and a group of the elders the morning after the coronation. The king, though disgusted that this Jew of York had repudiated Prior William and his baptism as a Christian, nonetheless desired that 'his' Jews should return safely to their homes.

The king was embarrassed, le Quatrebouches said, by the treatment they had received... On King Richard's orders, the constable at the White Tower had provided the Northampton-bound party with extra guards. Ursell had supplied the horses and a litter in which to carry Baruch, and a pack pony for their luggage (greatly reduced from formerly, as most had been lost in the fire which had ravaged Uncle Joseph's West Cheap house); and they left Baruch's grey stallion, Turstin, with the Quatrebouches, in return.

Two of the guards rode up ahead, followed by Uncle Joseph and his elderly servant Mordecai, then came Hanna and the sparrow-like Isaac le Docteur with Baruch's litter, while behind rode Serlo and Elias, trailing the pack pony, and then two more king's guards. Serlo remained tearful and Elias glum, both still wretched that they had not given Baruch protection when he needed it.

Three days had passed since the coronation, riot and fire. More of what happened had emerged the following day. Elias, too, had seen the Beast's squire, de Cuckney, in the mob, together with the red-headed Scot, Darrell. The king had sent his justiciar who was also York's sheriff,

Ranulf de Glanville, to quell them – but he came with so few men that there was nothing they could do. It was a Christian knight, however, one of Quatrebouches' friends, who had helped them at West Minster, hiding Rabbi Abraham, Deulebene, le Docteur, Uncle Joseph and Haim in an ante-chamber of the Hall until it was safe to put them in a boat taking them straight to the White Tower. The knight also supplied the horses for Ursell, Elias and their men to escape, and sent his own men with Serlo to look for Baruch, David and Reuben.

Reuben… he'd clung to Hanna, Ben as he thought, when she said goodbye, a small boy, without mother or sisters, alone with his grieving father. When Hanna woke up the morning after the riot, the burials were already over. She shut her ears to conversations about a dog found gnawing on a charred limb amid the ash-sludge. What now of her hopes of finding Da and Ben? Hanna wished she'd never left York, never stolen her Granda's book – 'here come the Jews with their enchantments'… But perhaps she could still put the contents of the book to good use – in helping to make Uncle Baruch better, for instance.

Though he was physically weak, Baruch's will remained strong and it was he, from inside the litter, who was insisting that they should travel as fast as possible, whatever the discomfort, so that he could be at his family's house in the town, with his older brother, Jacob, and Jacob's wife, Floria. Hanna had done little more than greet them at Baruch and Comtessa's wedding. She wasn't sure either she or Ben had made any sort of impression on them, when the twins had just been two children among so many. But she found she didn't care about whether they'd see through her disguise. She didn't care about anything; she was just numb.

Uncle Joseph was unfamiliar with the route that they were travelling. He seemed nervous and had developed a disconcerting twitch in the bag under his left eye. He seemed even less able than formerly to assert himself against his younger colleague, even though Baruch was the one who was ill. Mordecai, who scarcely looked in a better state himself, was solicitous in his care of his master.

Once again they were passing through forest, but Hanna scarcely gave a thought to wolves or robbers. The trees were tall, their leaves a pale, end-of-summer green. She felt so tired, dazed. During both of the past two nights she had been woken by nightmares which returned her to the coronation. 'Here comes the Jew to cast her enchantments!' she heard shouted again and again and she was rowing once more with Reuben on the Thames, straining to reach his home in time to rescue his mother and sisters, and each time arriving too late.

And now it was raining again, hard. Her pages of spells were dry inside their leather pouch, where she had also put a letter from Master Thomas which had arrived for her and Uncle Baruch shortly before they left London, regretting what had happened 'especially the unfortunate business with Prior William'; he did not yet know when he was returning to York. But Hanna herself was once again wet through to the skin. She hoped that the awning of the litter was enough to ensure that Uncle Baruch remained warm and dry.

Several times in that stretch of forest she had heard the bellowing roar of rutting stags and the clash of antlers as the rival males fought for supremacy. She cast her mind back to the day of the hunt with Uncle Baruch and the Beast. That day, it seemed to her now, was when everything had started to go wrong, when Baruch had been struck by the arrow — at Malbisse's behest, Hanna was sure, if not directly by his hand.

At least if Baruch had died that day he'd have been together with his wife and son. Now, his life lay in the balance as his body lay in the litter somewhere between London and Northampton. Le Docteur was checking on him frequently, but Baruch was still far from well. The wound in his chest from the hunt had opened up again during the beating he had received on the day of the coronation and his head and much of his body were covered in cuts and bruises. He had only escaped being kicked to death thanks to Prior William's intervention.

But that had led to what the elders were referring to as his 'apostasy' – the fact Baruch had apparently agreed to become a Christian – although he had recanted as soon as he was in full control of his faculties again.

Hanna had heard them discussing it long into their last night at the White Tower, even while they were sitting in mourning for those they had buried earlier that day.

'He shouldn't have done it,' said Crispin. 'He has brought shame on his family and will bring shame on our community in Northampton if you insist on taking him to his brother there.'

'What would you have done, Crispin,' Joseph had asked quietly, 'if you had been in his place?'

'I would have died rather than be defiled with their disgusting water, that much I know,' said Crispin. 'I told him it was foolish to go, but he wouldn't listen –'

'I don't think he was in a position to resist Prior William.' It was the quavery voice of le Docteur. 'He would have been in considerable pain, and may not even have been fully conscious.'

Nearby, there was the sound of strangulated crying. It was Serlo. Hanna was aware of Elias moving across, could hear quiet words of comfort.

'Now is not the time for this discussion, perhaps,' said Crispin. 'But there is something that I should tell you – I have already sent a messenger ahead to Northampton to tell them what has transpired.'

Hanna was glad that le Docteur was less concerned about Uncle Baruch's spiritual well-being than with helping him to get physically better. But she did not have the same confidence in Isaac's skills as she did in Granda and Da's. Isaac had bled Baruch both evenings, a practice Hanna knew they disapproved of.

Hanna thought longingly – and guiltily – of the spells inside the book hidden inside her tunic, but knew that even if she had mastered them that the current company would never agree to her trying one of them on her uncle and there would be no opportunity for her do so in secret. Yet she found the names of the angels running constantly through her head, *Nasargiel, Dotham, Kemnel, Tamiel,* while at the same time wondering if there were things she would have been able to do if she had watched more closely which medicines Granda had prescribed when.

The rain was easing now, though remained a constant drip-dripping through the leaves of the trees. Surely it couldn't be that much further to Northampton? If Baruch died, it would be her fault. But his condition was stable – if only they could get him safely to Northampton and into the care of his family... *Nasargiel, Dotham, Kemnel, Tamiel.*

'Come on Lief,' she murmured, 'just a little faster.'

Uncle Jacob's household was clearly expecting them – Crispin's messenger must have arrived. Baruch's family house was again built of stone, though not on the grand scale of Spen Lane. The servants and children took their horses to the stable and carried their small amount of luggage into the house. Hanna and Serlo helped to unharness the Quatrebouches' horses from the litter and then, with le Docteur, followed Jacob's men as they carried it, with Baruch still inside, across the courtyard to a room at the back of the house.

The room was freshly swept, with a mattress on the floor, and lit by a candle; dry but chilly. This wasn't where she'd put Ben if he were sick, and this were her house, thought Hanna. Between them, they manoeuvred Baruch off the litter and onto the mattress as gently as they could. He was barely conscious and didn't appear to have any sense of where he was or even who they were. Tears rolled silently down Serlo's face. Hanna felt cold, scared, alone.

Upstairs, in the main part of the house, the living room was lit by torches and candles and had a fire burning in a wall-built fireplace with chimney. Elegantly dressed in tunics of fine blue wool, Jacob and Floria greeted the travellers warmly, but asked nothing about Baruch. Uncle Joseph didn't make any introductions, and the couple appeared not to recognise 'Ben': 'he' was just another member of the party, in some way connected with Baruch. Hanna hid in the shadows.

Her Uncle Jacob was talking to Joseph, asking him if his wife Anna was any better. Jacob was tall like Baruch and his eyes grey like Baruch's and Ma's, but Jacob's gaze was less intense and his movements less definite than theirs.

'Anna, as far as I know, is no worse,' said Joseph. The muscle under his eye was twitching erratically. 'Thank you for asking. But I am so sorry, Jacob. Your brother, Baruch, is very sick.'

'Crispin's messenger arrived from London yesterday. He told us what happened.'

'Do you mean the riot? How he got his injuries?'

'Yes – and his conversion to Christianity.' Jacob's voice was quiet; Hanna could barely hear him.

'According to them, Jacob. We only have their word for it.'

'You deny that he was profaned with their bitter, accursed water?'

'He was too weak – too physically weak – to do otherwise.' Joseph hesitated. 'It was his friend, Prior William from St Mary's. You'd have seen him when you came to Baruch's wedding party?'

Jacob nodded. Joseph continued:

'I never liked Baruch's friendship with him – both far too fond of their material pleasures – but if it weren't for the prior then the mob would have taken him.'

'Better that he had died then, a loyal and honourable Jew.'

Joseph said nothing.

'As it is, he has brought shame upon his family and,' Jacob stopped and Hanna looked at him, fearing that he might break down and cry. Then he continued. 'The decision has been taken. He is no longer a Jew, and he is no longer a member of this family. He can stay here tonight. Tomorrow, he must go.'

'It will kill him, Jacob. He is your brother.'

'Not any more. The rabbi, the community – we went through it again and again.' He hesitated. 'They gave me little choice – my children, my grandchildren, I have them to think of –'

'What does your rabbi say? If Baruch wants to pray –'

'He will not come.'

Joseph stared at Jacob. He brushed at his eye with his hand, as if to stop its twitching.

'We should have stayed in London,' he said, eventually. 'It was your brother who insisted… If you had been through what we've been through… You will speak to him, surely?'

Jacob shook his head. 'I will not. He is already dead to me.'

Hanna crossed the courtyard to Baruch's room. Le Docteur was sitting next to him, his lips moving in prayer. Again, he held a bowl of bright red blood in his hands. Baruch lay unmoving, his eyes closed; his face was grey and covered in a light sheen of sweat, his beard knotty, unkempt. His tunic was open to reveal the festering wound on his chest – de Malbisse's work, thought Hanna.

'I just came to say goodnight,' said Hanna, standing in the doorway.

'That's all right, my boy, come in, come in,' said le Docteur.

Hanna went into the room and stood by the bed, feeling awkward and unsure of herself under the doctor's gaze. Tentatively, she took her uncle's hand.

'Goodnight, Uncle Baruch,' she said. There was no reply.

In her dreams she was again back in London on the day of the coronation, carrying the casket with David. Yet this time the leader of the mob was not de Cuckney but the Beast himself, his pale blue eyes flashing and his scar bright white against his skin. And the boy following behind him was Will…

She woke, drenched with sweat. It was dark in the room. With the room's door and shutters closed it was hard to tell what time it was. Someone come in. Whoever it was opened a window, letting in cold air, but still no light – it was not yet dawn.

'Elias, Mordecai, I need your help. Wake up,' said Uncle Joseph.

She sat up. 'I'm awake, Uncle. I can help.'

'I need you to wake Elias and Mordecai up, and send them to Baruch's room.'

Hanna had slept in the clean clothes one of Jacob's household had given her the previous evening. She gave Elias a shake, and Serlo, too – it seemed too disrespectful to do the same to Mordecai, but she gently called his name. All four crossed the courtyard to Baruch's room. Le Docteur and Joseph were standing outside. They both looked utterly exhausted.

'Ben, *Hanna*, – you must go away. You too, Serlo. Mordecai and Elias, you must fetch water and help me wash Baruch's body,' Joseph said.

So her uncle was dead.

She and Serlo stood together in the courtyard. He was shaking with silent sobs. Hanna put her arm round his shoulder, though it scarcely reached. She didn't feel old enough for this. Da and Granda should be here, Ma. Jacob was Baruch's brother, but he was nowhere to be seen. She thought of Ben – where was he? Maybe he, like Uncle Baruch, was dead. Still she did not cry. Behind her, she heard Elias and Mordecai drawing water from the well. She shivered.

'Come on,' she said, and led Serlo back inside to seek what warmth they could from the ashes of the previous night's fire.

Their funeral procession consisted of Elias and Serlo at front and back of the litter in which Baruch's body lay, with Uncle Joseph, who carried his prayer book, Mordecai, Hanna, who carried the spade, and Le Docteur following; Baruch's body was concealed by the litter's awning.

The air was cold and the stars and moon still bright in the sky, occasionally hidden by cloud. The cemetery where Northampton's Jews buried their dead was outside the town, as at York. Once at the place, the small procession continued on past its gate and into the open space beyond. The grass was long and wet with dew. They laid the shrouded body on the ground and took it in turns to dig the grave, Serlo, Elias, Uncle Joseph and Hanna; le Docteur did not have the strength. When the grave was deep enough they laid Baruch's body in it and then Uncle Joseph took his book and read: '*I say of the Lord, my refuge and stronghold, my G—d in whom I trust, that He will save you from the fowler's trap, from the destructive plague. He will cover you with his pinions. You will find refuge under his wings…*'

As Joseph spoke the words the pink light of dawn glimmered in front of him. Serlo sobbed, quietly. Joseph finished and again they took it in turns with the spade. When the body was covered and the grass clods back in place on top of the grave, the funeral party walked back to Jacob's house without talking; Serlo's sobbing was reduced to loud sniffs. By the time they reached the house, the sun was fully risen, but obscured by cloud.

Hanna felt for the notes she had made from Granda's book, still secure in the pouch hidden inside her tunic. Now she knew which spell to learn – one to avenge Uncle Baruch's death.

19. HOME

They entered York four days later, just before the gates were locked for the night. It was raining lightly and the streets were already empty. The ground underfoot was soft, deadening the sound of their horses' hooves. They made their way up Coney Street, past Joseph's house, and then Hanna was home. She said goodbye to Lief, scarcely listening while Joseph – the muscle under his left eye still twitching – spoke briefly with Granda. She then held Ma's hand tightly, leaning against Granda, and watched as Joseph, Mordecai, Serlo and Elias led Lief away to Spen Lane where they would break the news to Comtessa that Baruch was never coming home.

Hanna was too tired that night to give anything but the barest outline of the facts, telling Ma and Granda scarcely more than Joseph had – that Baruch had died from injuries received at the hands of Christian rioters. She didn't even mention the stranger Todros and her attempts to find out what had happened to Da and Ben. Jessie and Ma relit the fire and heated water for her to bathe.

Too tired to eat, Hanna went almost at once to bed, where she fell asleep encircled by her mother's arms. She didn't hear the knock on the outside door, and the messenger summoning Granda to go next door to Joseph's house to hear with Rabbi Yom Tov and the other men of the community Joseph's account of the events of the riot, their friend's apostasy, rejection by his brother and the Jews of Northampton, and death. They discussed long and sorrowfully into the night, and prayed. So she knew nothing of the bitter argument between Granda and the rabbi, in which Granda argued that their fellows in Northampton were wrong to reject Baruch, and the rabbi said that they were right.

When Hanna woke next day, sun was streaming into the room and Ma was already up. Hanna had slept without interruption. She stretched, and luxuriated – home. Maybe now everything could be all right, her misdemeanours with magic consigned to the past, her life as Hanna here in York to live. Except everything wasn't all right. Da and Ben were still away; her magic had provoked a riot in which people had been killed; Uncle Baruch, whom she had done nothing to help, was dead – yet she wanted to use that same magic to exact her revenge.

But still, she felt well. She got up, peed in the pot and splashed her face with the cold water that Ma had left her. There was no sign of Ben's tunic and leggings she'd stripped off the previous evening – Ma must have already taken them to wash – but the leather pouch lay on the floor. Hanna picked it up. She opened the chest at the end of the bed and scent of lavender filled the room – Ma had placed this year's flowers, fresh dried, between her clothes. She pushed the pouch to the bottom of the chest, pulled out her everyday, practical brown linen tunic and put it on.

Now, she was Hanna again – to whom none of these horrible things had happened.

'My poor, lovely girl,' Ma said. 'I should never have let you go.'

She put her hand on Hanna's. They were eating outside in the courtyard, shaded from the bright September sun by the trees whose fruit hung ripe and almost ready to pick. Ma and Hanna sat on the rush mat that Will's ma had woven and given to them; Granda, his limbs too stiff to sit comfortably on the floor, was on one of the low stools. Ma's face, arms and hands were a couple of shades darker than when Hanna left, from the hours she'd spent outside, picking the beans in their courtyard garden, which still lay in neat rows in the sun to finish drying for winter storage.

Granda, too, had apparently not spent all the time Hanna had been away shut inside with his books. The contrast between his shock of white hair and black eyebrows was all the more startling against tanned skin.

The tremor in his hands seemed worse, Hanna noticed, and wondered how he'd managed with treating his patients. He'd grimaced slightly when she'd asked how Leo, Muriel's grandson, had got on, and had mumbled his reply. She'd have to wait until they were working alone together again to find out.

'I'm fine, Ma, honest I am.' Hanna pulled her hand away. 'But Uncle Baruch…'

'We will go to sit with Comtessa in a short while, take them food.'

'I thank G–d that you are returned safe to us,' said Granda. 'We have missed you so much, Hanna.'

Hanna swallowed, managed a half smile. Being Hanna once more gave her hope. She was Hanna, returned from Rouen, where – their new story went – it was Ben's turn to stay with his cousins until Da returned. She had told Ma and Granda the events of the past three weeks in far more detail than the previous night, while still omitting so much that mattered, including her brief dockside encounter.

'Those unclean idolaters!'

Ma was still expostulating about the Christians and the riots. 'They are all the same. Why, only last week here in York, Muriel was telling me –'

'Have you listened to what Hanna said, Abigail? Everything she said told us that they are not all the same. Prior William rescued Baruch –'

'And made him forswear his faith! You said yourself their friendship spelled trouble.'

Hanna felt a sense of rising panic. Her parents' frequent disagreements rarely bothered her – they flared up, they made up – but the threads binding Ma and Granda together were so much more delicate.

'And other Christians helped Joseph and the others escape,' Granda continued. 'Joseph was emphatic on that point. Our Ranulf de Glanville and the king's soldiers might not have been much use, but it was a Christian knight who helped Joseph and the others escape to the Tower, Joseph said – and the mob that set the houses on fire were common criminals –'

'Common *Christian* criminals,' said Ma, standing up, her voice steely. 'Led, Hanna says, by one of de Malbisse's men. I am going to pack up the fruit and eggs Jessie's prepared to take to Comtessa's. Excuse me.'

'Abigail,' Granda began to remonstrate, but Ma was gone. He sighed.

'Don't worry, Hanna,' he said, 'she'll be all right. And your ma is right in one thing at least, Hanna – we should have kept you here with us. We could have lost you…'

'So many people joined in, Granda – people no different from our neighbours here.'

She paused, feared the answer to her question. 'Could it, could it happen here, Granda?'

He sighed again. 'It can happen anywhere, my dear.' He registered the panic in her face. 'People always fear difference, people from elsewhere – even your ma. You heard her just now. And Muriel can be a deeply stupid woman… People born in the town don't trust those from the villages. The English don't like the Scots. And when it comes to different religions – you've heard Da and Master Thomas arguing. We don't like Christians because they think they've found the messiah we know we're still waiting for – and then they blame us for Jesus' death, and much more besides. Rabbi Yom Tov saw things far worse than I did, in France…

'But sometimes, just sometimes, people do get along. In Cordova, when I was a child, and before I was born – Christian, Jew and Muslim – for a while, while everyone had enough to eat and times were good, we lived well together – even while thinking each others' beliefs were wrong.'

'But York isn't Cordova, Granda.'

'But it could be – there are people of learning here. And King Richard still needs us, not to mention the monks wanting loans to build ever grander churches – things will settle down, you'll see, once the king has been on the throne a while. So long as everyone has enough to eat. Come here, my dear.'

He opened his arms and Hanna went to him, let herself be hugged, breathed in the familiar herby, medicinal

Granda smells (and felt an acute pang of missing Da).
Then he put his hands on her shoulders and looked
intently at her.

'Our lives are woven together with those of our
neighbours like the rushes of this mat here, that Will's ma
gave us. Think of Jessie, who works with us every day.
We've helped them, saved their lives – think of Will – he's
been here to help with fish traps and to read with me, by
the way, while you've been away. Due to come again
tomorrow.'

Hanna started, moved away, suddenly seeing Will's
face as she had in her nightmares, his face distorted with
hate. Ma had given her a letter from him he'd written in
reply to the one she sent him before she left, but that
didn't feel as real.

'Not that I'm encouraging you to see Will, of course,'
Granda added. 'I don't want us back where we started
before you went away.' He stood up, grimacing, but
waving away Hanna's attempt to help him.

How would she feel when she met Will, Hanna
wondered.

Granda put his hand gently on her shoulder. 'Why
don't you go and check what your mother is doing? She'll
be glad of your help. I must go to prepare myself for our
visit to Spen Lane.'

20. WHARF

Beaumon opened a sleepy eye as two ducks flew, squawking, overhead – and closed it again.

'You're not the only one who's tired, old girl,' said Will, pulling on the oars with arms still stiff from scything the wheat and oats on the Acaster estate. His face, arms and upper body were all sunburned, his hair turned from mid-brown to gold. They'd been working flat out to get the harvest in before the weather turned. The crop was poor – there'd not been enough rain in the early summer. But with de Malbisse and his immediate household away at the coronation in London, the atmosphere on the estate had been relaxed, even while they worked as fast as they could.

The boat rounded the bend in the river and passed the convent's wharf. The late afternoon sun warmed Will's back while astern behind him Jack stretched out his wings to soak up the heat.

It was nearly two months since Will had seen Hanna. Once his uncle was up and about again Will had returned home to find her letter telling him that she'd been sent to her cousins' in Rouen to keep her out of trouble. He'd written to her in answer, leaving the letter with Samuel and Abigail to forward, but had heard nothing further. Maybe it was time to put an end to their experiments with magic, he'd thought – though he hadn't said so in the letter. But he missed her, in a way that made him find the flirtatious, teasing girls on the estate irritating.

It was ten months since he'd seen Ben. Last year he and Hanna had come to help with the harvest at Acaster. Will missed them both.

Will pulled on the oars and a family of swans, their mottled grey cygnets nearly fully grown, bobbed gently up and down on the swell. He was looking forward to studying again with Master Samuel, who'd never mentioned the night in the woods, just asked Will if he was ready to read with him when he'd come to empty the fish traps for Ma. One day, Will thought, perhaps he too could put quill to vellum and write stories that others might read. He wanted to do more than simply list quantities of wheat and oats and the money each was worth. And turning words into stories and writing events into existence was itself a type of magic.

He passed the junction of the two rivers and the king's landing place busy with boats unloading sacks of grain and reached the wharf for Joseph's house. From there he could hear the buzz of voices and there seemed to be smoke from several cooking fires – was Joseph back, perhaps?

All was quiet at Hanna's. He secured the boat, pushed the oars out of sight and held out his arm for Jack to hop onto his shoulder. Then, with Beaumon, he jumped out on to the grassy bank and up to the familiar gate in the grey stone courtyard wall.

'Hello! Mistress Abigail! Jessie!' he called. There was no reply but the gate opened almost at once.

In front of him stood Hanna. She looked taller, thinner, her face pale, but her dark curls still fought to escape her red headscarf. She smiled, and the deep dimple appeared in her cheek.

'Will!'

'Hanna!'

He pushed his hair back from his face in that familiar gesture and his eyes crinkled as he smiled. She needn't have worried: Will was her friend and she felt only relief and pleasure to see him. How could she have doubted him?

They stood for a moment, awkwardly. The jackdaw, quiet, looked from one to the other. Beaumon, on the other hand, had no inhibitions in expressing her pleasure at seeing an old friend again, going down on all fours with her head on the ground and wagging not just her tail but her whole rump from side to side, and whining excitedly.

Hanna and Will laughed and the dimple re-appeared. She knelt down beside the dog and hugged her.

'Did you miss me, Beaumon? Did you miss me? I missed you,' she murmured.

'How was Rouen? When did you get back?' Will asked.

'Yesterday. It – it was fine.' She replied without looking up, nuzzling Beaumon's neck.

'How are you?' she asked. 'Ma told me your uncle is better.'

'He is. We've been harvesting, just finished. I – I was coming to see Master Samuel, to read.'

Hanna stood up and met Will's gaze.

'He's not here, I'm afraid,' she said. 'He and Ma have gone to see Comtessa again, to Uncle Baruch's house – I was supposed to go, I did yesterday, but then Ma and Granda said to stay here, to rest – oh, Will…' Her voice broke, she put her hand to her face and turned away. She really didn't want to cry.

Will stepped inside the courtyard and shut the gate behind him. A pot was on the cooking fire but there was no sign of Jessie. The hens and goats were busy with a pile of vegetable peelings. Jack flew down to join them.

'What's the matter, Hanna?' Will said.

Hanna took a deep breath and turned round.

'There's a lot to tell you. My uncle Baruch is dead.'

And it was a lot for Will to take in. She began at the beginning, the fact she'd lied about Rouen, had been made to disguise herself as Ben in order to take the role of Baruch's clerk and had ridden in the hunt with him at Acaster.

'You went as Ben?' Will kept saying, 'you pretended to be Ben?'

He was at least able to reassure her that all four of the dogs had returned safely home after the hunt. Then it was on to Baruch's injury, possibly on the orders of the Beast, and the riots in London, the Beast's men among the mob, and Baruch's conversion, rescue and death.

'But there's more, Will, things I haven't told you, things I haven't told Ma and Granda — haven't told anyone.' Will could hear the anguish in her voice.

'So tell me then,' he said.

'It's the spells, Will — I copied them out of Granda's book before I left and took them with me.' Will frowned and looked troubled.

'So what happened?'

'I think they worked, Will — they did, honestly, I'm sure they did. But' — she hesitated.

'Go on,' he said.

Will felt Hanna's excitement, despite himself, as she explained how first the spell to ensure she had a good trip worked ('You trusted a lettuce?' Will asked. 'You don't just think, of course its leaves stayed open — why would they shut?' 'Just listen,' Hanna replied) and then recounted the hold-up by highwaymen armed with bows and catapults, how she had begun to say the spell she'd learned that morning to dispel enemies, and it had summoned wolves who had attacked the highwaymen, but left the others and their horses alone, enabling them to escape.

Will listened, was thinking, said nothing.

'But' — she hesitated.

'What?'

'There was a boy, Will. It was his da who was attacked by the wolf, it bit his throat. The boy was crying for his da... And if I summoned the wolves, it's like I killed him. We just left, Will — rode off and left them.'

'That's grim,' Will said, then paused. 'You don't think' — another pause — 'that the wolves coming was just a coincidence?'

Hanna flushed red with anger. 'No, I don't, Will. You weren't there. I could tell. And' — again she hesitated — 'Then somehow the crowd knew at the coronation. They could sense my powers — "Here come the Jews with their enchantments", they said.'

'Are you sure?' said Will. 'Isn't that just one of the things that people say? I've heard my aunt, people here in York...' He stopped, silenced by the anger flashing in Hanna's eyes.

'I'm sure, Will. So do you see, it was all my fault – if I hadn't been there, none of it would have happened...'

She gulped, swallowed a sob, still determined not to cry. 'And I want to try to put things right. I can use my magic –'

'How?'

But there was shouting coming from the front of the house.

'Abigail! Hanna!'

Hanna and Will stood up, startled, as Muriel burst through the back door and into the courtyard. She looked momentarily askance at finding the two of them there together, but was undeterred from delivering her message.

'The boats,' she said, out of breath, 'they've passed Acaster. Ours is among them – Manasser paid a man to ride from Acaster to come on ahead and tell us.'

All thoughts of Baruch, the Beast and magic vanished. 'Da – my da, and Ben,' said Hanna. 'Did Manasser say anything about them?'

'No, child, he didn't,' Muriel said.

'But maybe he has letters? He wouldn't necessarily tell you that.'

Hanna felt a surge of hope. This time, surely, Da would have sent them news, even if he and Ben were still unable to return themselves, for whatever reason. And if they sent letters, her meeting with Todros would be irrelevant, it wouldn't matter that she'd lost him.

'He didn't, no,' said Muriel. 'Is your ma at Comtessa's?'

'Yes.'

'Then you go and fetch her. Tell her to come to the quay. That's where I'm going now. Gentill and the children have already gone. I'll see you there,' and with that Muriel was gone.

Hanna looked at Will expectantly, caught up in Muriel's sense of urgency, seized by a welcome rush of excitement, of impatient purpose. 'Come on, Will, let's go!'

The boats were just approaching the wharf when Ma and Hanna got there. Will, it turned out, was needed at his aunt's bakery, and glad to avoid further discussion with Hanna of spells and magic. Gentill, Leo, Hakelin and Flo were already at the wharfside, waiting with Muriel – Flo, who'd only just been born when Manasser left on his trip.

'The sheriff's man will take a look at the goods here,' Muriel told Ma as she arrived. 'Then we can take the boat upstream.'

Hanna recognised the boy in charge of the small boats that were waiting to unload. It was Abe, youngest son of Levi, the carpenter, only a few years older than Hanna and Ben. He was stocky, broad chested. They'd played together when they were little but now, Hanna realised with a jolt, he was already married and a father. No wonder Muriel was putting pressure on Ma about her and Ben. Hanna returned Abe's friendly wave and smile, but it didn't seem the time or the place for a chat.

'Hanna – daddy's home!' cried Hakelin, Gentill's middle child, grabbing Hanna's hand.

'And maybe with news of mine,' Hanna thought.

Leo waited quietly at his mother's side, his baby sister Flo in her arms.

Also waiting were three monks who, judging by their dress, were from St Mary's, and several raggedy boys with handcarts who were vying with each other to be of service to the disembarking passengers. The 'sheriff's man', it transpired, was Aelred, on other occasions 'the constable's man', the spindly, blonde youth who had come to fetch Samuel to the castle that day, in another lifetime, to tend to the man with the fractured skull.

The boats were only three – others had docked south of the town at the convent's wharf. Here, there was a small wherry, all of whose passengers seemed to be monks, presumably coming to visit their spiritual brothers who were waiting on the quay; a boat containing a grim-faced peasant and what appeared to be a whole flock of sheep; and then, at their head, the boat which brought Manasser back to his family, together with the goods paid for by Muriel and Ma. Twice the size of each of the others, the boat lay low in the water, weighed down with its cargo. It was like the one in which Hanna had crossed the Humber on the way to London: flat-bottomed and with blood-red sails, it had made its way across the sea, negotiated the capricious currents of the Humber and then patiently ridden the high tides up the Ouse to York.

Two of its crew leapt out as they drew close and hauled on the heavy ropes which they wound round the posts alongside the wharf and tied with knots Hanna had yet to fathom. The others took down and secured the sails, while their captain remained at the helm.

Manasser stood at his side, upright and dignified in a dark blue tunic. He looked just as Hanna remembered, now smiling in the depths of his beard; despite the dark, bushy growth he looked just like Muriel. Standing between Ma and Hanna, she was dabbing at her eyes with her handkerchief, caught between laughing and crying. Gentill was concerned with ensuring that Leo and Hakelin didn't fall between boat and wharf in their excitement to see their father.

All Hanna could think of was the possibility that Manasser might be bringing letters from Da, or at least certain news of his whereabouts.

Manasser disembarked from the boat, and the greetings began. Aelred was hovering, however, unmoved by the family reunion and apparently just about to board the boat. Muriel and Ma went into the hold with him to check its cargo, leaving Manasser embracing his wife and Flo while Leo and Hakelin danced around them.

The party of three re-emerged from the boat's hold even faster than Hanna had expected. Aelred waved a cheery goodbye and left them alone on the quayside.

But there was no news of Da and Ben. Ma asked Manasser while they were unloading and sorting the goods. He had met with traders from the south, one in particular who was his source for almonds and, often, for news about Da's sisters. But there had been no update, no word at all about either Da or his sisters, and no mention of any trip to Sicily.

Muriel apologised to Ma and Hanna that Manasser hadn't brought her grandson, Elchanan, with him from Rouen – apparently he was now promised to a lovely girl there. Hanna, who had forgotten all about him, wondered why Muriel was even bothering to tell her, when there was still no news from Ben and Da... She saw the back of Todros's dark head and black cloak disappearing among the wine sellers and drinkers of the port of London, and the thick-set men hunting him down – taking with him her twin's and father's story. Ma, too, remained silent.

There was one arrival none of them had noticed. A monk disembarked from the same boat as the farmer and his flock of sheep. The monk, of indeterminate age, fair skinned, eager-eyed, was dressed in a white surplice, unlike any of the other monks in York. He spoke to no one but, throwing his small bag over his shoulder, strode purposefully from the quay in the direction of the town.

21. REVENGE

The cooking fire was still warm from the preparation of their mid-day meal. Hanna placed a few more lumps of charcoal on the glowing embers and knelt down to blow on them until the new pieces caught. She placed on the fire the pot which she and Ma used to melt down the stub-ends of their Shabbat candles to make new. Hanna had taken as many as she dared, hoping that Ma wouldn't notice; it wasn't holy candles that she was making.

She placed another, larger pot, of cold water, next to the fire. Alongside lay a pile of small nails, together with the leather pouch and the notes she had made from Granda's book. So far, so good. Jessie had gone home for the day, and Ma and Granda had again gone to visit Comtessa. They would be back in time for evening prayers, but that was still an hour or so away. Hanna had pleaded another headache, and they had left her behind to rest. She shivered. It was a sunless day and there was a brisk breeze that had brought down the last apples left on the tree to ripen. They lay underneath it, bruised.

Taking up her notes, Hanna read again the list of angels' names: *Af, Hemah, Meshabber, Barakel, Gadriel, Leliel… These are the angels who are full of anger and wrath and who have been put in charge of combat and war and are prepared to torment and torture a man to death. There is no mercy in them but they wish only to take revenge and punish whoever is delivered into their hands.*

The molten wax smelt of honey. Hanna wrapped her hands in the cloth and took the pot from the fire, pouring the wax at once into the pot containing the cold water. Quickly putting the first pot down, she shook the cloth from her hands and plunged them into the cold water to take hold of the wax while it remained soft enough to mould. But the wax was still hot inside and as she squeezed it with her right hand she burned her palm and fingers. She dropped the wax back into the water, and held her hand submerged, waiting for the pain to pass... She couldn't afford to leave the wax any longer. She pulled it out with her left hand, dropping it into her lap. Ignoring the pain, and the large blister already risen on her palm, she used the tips of her fingers to pat and shape the wax into the form of a man – body, head, arms and legs – then pinching out a nose and ears on his head. Tipping the nails onto the ground, she carefully laid the wax figure on the piece of wood. She pressed her little finger nail into the left side of its face to scar it.

She quietly intoned again the names of the angels and then the words of the spell itself: 'I deliver to you, angels of anger and wrath, Richard de Malbisse, that you will strangle him and destroy him and his appearance, make him bedridden, diminish his thought and his knowledge and cause him to waste away continually until he approaches death.'

As she read, she picked up the nails one at a time and pushed each in turn into the small wax body, one in its head, another in its chest, then the stomach, and then, very gently, each of the arms and legs, taking the utmost care just to pierce the wax, not break it.

She finished saying the words and found she was shaking, with tears rolling down her face.

'Uncle Baruch,' she sobbed, 'I am so sorry.'

A scuffle breaking out between two of the chickens brought her to herself. She picked up her notes, the pouch and the piece of wood with the wax effigy of the Beast and took them up to the room she shared with her mother. She opened up the chest at the end of the bed. The scent of lavender – what would Ma say if she knew what she was doing? Ben's clothes, fresh washed, were at the top; her own, underneath. She pulled them all out, then laid Ben's at the bottom. She put the notes back in their pouch, placed it and the effigy on top of Ben's clothes, covered them with her own, then shut the chest.

There, it was done, and she was powerless to do more. She could only wait for news of the Beast's death.

She went downstairs to find some of Granda's ointment to put on her blister and to ensure she had left no traces in the courtyard outside that would betray her. She'd say nothing of it to anyone, not even Will.

New Year was approaching and Hanna tried to take pleasure in the new clothes being sewn for her from the fine Florentine cloth that Manasser had brought.

Outwardly at least their preparations took the same course as they did every year. Muriel was clearly trying not to gossip and she and Ma rose even earlier than usual each morning to go to pray, usually waiting for Comtessa before they entered the synagogue together. Granda kept to his familiar routine, preoccupied with his patients, books and translations, and talked of Da and Ben's continued absence with a determined cheeriness – 'if something bad had happened, we'd have heard,' he said. Both he and Ma were clinging to the hope offered by Hanna's account of her meeting with the mysterious Todros.

Hanna felt detached from it all.

Granda knew from conversations with the constable and others in the town that news of the events in London had also reached York's Christians. It seemed that the priests in York's many churches were doing nothing to incite their parishioners to violence – but York had so many churches and Granda did not have friends in every congregation. They missed Master Thomas. Yet Will still came for his lessons, their Christian neighbours still sought out Granda's medical skills and bought smoked fish from Ma. The Cistercian monks from Fountains, Rievaulx and Meux transferred to Joseph the dealings in wool and grain and gold they had had with Baruch, and housewives still came to Ma and Muriel to buy cloth and spices. Apparently, their lives continued as they always had.

It was evening and Hanna was writing out a fair copy of Granda's translation. She was soothed by the smells of their medicines and the oil lamp, the gentle hiss of the wick as it burned and the warm colours of the hangings on the walls and rugs on the floor. But still she found her mind wandering to Da and Ben – she missed her twin's reluctant presence – and then to Uncle Baruch and his brother, Jacob.

'Why did Jacob treat Uncle Baruch like he did?' she said.

Granda looked up, his black brows meeting in a fierce frown at the interruption.

'What?'

'I'm sorry. I didn't mean to disturb you,' Hanna said.

'Well, now you have, what is it?'

Hanna repeated her question. Granda sighed and this time spoke more gently.

'I don't know, Hanna. Sometimes' – he stopped, then started again – 'he obviously felt he had to agree with his community.'

'He could have left, he could have brought his family to live here in York,' said Hanna.

'Who's to say that people feel differently here?'

'What do you mean?'

Granda shrugged. 'Rabbi Yom Tov thinks the Jews of Northampton were right. Joseph, too – even Manasser.'

Hanna was shocked. 'Why?'

'It's difficult, Hanna.' He paused. 'Maybe, it's – it's how a religion protects itself, stays strong when it's under attack. If Baruch were allowed to become a Christian, and still be buried on Jewish sacred ground, what's to stop anyone else doing the same when their faith and life are under threat?'

'But his own brother,' said Hanna. 'I could never do that to Ben.'

'And I hope you're never put in the position where you have to choose,' said Granda. He reached across and placed one of his hands on top of hers. 'Baruch – I didn't always agree with him, but I miss him. We were stronger when he was here.'

'What would you have done, Granda, in Uncle Jacob's place?'

'I think G–d teaches us that we should forgive the brother who has wronged us, if he repents…'

He picked up his pen again. 'But I honour G–d
through our studies and quest for His truths, His reason,
my dear.' He smiled at her, squeezed her hand in his and
returned to his writing.

22. ATONEMENT

The celebrations for New Year were muted. The previous year Baruch and Comtessa had welcomed the whole community to Spen Lane – Da and Ben had been there – and it had seemed that all could be well. Now, once more, there was a shadow hanging over them, and a collective shadow this time, not just a personal grief. And their sorrow over Baruch divided them rather than bringing them together. Uncle Joseph only left his house, where his wife, Anna, lay sick, to go to pray at the synagogue. Rabbi Yom Tov's eyes burned with a new fervour as he preached his sermon reminding his congregation of the martyrs of Masada, who had taken their own lives rather than yield to the Romans, and those he himself had seen burned at the stake rather than renounce their faith.

Then, it was the dark days leading up to the Day of Atonement. As a small child, Hanna had always liked their intensity. She and Ben had counted up their wrongdoings – not studying as hard as they should, dodging out of domestic tasks, teasing their less hardy cousins, making fun of Muriel, not listening during the sermon – and happily repented of them in the synagogue, not thinking at all about whether they were going to do exactly the same again in the coming year. And the day itself was defined by a sense of solemnity and peace.

This year, the festival coincided with the Christians' Michaelmas – which not only marked St Michael the Archangel's defeat of the devil, but also the end of the agricultural year, when tithes and taxes were collected according to the quantity of crops harvested. It was a busy time for Hugh, Will's dad, and for the sheriff's men, reckoning and collecting what was due to the lords, church and king.

Hanna, for whom the reckoning was solely spiritual, looked at the sum total of her deeds and found herself wanting. This year her wrongdoings really were serious and she had done things for which she could not forgive herself. The crowd in London had rioted and Baruch had died, Benedict le Puncteur, too. Reuben had lost his mother, David had lost his father, Uncle Joseph's daughter her husband. The wolf at the highwayman's throat, the boy crying for his da… Moreover, Hanna was continuing to use those same offending magical powers; the nail-pierced effigy of the Beast still lay hidden in the lavender-scented chest at the end of her bed.

9 Tishrei 4850 / 29 September 1189

In the morning, Hanna went to Uncle Baruch's house in Spen Lane. Serlo opened the gate, obviously pleased to see her, but rueful. The fact of Baruch's death lay heavily between them. But he came with her to the stable and stood with her as she fed Lief the vetch she had picked for him at the river bank.

Then she went to find Comtessa and Cresselin. They were the ones – in York – whom she had wronged the most.

'I'm sorry,' she said. 'I'm sorry that Uncle Baruch died and that I didn't help him.'

'What could you have done, my child?' Comtessa asked, and held out her arms. Their embrace was made awkward by the bump of Baruch and Comtessa's baby, due in just a few months' time.

Hanna didn't tell Comtessa about the spells she had carried in her soft leather pouch that day, nor that she was still using them, to avenge Baruch's death.

Once home, she went with Ma to the miqveh to bathe in preparation for the festival. Afterwards, sanctified, refreshed, as they crossed the courtyard between synagogue and mikveh, they heard music – pipes, and the banging of drums. Hanna knew it sounded familiar and that she didn't like it – but what was it?

She stepped out into Coney Street and there, coming towards her, was her answer. She flattened herself against the wall to avoid being crushed. Wave upon wave of townspeople passed her, some on foot and others on horseback, each craft and guild ordered in rank, with horns and drums and pipes, among them a small man on a large horse whom she recognised as the new sheriff, John Marshall, and now a cart on which cavorted a collection of small devils, clad in black, their faces red and snarling, under curling red horns.

In their midst writhed a dragon, with a horned devil head, being speared, even as it passed in front of them, by the warrior archangel Michael, who towered above them like an avenging giant bird, huge white-feathered wings at his back. A small blonde boy stood at his side, grinning, and holding a set of scales. And then came the priests, their heads deep in their silken hoods, faceless, followed by the boys no older than Hanna who carried buckets of water and swung incense burners... Its intense, heady scent filled her nostrils.

Then, before her, terrifyingly, she saw a group of men dragging a body. His head was all bloody and his scarlet robes torn. It was Uncle Baruch. Cries filled her ears. 'Kill the Jew! Kill! Kill!' Prior William cut through the crowd on his dark bay horse, his sword held aloft...

'Hanna, Hanna!'

She was lying on the ground and Ma was shaking her. She sounded angry and scared. The drums and pipes had gone and Hanna was aware of the feet and legs of a crowd gathering round her and the cold damp of the muddy street seeping through her tunic.

'What happened?' asked Hanna.

'I don't know, I was standing next to you, squeezed against the wall to let the procession pass, and then you collapsed. You've got to get up. People are staring, Hanna. Let's get you home.'

The procession, yes, Hanna remembered – there was the angel vanquishing a dragon, but after them came the priests and the boys with their incense burners – and then she'd been back in London on the day of the coronation, watching Uncle Baruch carried away by Prior William all over again…

Her head throbbed.

She struggled up onto her feet and, holding onto Ma's arm, unsteadily walked the short distance home.

That evening Ma lit a candle for all their relatives, alive and dead, including Da and Ben and Uncle Baruch, which is when Hanna cried.

York, 10 Tishrei 4850 / 30 September 1189

In the candlelit warmth of the synagogue next day, squashed in between Ma and Muriel, Hanna was merely conscious of feeling sleepy and heavy-headed. She could hear the laughter of the children, Muriel's grandchildren among them, out in the courtyard, and wished she were still one of them, too young to fast and play a full part in the service. She could understand that G–d might forgive her for not being able to rescue Uncle Baruch, but why should G–d forgive her for using spells not of His teaching in the first place, when she was still using them against the Beast?

Rabbi Yom Tov preached of the rewards of martyrdom. 'Happy is he who is slain or slaughtered and who dies attesting the Oneness of His Name. Such a one is destined for the world to come, where he will sit in the realm of the saints,' he told them.

There was some muttering among the congregation afterwards as they broke fast together that perhaps the rabbi hadn't struck quite the right tone for that particular day.

Hanna took comfort in Granda's anger – 'What good are we to anybody, dead?' he said as they made their way home in the dark.

They could just make out the shape of a man on horseback outside their house. But it was a messenger on his way to St Mary's abbey, bringing a letter from Master Thomas – not news of Da and Ben.

'My eyes are too tired. You read it to us, Hanna,' Granda said, once they were inside. He broke the seal and handed the letter to her.

'You can tell me Thomas's news later,' said Ma. 'I'm just saying hello to Jessie. But you stay and help your Granda, Hanna.'

'If you're sure, Ma,' said Hanna. She began to read:

Bermondsey Abbey, London
The feast of St Lupus of Lyons, 1189

My dear friend, Samuel,

I hope that this letter finds you and your family safe in York, after the terrible events of the coronation. I was so sorry to hear of the death of our fellow townsman, Baruch, and that the attempts by my brother monk, William, to save his friend's life (and, as he thought, his soul) merely resulted in Baruch being lost to all. The accounts I have heard of his death and subsequent burial in Northampton are garbled, but all sad. You and your family, Comtessa and her son, Elias and Serlo, and the rest of Baruch's household are every day in my prayers.

I have to tell you of another death. (At this Hanna started – already? But her hopes were at once dashed.) *Prior William fell from his horse while hunting with friends in the forest at Richmond. He dislocated his kneecap, which lodged itself at the back of his knee. Several doctors attempted and failed to return the kneecap to its rightful place. The leg festered and a fever set in. By the time I received word it was already too late. I reached him only in time to arrange his funeral. William and I disagreed about many things, but I had known him since I was a boy and first arrived at St Mary's; I am bereft.*

I was not the only man from York at his funeral. There I also saw Richard de Malbisse and others of his party – young de Cuckney and the Scot, Marmaduke Darrell, the diminutive John Marshall and de Malbisse's daughter, Emma. There was talk that she is to be married.

But our Yorkshire noblemen make me uneasy, Samuel. They were complaining that Baruch's death has not freed them from their debts, for which the promissory notes remain in York. And they have royal backing: King Richard has appointed John Marshall as sheriff. The king is insisting that Ranulf de Granville accompany him to the

Prior William and Uncle Baruch, both dead. They were both younger than Da, and just as full of life – or had been…

Granda said nothing for a while after Hanna finished reading the letter. He held his hands in his lap and watched himself rub one thumb against the other as if easing a pain, and Hanna wondered if he too was thinking of Da.

'Sad, very sad,' murmured Granda eventually. 'I must share this news with Joseph, but not now. If you'll excuse me, I am just going to rest for a while.'

He stood up stiffly just as Ma returned, but left the room without speaking. She turned to Hanna.

'What news, then, my love? Is it bad?'

Hanna told her what Master Thomas had said, about Prior William's death, Malbisse and his fellow men of York, and Thomas's delayed return to York. Ma listened, tight-lipped, though with a sharp intake of breath and slight shake of her head at her half-brother's name.

'What do you think, Ma? What does it mean for us?' Hanna asked.

'I don't know, Hanna. I just know that there's work to do and I want your Da and Ben to come home.'

And so Hanna tried to lose herself in the rhythms of everyday life. Ma made fewer domestic demands on her since her return from London; she paid Jessie to work longer hours and called on Leo for help with smoking the salmon whose season it was to swim upstream and which leapt so readily into the nets Ma cast from the wharf behind the house. So Hanna was free to help Granda with his patients, the writing-up of their case histories, and the painstaking yet somehow liberating work of transcribing his translation of the medical texts on which he relied. 'Let's have it ready for when Thomas returns – and Da,' he said. Frequently now, she wrote while Will read (and also wrote) with Granda. She no longer acted simply as Granda's scribe, but helped him with the trickier passages, able to draw on her own growing medical knowledge to be able to make sense of what the earlier Arabian physician wrote.

Her medical skills were instinctive, a gift from G–d, Granda told her. 'You have forebears,' he said, and told her of the women doctors who practised in the far south next to the Mediterranean Sea, who had even written books about their work. Often, Hanna could ease a patient's symptoms simply by resting her cool hand on their forehead, even before deciding which of Granda's ointments or tinctures to prescribe.

So Simchat Torah succeeded Sukkot and the Christians too thanked G–d for the harvest, then prayed for All Souls. The leaves fell from the trees and autumn turned into winter and the people of York staved off the misery of cold weather and short days with preparations for Chanukah and Christmas. Malbisse sent word that he would not be returning to Acaster until the Christians' New Year and John Marshall announced in the marketplace that King Richard had sailed for France, on his way to Jerusalem.

23. WINTER

Still Malbisse did not return. The manor house at Acaster remained shut up, the scaffolding swayed and slipped in the winter gales and the green oak lay unused and mildewing on the ground. Will's and the other families on the estate tended to the dogs, hunting birds and horses but spent the greater part of their time on their own plots, brewed beer, sang and danced – and enjoyed the sense that their time and effort was spent on their own account.

Hanna was no longer a visitor there, her days of tree-climbing and bareback horse riding seemingly over, although Will continued his visits to the house in Coney Street to study with Samuel. Hanna no longer thought of magic as fun, no longer thought of magic much at all, it seemed, instead caught up with her work with Granda and their patients in the morning and with their translations in the afternoon and evening.

So she spoke to no one of the wax figure in the lavender-scented chest at the end of her bed and kept her memory of it firmly locked away, too. Every once in a while she would wonder briefly if Malbisse was sick, dying, and if that was why he did not return, but she chose not to think of her role in his demise.

She also tried not to examine too closely how much she looked forward to Will's weekly visits and the hours she spent near him, his brow furrowed in concentration underneath his fringe, and their chatter about this and that while they walked with Beaumon and Jack through the bare-treed woods in pale, wintry afternoon sun.

And the anxiety she shared with Ma and Granda about Da and Ben – where were they? Why hadn't they sent word? – that, too, she pushed away, held at a safe distance. Sometimes she allowed herself to plan how to steal away in a boat, down the Ouse, to the Humber and out to sea, to foreign lands, in search of her da and twin — but most of the time she felt as if held in suspension, like one of the leaves immobilised in the ice of the frozen water trough in the market place.

The Foss and Ouse froze briefly, too, then flowed black between their white, snow-covered banks; travel and trade were hard. Grain was scarce in the market place and the price of bread went up, and up again and then up once more and people in the market and at the mills and at the bakers' were complaining because their loaf of bread cost them three, four, five times what it had cost them in the autumn and times were hard and there must be someone to blame.

It was not long after the turn of the Christians' year that the white-clad monk began appearing regularly in the town. 'Down with the enemies of Christ!' he kept shouting, apparently not caring whether anyone was listening or not. His eyes burned with the same intensity as Rabbi Yom Tov's when he spoke of martyrdom. His robe was muddied and dirty, his hair all awry. To Hanna he looked quite mad, yet others in the market place appeared to regard him without concern. She was sure that she had seen him before, but she couldn't place where.

When the snow was still on the ground, Mordecai, Joseph's loyal, ancient servant, died and was mourned and buried. A week later, Uncle Baruch and Aunt Comtessa's baby was born, Cresselin's little brother, baby Baruch. He had the square chin and grey eyes of his father and his mother's fair skin. Her tiny cousin grabbed and held fast to Hanna's little finger and Hanna wished that her uncle was there to see them, Da and Ben, too. After the circumcision there was a party, at which the guests were both happy and sad. Serlo and Elias kept a fierce watch. Soon after, Elias and his family moved to Uncle Joseph's house, who felt in greater need of his services.

A week or so later, just after the Christians had celebrated Candlemas, Malbisse finally came back to Acaster. Will was with the dogs in the kennels when he heard the sound of hooves approaching. It wasn't the Beast himself that day, but an advance party consisting of de Cuckney and Darrell and their servants, demanding that Will's ma and da and the other families of the estate prepare at once for the arrival of their lord, due in a couple of days by river from Selby.

'Two days?' grumbled Will's ma. 'We'll never get it all done.'

But they did, or thereabouts.

'He's back,' Will told Hanna, when he arrived for his next lesson with Granda.

At first Hanna wasn't sure who he was talking about, so firmly had she closed the lid on that particular thought.

'Who?' she asked.

'The Beast.' Hanna felt suddenly cold, thought she might vomit.

'How is he?' she asked.

'You're all of a sudden concerned for his welfare?' Will laughed.

'No, but, you know what I mean,' said Hanna.

'He's not changed,' said Will. 'Ordering everyone about, angry that the place is still a mess, the building work uncompleted. Some of the tenants, hearing that he was back, came to petition him for extra grain. He didn't want to know – threatened to beat them if they came to ask him again, told them to come and beg in the town – while his store is nearly full.'

'What about Emma?'

'Now that's the real bit of news. She's married. To a wealthy landowner, Robert de something or other – that was the reason, or the main one, that the Beast had stayed away so long, apparently.'

After Will had gone, and Ma was chatting with Muriel and Granda had gone to his study, Hanna went to the chest at the end of her bed and took out the wax effigy of de Malbisse, together with her notes of the spell. She sat with them on her lap for a moment, looking at the figure's crudely made head, body and limbs all stuck with horseshoe nails and the fingernail scar on its face. She pressed the nails to make sure they all remained firmly embedded. Her fingers hesitated on the nail which pierced the doll's rib cage and saw again the wound that had gaped and festered in Uncle Baruch's chest. Then, in her head, she sat firmly on the lid of the box in which she locked those memories, lest one escape again. She read once more from her notes the names of the angels and then the words of the spell itself:

> *I deliver to you, angels of anger and wrath, Richard de Malbisse, that you will strangle him and destroy him and his appearance, make him bedridden, diminish his thought and his knowledge and cause him to waste away continually until he approaches death.*

Just because the spell had not worked so far, did not mean that it was never going to work. If her powers of magic were sufficient to overcome wolves and thieves, they might yet be strong enough to exact revenge on de Malbisse.

24. LYNN

A couple of days later, Hanna was in the marketplace. The afternoon was grey and the wind icy. The few stall holders in the market were already packing up, their meagre goods sold or else beyond selling. But there was still a queue outside Will's aunt's bakery. The women waiting looked worn down, hungry. Hanna wondered if any of them were those the Beast had sent away – their faces were unfamiliar to her. When Jessie had let slip that she was finding it hard to afford bread for her children, Ma had put an extra penny in her weekly wage. This year's wheat was late in being planted as the weather was still so cold, and prices wouldn't fall until the next harvest.

Just ahead of her a group of young men fell out of the tavern on the corner of the market square. They all bore the sign of the cross on the back of their tunics. With life in the surrounding countryside so difficult, it was easy for John Marshall to find more recruits to follow the king to France. These ones were lairy and loud, full of drink.

'Down with the enemies of Christ!' shouted the mud-bespattered, white-gowned monk, who appeared suddenly from the alley next to the tavern.

'Down with the enemies of Christ!' several of the recruits slurred back at him. It wasn't clear which particular enemies they had in mind. Hanna pulled her hood forward to cover her face and walked home as quickly as she could without actually running.

As she turned into Coney Street she heard hooves behind her. She turned in terror, fearing one of the would-be soldiers. In relief, she recognised Elias on his familiar large bay. The horse was covered in a froth of sweat and Elias looked exhausted.

'Elias,' she said. 'Are you all right? Where have you come from?'

'From Lincoln. Joseph had sent me there with letters, but while I was waiting to return a messenger came from Lynn, with news both for Lincoln and us here in York. From Deulebene, do you remember? We were with him in London. I'm to give the letter to Joseph and Rabbi Yom Tov. Do you know if they're in?'

'I don't, no, sorry – you'd have to go and see. Anna will be there, though she's still not well.' She hesitated a moment. 'Is the letter anything bad?'

''Fraid so. There's been trouble at Lynn. Some killed.'

'Trouble? What sort of trouble? You mean like in London, at the coronation?' Hanna felt faint. She held onto the wall. Its damp chill took the faintness away.

Elias grimaced. 'Yes,' he said 'I'm not sure of the details. Don't you be worrying though, Miss Hanna – Lynn's a long way away, and it's not like here. It was others from across the sea that caused the trouble, I think – you'll see.' He smiled at her, and gave his horse a gentle kick in the ribs to encourage him to trot the final few feet to Joseph's house. 'I'll see you later.'

A long way away. Lynn was far away, that was true – it was where Uncle Baruch had gone, to fetch his Norwegian falcons. But why was it happening again? And after the monk and recruits' cries in the marketplace, what was to stop it happening here?

The letter was read out at the synagogue that evening, punctuated by the coughing and clearing of throats of a congregation sharing their winter maladies.

From Deulebene of Lynn, 12th of Sh'vat, 4950
Lynn Castle

Jews of York, may the Rock guard you, I have bad news. Several of our fellows – Moses, Solomon le Chat, Benjamin and Vives – have gone to Paradise: they were murdered. Many of our houses have been destroyed, almost all plundered. Many of us are now dispersed to neighbouring towns and those of us who remain, like myself, are staying in the castle under the king's protection.

It happened like this: one of our fellows, David, had converted to the Christian faith. Angered, some of our community set upon him in the street. He took refuge within a church and those who pursued him were banging on its doors to make him come out. Those Christians within the church with this David shouted for help, which drew others within the town who came, armed, to their defence – in particular, a group of young men from across the sea. It seems that our own Christian neighbours, those with whom we work and live, were reluctant to attack us. The foreign assailants chased the Jews from the church and those I have named above – may their memory be blessed – were slaughtered. Then these same Christians attacked and burned our houses.

The following day Isaac le Docteur – may his repose be in Paradise – arrived from London. Though a very old man and much respected by Jew and Christian alike, when he voiced his outrage at the way we had been treated, the Christians seized him and killed him.

The young men who had led the initial attack took the goods they had stolen to their ships and left before they could be caught by the king's officers. Our Christian neighbours in Lynn put all the blame on these young men.

I urge you, take care. Be in good health,
Deulebene of Lynn

At home afterwards, Granda, Ma and Hanna ate their meal in silence. Hanna was waiting for Ma to begin to rail against the Christians again, and was relieved when she didn't. Her memories of the sparrow-like doctor and images from the coronation were crowding in on her and of the men with the crosses on their back in the town that morning. She pinched the skin on the back of her hand hard, to make them go away.

'Can we go to the castle here, Granda? Ma? Can't we go now?' asked Hanna.

'You know we can't leave now, Hanna,' Ma said, 'or even next week. Lent – it's our busiest time… No Christian will be eating meat until after Passover. This is when our fish earn us enough money to keep us the rest of the year.' She pushed escaping locks of hair back under her scarf. There was grey, Hanna noticed, newly straggling through the dark brown.

'Your Ma's right, Hanna – don't rush us in there,' said Granda. 'Once we're there, we're prisoners, my child. All of us, together. That's a lot of people in a small space...' He frowned, looked pained. 'Things will be fine, you'll see – the Christians here in York are different, too much habituated to us. We're so far north, it's different here.'

But there was doubt in his voice.

Hanna was still thinking about Lynn, and what Master Thomas had said in his letter.

'There are plenty of new recruits in town,' she said. 'And those who owe money – Malbisse is back... And the new sheriff, John Marshall – he borrowed money from Uncle Baruch, too.'

'We will be fine,' Granda repeated, 'you'll see.' He paused. 'Though I do wish Master Thomas was here – I could give him my books to look after, if we did have to shift,' said Granda.

'You're not planning to leave us, Master Samuel, are you?'

It was Will, his head appearing around the door, smiling.

'Hello, Mistress Abigail, Hanna.'

Hanna's stomach did that disconcerting somersault. But even if going to the castle meant she would be unable to see Will, she still wanted to be within its walls.

Will, it turned out, was also nervous. He'd been accosted in the town by John Marshall and some of his young men, who'd wanted to know why he hadn't signed up to go with King Richard to Jerusalem; they were unimpressed by his excuses.

The next morning, just before dawn, Hanna was woken by the rumbling of wheels and horses' hooves. It was several minutes before the noise faded into the distance. When she got up a bit later Ma told her that Joseph's two daughters, their husbands and children, had all left.

Muriel came round in the afternoon.

'They're headed for Rouen,' she told them. 'And they've taken Anna with them – she said she was too ill and would rather die here than between here and there, but the others insisted.

'I've been trying to persuade Manasser and Gentill to go to my sister's, but they say they won't leave me behind – and Manasser is still buying goods to take on our next trip.'

She looked defiant. 'I'm not going to change my mind. This is where I lived my life with my Abraham, may his soul rest in Paradise. But I'll have another good go at changing theirs. And you, Abigail, you wouldn't go to your sister's across the sea?'

'How can I go anywhere?' said Ma. 'I've fish to sell – I've my share of Manasser's merchandise to pay for, remember, as well as a family to feed – and what if Moshe were to return, and find me not here?'

'Hmph,' said Muriel. 'And what about me? I was thinking you might say that you couldn't leave me here…'

Ma laughed and placed her hand affectionately on Muriel's arm. 'Oh, you old fool, Muriel. That as well – how could I possibly up sticks and leave, with you still here?'

Then their talk turned to how best to store securely the cloth, tools and wool which awaited shipping with Manasser.

Hanna went to Granda's study to lose herself in the certainties of Latin and found him shakily dosing himself for a sore throat. 'Nothing to fuss about,' he insisted, 'it happens every year – it'll soon pass'

25. BREAD

The Christians' Shrovetide came and went – a blast of wanton excess before their Lenten fast. When they were little, Will, Ben and Hanna, together with all the other children they knew, would roam wild round the town, on the tail of a ragged regiment of youths armed with cudgels, stones, banners, trowels and handstaves, taking in the bloody cockfights, the bear-baiting and the epic football game in the meadows by the Ouse – one year the three of them even took part for a heady, life-endangering half hour – but this time she and Will remained firmly indoors, each with an equally strong sense that the town was not safe, no longer theirs. They read and wrote alone together, as Granada was still sick, laid low with phlegm on his chest that this year he couldn't shift, however violently he coughed. He was unable even to look at his manuscripts and Hanna reluctantly also shut their door to the town's unwell.

14 Adar 4950 / 1 March 1190

When it came close to Purim a couple of weeks later, Granda had recovered sufficiently to leave his bed and sit with Hanna in the mornings while she dealt with those who sought their medical advice; he spoke only when she was unsure of a remedy and asked for his opinion. Afterwards, with a blanket wound round his shoulders, he spent time at his translation, periodically seized by a coughing fit during which he had to lay his quill down rather than splatter ink across the manuscript.

Hanna was determined to shake off her feeling of dread. When she was little, Purim was her favourite time of year. She loved the making, giving and especially the receiving of sweet gifts, the sense that winter was oh-so-nearly over and the story of brave Queen Esther who saved the Jews of Persia from annihilation by the wicked vizier, Haman. This year, as usual, she and Ma and Jessie spent the day beforehand baking together, with honey and almonds and poppy seeds, so that they had generous amounts to share with Jessie's and Muriel's families and at the synagogue and also to send to Will's Ma and Da at Acaster and his aunt and uncle in the town.

At the synagogue, later in the day, Simeon, Rabbi Yom Tov's nephew, had been chosen to read Esther's story, which he did well enough, but no one brought it alive in the same way that Da used to, with his skill in doing all the voices – oh, how Hanna missed him, acutely conscious that neither he nor Ben were sitting in their places with the other men.

The sanctuary was bright with candles and warm, too, especially with the press of bodies. The light reflected off the gold on the pages of the book of the Torah from which Simeon read, scribed some 200 years previously by the Sea of Galilee, and brought out each year at the feast of Purim. But each time Simeon mentioned the self-satisfied, hateful Haman at the centre of the story, it was Malbisse's face Hanna saw, cold blue eyes against pale skin under white-blonde hair, and the jagged scar that stretched between his mouth and right ear. Dully her thoughts turned to the scar-faced effigy that lay in her clothes chest, its form pierced by nails…

There was the sound of a horse and shouting outside, but Simeon read on: 'Then Haman said to King Ahasuerus: "There is a certain nation dispersed among the other nations of your empire. They do not keep your majesty's laws. If it please your majesty, let an order be made for their destruction–"'

Just then the door to the synagogue swung open. Everyone turned to look. Hanna didn't recognise the man who stood in front of them, though from his clothes he appeared to be the rider whose horse they had heard. From the look of sweaty, mud-spattered exhaustion on his face, he had travelled a long way, fast. He was holding a letter in his hands.

'I come from Norwich. Those who sent me said I should not delay in giving you their news,' he said, 'whether feasting or at prayer. Forgive me.'

A murmur of consternation swirled through the congregation. Hanna felt sick. Ma reached out to put a hand on her shoulder, but Hanna brushed it away. Simeon looked at Rabbi Yom Tov, unsure what to do, his uncle looking equally shocked and unsure next to him. Uncle Joseph stood up, somewhat unsteady on his feet. The muscle under his left eye was twitching.

'Welcome, my friend,' he said as he stepped forward to greet the stranger, 'Let us talk first. Samuel, will you come with us?'

Granda also got up from his seat, gave a quick half-smile to Hanna, and together with Uncle Joseph ushered the messenger outside.

Rabbi Yom Tov raised his voice above the hubbub which ensued. 'Let us continue,' he said. 'We will welcome our guest to our feast when we are finished here, and learn his news then.'

But Hanna scarcely heard a word of the rest of Simeon's reading and the revenge exacted by the Jews on their enemies. Surely the arrival of the messenger could mean only one thing…

And she was right. The letter, which Uncle Joseph read out to them once prayers at the synagogue had finished, said that violence had erupted in Norwich soon after the news reached the city of the attack on the Jews in Lynn. Those Jews who reached the safety of the king's castle in time had survived; those who did not were killed.

'Please now can we go to the castle?' Hanna asked again, when she, Ma and Granda were alone together at home.

'What's the point of going to the castle now, when we'll go hungry in the end anyway, if I've not sold my fish?' said Ma. She sounded angry.

'This is York, Hanna,' Granda said, then stopped, his shoulders shaking as he was seized by another coughing fit. Hanna fetched him a cup of water, and he took a couple of sips. 'Just because bad things have happened in other places does not mean that they will happen here. But I will talk to Joseph – so long as we are prepared…'

And so they did not go. Finally, a few daffodils were opening bright and yellow in the woods down by the river. The first shoots of garlic and poppy were poking through the soil in Granda's courtyard garden. But the wind was still cold and the price of bread going up, and Granda still couldn't shake off his cough.

A week later, Hanna and Granda were making their way through the market, stepping carefully around the dirty puddles as there'd been a fierce shower while they been at Comtessa's. Baby Baruch and Cresselin were unwell and Comtessa had sent word asking for Granda to call. It was the first time he'd been out to see patients since his own illness; the cold air made him wheeze and he was walking with a stick. The children's illness was nothing serious – Comtessa, perhaps understandably, was inclined to fuss and liked the reassurance of her late husband's physician. Hanna's cool hands on Baby Baruch and Cresselin's foreheads had soothed them, after she and Granda dosed them with rosehip syrup. Serlo had been particularly glad to see her. She'd also checked on Lief in the stable before leaving.

Now, though, there was a crowd outside Will's aunt's bakery on the other side of the square. As they approached, Hanna could hear someone shouting angrily above the general hubbub.

'How am I supposed to feed my family when you've put the price of bread up again? You're a thief! Stealing the bread from my children's mouths!' She was shaking her fist, her face screwed up in hate. It was the woman from the castle, Mary, the wife of Unwin, whose shattered skull Granda and Master Thomas had mended.

As she drew nearer, Hanna saw how thin the woman's arm was. The shutters to the bakery were firmly closed.

'How come yesterday you were selling it for three pennies and now it's four! And I've only earned two pennies since last week!'

The woman banged her fist on the shutters. Two small children were hanging on to her tunic, crying, one scarcely more than a baby. Their clothes were rags, their bodies just skin and bone. Hanna realised with a shock that they were the babe-in-arms and toddler who'd been with their mother on the afternoon of their father's injury.

'That's Will's aunt and uncle they're shouting at, Granda – I'm going to see they're all right,' Hanna cried. Granda reached out his hand to stop her, but was too late, and she ran ahead of him towards the crowd.

But just then, from the opposite direction, a group of men on horseback rode into the crowd, nearly knocking over the women outside the bakery. The mighty chargers towered over them and a couple of their riders, the sign of the cross on their backs, had their swords raised above their heads. The women's angry shouts turned to screams of fear as they backed away – all except for Mary, Unwin's wife.

'My children are starving!' she shouted, her eyes huge in her gaunt face. 'What are you going to do about it, so fierce and brave on your big horses?'

The horse in front of her reared up – for a moment Hanna thought the rider intended to cut the woman down – but the horse's sharp hooves just missed her. The woman stood her ground, her children hiding behind her, screaming, and her companions, fear in their eyes, regrouped around her.

'Bread! Bread! Bread!' they chanted. 'Bread! Bread! Bread!'

The young men on horseback conferred briefly. 'Open up!' one of them shouted, leaning over to bang on the bakery door. 'Open up!' he shouted again. 'Give these women bread! For free!'

The top shutter opened and Hanna could see Will's aunt's terrified face.

'I can't give it you for free,' she said. 'This grain – there's plenty now – but we've paid double for it.'

'Give us what you've baked,' shouted the same young man, 'or we'll beat your door down and you can take your chances with the crowd.'

'Bread, bread, bread.' Some of the women were near sobbing now, exhausted by their efforts and hunger. Hanna watched as Will's aunt disappeared from view for a moment and then reappeared with an armful of loaves.

'Here you are,' she said, throwing them towards the women and herself near tears, Hanna thought. 'I'm ruined,' she shouted at them, hurling the last loaves into the crowd.

Before Will's aunt could bang the shutter shut, another of the young soldiers of the cross tossed a couple of coins in through the window.

Granda, wheezing badly, had caught up with Hanna by now and she put her hand into his. He gripped it tightly as together they turned for home.

26. FIRE

That night, Hanna woke with a start. There was shouting in the street below. She got out of bed and opened the window shutters to look. There was an ominous orange glow in the sky and plumes of smoke... She couldn't see enough to tell exactly where the fire was – but, from the yelling below, something was definitely happening in Coney Street. Hanna thought she could hear Granda's voice. Ma was asleep next to her.

'Ma! Ma! Wake up!' Hanna cried, at the same time pulling her tunic on over her head.

'What, what is it?' asked Ma, still half asleep.

'Fire, Ma – in our street. I'm going to see – I think Granda is already out there.'

'Whose house?' Ma asked. 'It's not Uncle Joseph's, is it?'

It was clear as soon as they went outside that it was not, but rather the collection of poorer wooden houses, further down the street towards the castle. Their inhabitants were safe, but desperate to save what they could of their homes and belongings.

It was blustery, gusts of wind sending showers of sparks up into the night sky, so there was a risk, too, of the fire spreading. They and all their neighbours, it seemed, were in the street in various states of undress and distress, including Jessie and her husband, while Rabbi Yom Tov and Granda were among those helping to organise human chains to get water from the river to douse the flames.

Hanna went to check Granda was all right.

'I was awake when it started,' he said. 'I'd heard voices, people outside in the street.'

'The smoke – it will make your cough worse,' said Hanna.

'I'm fine for now,' he said, leaning on his stick. 'You go back and fetch more containers, our buckets, bowls — I'm all right here.'

Hanna did as he told her. Ma was with Joseph and Rabbi Yom Tov outside Joseph's house. Both had clearly just been roused from their sleep; Joseph looked so old, so vulnerable. Ma was taking charge, persuading them to go back inside, that there was no danger to their house and the synagogue. Hanna left her to it. Compared to Hanna's memories of the fire and storm in West Cheap, it all seemed very contained — but the sky was glowing up towards St Mary's as well, so perhaps fire had already broken out elsewhere. But at quite a distance from Coney Street — could it really be sparks blown by the wind?

'Hanna! Hanna! Are you all right?' It was Will. 'I thought it was your house or Joseph's that was on fire — that you were under attack. But there seem to be fires all over the town.'

As he spoke, Hanna became aware of a further orange flickering in the sky behind him, lighting up the cranes of the new St Peter's. They looked at each other.

'Spen Lane!' they said simultaneously.

Hanna hadn't been able to help Uncle Baruch in London, but she could help his family now. She and Will started running. She could hear panting behind them and looked back — it was Abe, Levi the carpenter's son, doing his best to keep up. They ran through the centre of the town, across the market place and into Spen Lane.

As they came round the corner into it, they were nearly knocked over by two men on horseback, galloping at full pelt, then had to flatten themselves against the wall to let a horse and cart pass — a horse and cart, in the middle of the night? — with its load covered with canvas. The smooth-featured young man who was holding the reins met Hanna's gaze fleetingly. De Cuckney.

Will and Hanna sprinted the last few yards holding their sleeves over their faces as the air was hazy with smoke.

The house was not yet fully ablaze. Flames were leaping freely from the roof. Several of its beams were already exposed and they were on fire. Flames were also curling round the sides of the shutters on two of the windows, but it seemed that the fire had not taken hold of the rest of the house. A crowd was gathering... Hanna couldn't see anyone from Baruch's household among them. Perhaps they had already escaped to safety...

Then she heard a wild whinnying from inside – the stables, Lief...

The gatehouse's huge door hung askew on its hinges, its bolts prised loose. The falcon head was gone. Hanna pushed her way through, Will following.

'You get the horses, Will!' Hanna shouted.

She ran across the courtyard, wrenched open the door of the house and went in. Where was Serlo, surely he'd have stopped any intruders?

The fire appeared to be contained in the upper floor, but the smoke now was dense. She pulled her tunic up to cover her mouth and nose. She was aware of Will on the stairs behind her and of flames in the ceiling above the stairwell.

She hurled herself against the door on the left of the landing, where Comtessa had slept with Baruch and now with Cresselin and Baby Baruch.

The heat and light as the door opened were intense. The flames feeding on the canopy above and the hangings around the bed flared up in the influx of air.

The hangings tore, half falling onto the bed and the bodies which lay on top of it. There, their faces glowing orange in the fire's light, were Comtessa, Cresselin and baby Baruch.

It was only as Hanna stumbled forward and reached through the hangings to wake them that she realised that each was lying in a pool of blood which had spilled from the jagged cuts in their throats.

There was a tearing sound above her as the hangings fell and knocked her to the floor.

'Hanna, Hanna – you must wake up now.' Then coughing.

Hanna opened her eyes. She was in her bed at home. Ma was not next to her. The shutters were half open and it was daylight, but she couldn't tell what time of day it was.

Her throat was sore, like she'd swallowed brambles, and her eyes prickled, too – as if full of grit. She remembered Comtessa, Cresselin and baby Baruch, the blood and the fire and felt sick. They had not been safe in their bed, so how could she be in hers? And she thought she could still hear the screaming of the horses. Was that Lief?

'Ah, you're awake, my dear. It's late morning – you must get up.' It was Granda, standing next to her bed, holding a cup out to her with his trembling hand.

'Here, drink this,' he said. 'It'll make you feel better.'

The cup held a drink of ginger and honey, the liquid itself cool, yet warm with the heat of the spice. He looked haggard and old, his eyes bloodshot. He turned away to cough momentarily, but smiled at her reassuringly as he sat down next to her on the bed.

'How did I' – she was too weak to talk.

'Will and Abe brought you home. They told us what happened, what you found. You should never have gone in there – but there's no point in telling you that now.'

'And Will?'

'He's fine. He went back to his aunt's to get some rest, but has already been here this morning to see how you were. He said to tell you that Lief is all right – Abe followed you both in, and got the horses out – and they're safe with his da at Acaster.'

So Lief was alive. 'But Baruch's household, Serlo – were they all…'

'Dead? Yes, Comtessa and the children, slain in their beds. Serlo's throat was cut, too, his body dragged into the stables – Abe found it. Everyone, dead.'

Granda sounded matter of fact, dispassionate. His gaze held Hanna's, steady.

'And whoever did it took whatever they could find of value – Comtessa's jewels, all the silverware, the wall hangings… Then they set fire to the house – or so it seems.'

Hanna remembered the cart with its load covered in canvas. The attackers must have just left, just set fire to the house. But first they had murdered Serlo, Comtessa, Cresselin and baby Baruch. And it was one of de Malbisse's squires driving the cart…

'We buried their bodies, first thing…' Now Granda's voice cracked and his eyes filled with tears. He put his hands to his face.

'You should have woken me…'

'We left Jessie to watch over you.'

Hanna turned away, shut her eyes, only to see the flames burning the bed hangings of the bed on which Comtessa and her children lay and the jagged red smiles of their throats.

Granda was speaking again. 'But we need you to get up, Hanna. We're going to the castle today' he said. 'Joseph has spoken to Fitzhorn and it's all arranged. Your ma is packing.'

'But is it safe to be out on the street?'

Granda pulled a face, shrugged. 'Will has offered to take us there in his boat.'

'With all our things? Your books? What about your manuscripts and all the medicines?'

'Will has already taken them. He has been a good friend to us. Now, you need to eat something,' said Granda. 'Let me go to tell Jessie you're awake — she was warming some water for you to wash with, and making soup. We've not got long till we leave. I'll send her up.'

He left the room. Hanna felt numb. She felt wretched and yet felt nothing. Her mind was functioning clearly, clearer even than usual, perhaps.

She pictured herself opening up the chest in which she had locked the memories of the riot in London, the burnt out houses, the charred bodies, Baruch on his death bed — and placed in there with them, alongside a nail-pierced effigy of Richard de Malbisse, the flame-licked roof, screaming horses, throat-rasping smoke, burning hangings, blood-soaked sheets, the glowing faces and gaping throats of Comtessa, Cresselin and Baby Baruch. Then she lowered the chest's lid and fastened its clasp.

There was a rumbling of cart wheels now, and the clip-clopping of hooves in the street below and she hauled herself up to the window to take a look.

Just pulling away from Joseph's house was a cart pulled by two of his horses, surrounded on all sides by guards, some armed with pikes, others with crossbows, some in the colours of Joseph's household and others the constable's own men. Then Elias came out, on Baruch's bay horse. They overtook the cart and set off south at a gallop.

Their preparations were complete. Granda's rug and wall hangings, together with the goat and chickens, baskets of smoked fish, dried beans, and most of the kitchen utensils, they had entrusted to Jessie's family.

'We'll take good care of them, don't you worry. You'll be back soon enough,' Jessie said. 'We'll watch the house. My Godwin will stay here, with a couple of his friends.'

'Thank you, Jessie,' Ma said. 'You take good care of yourself.' She handed her two leather pouches stretched tight over the coins inside each.

The courtyard was quiet without the chickens and goats. Three bundles of clothing lay on the floor, together with Granda's medical bag. Hanna's concealed a misshapen wax figure and a pouch holding spells inscribed on vellum.

Granda stood by his myrtle plant against the south wall, fondling its dark, glossy leaves, looking at the rosemary, thyme and sage and the fruit trees that he had planted and tended with love, their roots reaching down into York's fertile soil, and the raised beds already green with garlic and poppy.

'Will you keep an eye on my garden, too, Jessie?' he asked.

'Don't worry, Master Samuel, I will.'

There was a knock at the riverside gate. 'Mistress Abigail, Hanna!'

It was Will, with Beaumon at his side. 'Your books and manuscripts are already safe inside the castle, Master Samuel,' he said, 'but we must go. The tide will turn shortly and there's people planning to come to Joseph's and the synagogue to take what hasn't been moved to the castle – and to see what's in your house and Muriel's. There was talk at King's Staithe as we passed – my aunt's gone to see who's left at Muriel's.'

Hanna grasped Ma's hand tightly.

He jerked his head towards the three bundles and Granda's medical bag.

'Is that everything?' he asked.

'That's it,' said Granda.

'Come on then,' said Will.

They shut the gate to the courtyard behind them – for the last time? wondered Hanna – and climbed into Will's boat.

Drops of rain fell softly into the water, each then trapped within its own concentric ripples. Hanna steadied the boat as Will helped Ma and Granda get in, Beaumon watching each attentively. They manoeuvred themselves into the boat's bottom with their bundles, Ma without too much difficulty, Granda more awkwardly.

'Travelling like one of my own baskets of fish,' muttered Ma as she hunkered down.

Granda grimaced, said nothing. Hanna squeezed in next to them and Will passed in Granda's stick, then covered them with the canvas. It was dark and airless underneath. Hanna was aware of Granda trying to stifle his cough. She concentrated on picturing what was happening outside…

Now they would be passing Joseph's house and the synagogue, now King's Staithe, the barges waiting to sail south and the small boats preparing to return to villages up and down stream; Will's arms would be pulling strongly and easily on the oars, his fringe flopping down over his eyes, Beaumon keeping look-out at the bow. Then there was the long haul down past the castle and its moat, its tower both threat and promise on the skyline… where soon she would be shut safely inside.

Now she could feel the boat turning and Will directing it towards the castle's riverside entrance where the flow from river to moat was regulated by a sluice gate.

There they could climb up onto the bridge that held the sluice gate and cross to enter by the castle's southern gate, unseen from the town. Hanna was jarred by the thud as the first oar struck the bank to steady the boat and soften its impact as it too struck. There was a pause while Will was securing the boat, to one of the bridge's timbers, and then he was already pulling the canvas off them.

'We're here,' he said. 'Go quickly. It's quiet, no one around.'

Ma climbed out of the boat onto the bank and stretched out her hand to help Granda. The sluice gate to the moat was open and the river was choppy where its flow met the water of the moat. Will grabbed onto the bridge to steady the boat as Granda joined Ma on the bank. Hanna passed them the bundles of clothes and Granda's medicine bag and stick, then clambered out herself.

'Thank you, Will,' said Granda. Tears were rolling down Ma's face. She and Granda turned to go.

'Hanna – I'll write,' said Will.

'How?'

'With pen and ink. Are you doubting my ability?' How could he tease her at a time like this? 'And then Jack will find you.'

Of course, Jack. Hanna briefly held Will's hand in hers, not trusting herself to meet his gaze.

'Bye, Will.'

'Bye, Hanna.'

Then she turned to follow Ma and Granda across the bridge to the castle.

27. CASTLE

The guard at the gatehouse appeared to be expecting them, let them in at once and again Hanna was inside the castle walls. She wrinkled her nose – the air was thick with the smell of yeast from the brew house. The heavy gate shut behind them. Hanna put her arm around Ma and hugged her. Ma hugged her back but didn't smile and her body was tense under Hanna's embrace. Granda, just ahead of them, put his bag down heavily on the ground. He leant awkwardly on his stick, balancing his medical bag on his hip, coughing.

The castle's lower bailey was as Hanna remembered it – the smithy and stables, the brew house, the long hall, and the timber keep on its mound on the far side of the inner moat. It seemed preparations were being made for more building: there were huge timbers piled up against the wall. This time Hanna was going to cross the inner moat and seek the security of the keep above.

With her bundle again balanced on her shoulder, she managed to dodge the geese, goats and chickens, but then – 'Hanna!' She felt herself gripped around her hips from behind. It was Hakelin, Muriel's younger grandson, closely followed by his big brother Leo, and then Muriel herself, holding baby Flo by the hand.

'See her now, she's walking!' said Muriel proudly. Flo held out her arms for Hanna to pick her up and Hanna put down her bundle so that she could, burying her face in the warmth of the toddler's neck.

'What took you so long? We were worried. We left straight after the funeral – may their souls rest in paradise' – Muriel's voice faltered – 'the children were asking where you were. Gentill has started preparing the evening meal with the others – you're about the last to arrive.'

'Have you seen our Dinah and Leah and the children?' It was Levi the carpenter, with his son, Abe, at his side. His voice was harsh and both their faces were tight, drawn, but Hanna could sense Ma and Granda bridle at the lack of a greeting.

'No, we haven't, Levi,' Granda said. 'But we came by the river.'

Abe turned to go. 'That's it, Da,' he said. 'We're done here with waiting – we must go back to find them.'

Levi turned with him and the father and son ran towards the castle's northern gate which led directly back to the town.

'Without so much as a goodbye,' said Muriel. 'But still not here… Levi and Abe came on ahead, the rabbi and Joseph needed some help with something – I'm sure Manasser could have done it just as easily – Dinah and Leah were going to follow on with the children – you'd think they'd have been here by now. Why they didn't all come along together –'

'We should go in,' said Granda abruptly. He picked up his bag and set off across the bailey.

Hanna and Ma mutely picked up the bundles of clothing and followed. Muriel talked as they went. 'It's not so bad inside – you'll see. But there are a lot of us, and keeping all the children in order… And that Fitzhorn, the constable, he's been a bit tricky. He's always got a mug of beer in his hand – testing the latest brew, he says. There's some as says we shouldn't trust him. He's gone off into the town now, left with a gaggle of his men to do who knows what…'

But, once across the drawbridge over the inner moat, she was silenced by the steep climb up the steps to the keep.

Wheezing, Granda banged on the gate to the upper bailey. It was opened by Caleb the butcher and his brother Aaron, together with a man in the constable's red and grey, one of Fitzhorn's sergeants, Hanna supposed. Caleb and Aaron looked bright-eyed and fierce, keyed up. She knew them well – as well as slaughtering the community's animals for eating, they also prepared the parchment on which she and Granda wrote – but found it hard to shake off her childhood fear of Caleb's knife, about whose sharpness and purity he loved to boast. He wasn't holding it now, but the brothers immediately shut and locked the gate behind them, not leaving it to the sergeant.

The upper bailey was narrow – no outbuildings, just a sole rowan tree among rocks against the far wall – and the weathered wooden walls of the keep rose up almost directly in front of them. Its three storeys looked strong and safe. Hanna could hear people up on the battlements, though she couldn't see them. She felt queasy and light-headed, the events of the previous night still flickering luridly through her mind despite her best efforts to lock them away – but here, surely, she and her family would be beyond the reach of their enemies.

Like Granda said, when all the fuss died down, once the Christians were done with their Easter, they'd be able to return home and mourn properly the death of their friends – wouldn't they?

The steep wooden stairs were narrow and dark, their torch holders empty. Hanna was scared, but she had to escape the fetid, tense atmosphere inside the tower. She steadied herself by keeping the fingers of one hand pressed lightly against the wall. She passed the hall on the second storey where the women and children were to sleep, and then the men's rooms above. The air here was already colder, the wind whistling as it blew through the tiny gaps between the walls' timbers.

After just two more turns, slightly breathless, she stepped out onto the battlements. There was no one else there – finally, she was alone. Buffeted by a gust of wind, she clutched at the wall behind her, momentarily blown off balance. Clouds scudded across the darkening sky; it was almost night. She had never been up so high. She stood for a moment, savouring the cool, fresh air. Down below she could see Caleb and Aaron still keeping guard at the gate. The bridge across the inner moat was now drawn up, so that the keep stood isolated on its own small island.

Levi and Abe had returned, alone, save for Little Levi, Abe's oldest son. Leah, Dinah and the other children were dead, slaughtered by soldiers of the cross. The soldiers, recently recruited and new to the town, had challenged the women to convert to Christianity. Their neighbours tried to intervene, and the soldiers threatened them, too. When Dinah and Leah refused to convert, the soldiers killed first them and then the children. Little Levi, no older than Gentill's Hakelin, had made a run for it, and was sheltered by neighbours while the soldiers went to drink at the tavern, disappointed to find that the house of Levi the carpenter contained no chests of jewels.

They couldn't even honour Dinah, Leah and the children with a funeral and burial as rushed as that for Comtessa, Cresselin and baby Baruch. Rabbi Yom Tov said prayers as Levi, Abe and nearly all of them wept, but neither the rabbi nor anyone else had any words of comfort to offer. How could they? Levi and Abe were sitting in mourning in a corner of the king's chamber, while their fellows took it in turns to sit with them.

They were so many in the keep's confined space, all on top of one another. The castle was built to defend and control a city, not house 150 children, women and men. Fitzhorn had given them full use of the three floors: the garrison's stone-built quarters at the bottom of the tower, which had two fireplaces, where they could cook, then the hall and finally the king's chambers above, where King Henry had stayed when he visited York, though now bare of wall hangings and furniture.

As for provisions, they were able to use those in the garrison's storerooms on the ground floor, as well as whatever each household had managed to carry in, which included a dozen or so chickens and whatever eggs they might lay. But the supplies were low – what was sufficient to last the garrison of five sergeants and three watchmen up to a month didn't go far when feeding so many. The women had squabbled about how best to ration the food when preparing the evening meal and Hanna had slipped quietly away.

That wasn't the only difference of opinion. There had also been an argument with Fitzhorn the constable, which had resulted in him – and his small garrison – being refused entry to the inner castle. Hanna wasn't sure how it had happened, as she had been down below in the kitchen. She hadn't taken much notice of Muriel's comments when they'd arrived, about some of their number not trusting the constable, but it seemed that Rabbi Yom Tov was chief among them.

Fitzhorn had been drinking all day and was thoroughly drunk. He'd gone out to sample the other ales of the town and by the time he'd staggered back to the castle and demanded entry to the upper bailey, it had been agreed not to let him in. Granda had done his best to convince Joseph and allay the rabbi's and others' fears, reassured them that it was perfectly normal for Fitzhorn to leave the castle, go about the town, even to talk to the sheriff – they did, after all, both work for the king.

But people were tired and frightened, reeling from the loss of Baruch's family and now Levi's. Joseph was reduced to a state of near panic and, with the rabbi on their side – 'it won't be the first time that we've been betrayed' – it was the voices of fear and mistrust that had won. Muriel had been loudest among those urging that they shut Fitzhorn, his watchmen and sergeants out of the keep. Amid much shouting and kerfuffle, the bridge across the moat was drawn up, the Jews were locked in, the king's constable locked out, and now they waited.

Hanna pulled her cloak tighter against the wind and eased herself around the central wall, keeping well away from the edge of the battlements. The moon had risen. The lower bailey lay quiet, all shut up for the night. The king's fishpond to the east glimmered silver, and the river, too, as it flowed south beyond the castle towards Acaster and the king's forest… Occasional golden dots of light punctuated the darkness of the town to the north. She wondered whether she'd be able to see her home in the morning, when the sun rose. And she wondered where Will was, what he was doing, hoped he was safe.

Hanna heard steps and a wheezing cough behind her and turned in alarm. It was Granda. He placed a hand on her arm, still coughing.

'Granda, are you all right?' Hanna asked.

Granda nodded his head, unable to speak, but doing his best to smile and reassure her. Hanna looked on, anxious. Finally, he got his breath back.

'I don't think I'll be climbing up those stairs again if I can help it,' he said. 'But Ma said you'd gone for some fresh air and I'd already looked outside the keep – nearly tripped over someone's wretched chickens. But oh my dear, what have we done?'

'What do you mean?'

'Banning Fitzhorn and his men from the keep! What are they supposed to do? We've effectively taken possession of the king's property!'

'What will Fitzhorn do?'

'I don't know, my dear. I've talked to Joseph again. He'll talk to the others during the course of the evening, to try to talk them round, to let us talk to Fitzhorn again as soon as he comes back. It was the fact that he had all his sergeants with him earlier, I think, that upset everyone – not to mention the fact that he was drunk and singing –' Granda stopped, seized by another bout of coughing.

When it had passed, he went on, 'But at least our books and manuscripts are safe in the storeroom, together with the Torah and lamps from the synagogue – Joseph transported them here.'

They stood in silence a while, staring out at the darkness. 'We could build Cordova in York' – Da's voice in Hanna's head. Once this was over, and she knew Ma and Granda were safe, then she would find Da and Ben. Maybe Will could help her… if he could be persuaded to leave his parents. Together, they could go down the river – maybe convince Manasser to let them travel with him on his boat…

'The food is ready. It's time to eat.' It was Ma come to fetch them.

28. SIEGE

In the night, Hanna was woken by her own screams that she mistook for those of Leif and the other horses at Spen Lane. Her sweating palms seemed to her wet with the bright red blood in which Comtessa, baby Baruch and Cresselin lay. Trembling, she felt Ma wrap her arms around her, and let herself be soothed back to sleep.

It was early morning when she was woken again, by Flo crying. She could also hear noises outside – a cock crow, but also voices, and the whinnying of horses, a dull thud of hooves, the jingling of bridles. She pulled on her tunic, stepped over Ma's still sleeping body and stood on tiptoe to look out of the window next to which they'd secured a space the previous evening. Her nightmare fears had gone, as if they belonged to someone else.

The light was grey, the sun not long risen. But it was no good: she was facing north, and could see the town, with the towers of St Mary's and St Peter's – even, perhaps, a glimpse of Coney Street – but nothing of the lower bailey or the entrance to the keep.

Half-waving a greeting at Gentill, who was now feeding Flo, Hanna made her way over the other bodies in her way, and again climbed up the staircase, past the king's chambers where she could hear the sound of prayers being said, and out onto the battlements.

Once more the height of the keep took her aback. The river barges making their way south with the tide were tiny.

A horse neighed below. Hanna needed to find out what was going on. She moved to the edge of the battlements and peered over.

The noises were coming from the lower bailey. There were as many men dressed in the red and yellow of the sheriff as in the constable's red and grey. She could make out the profile of the sheriff, John Marshall, whom she'd met with her Uncle Baruch not so many months previously and whose debts to Baruch were now owed to Uncle Joseph… Marshall looked even smaller today, his tiny stature accentuated by the size of the gleaming chestnut charger on which he rode. Gospatric Fitzhorn, the constable, was next to him, with a couple of other men on horseback.

Hanna also recognised among the crowd the young men on horseback wearing the sign of the cross who had been at the bakery that day – and there was Aelred, too. While his commander looked too small for his horse, Aelred, still skinny, looked far too tall for his dainty grey palfrey, as if his feet would touch the ground if he took them out of his stirrups. Hanna wished Will were there, to laugh at how absurd Marshall and Aelred looked together, to contain her fear. She leaned further over the wall, craning for a better view.

Then, at a word from Marshall, the men dismounted, and made their way to the gate in the lower bailey that opened onto the bridge across the inner moat. But the gate remained shut and the bridge drawn up.

The eyes of everyone below were on the keep, it seemed. Hanna ducked down.

'What are you doing up here, young lady? This is not your place.'

It was Uncle Joseph, almost choking on the words because he was so out of breath, emerging stiffly from the staircase. He was followed by Rabbi Yom Tov and Simeon. Hanna felt stung – notwithstanding his disapproval of her, Uncle Joseph wouldn't normally speak to her like that. Neither he nor the rabbi looked as if they'd slept, the bags under Joseph's eyes even baggier, the rogue muscle twitching on the left, and the shadows under the rabbi's eyes as dark as his beard. Both looked hunted, strained.

She squeezed past them to get to the stairs, too angry to apologise.

'We will not open up,' she could hear Uncle Joseph straining his voice to shout as she descended, 'until we have proper assurances from King Richard that we are safe.'

The morning passed. When Ma wasn't kept busy with tasks, she was kept talking by Muriel who clucked away like one of the chickens pecking for insects in the scant grass of the upper bailey. Granda was doing his best to remain in a world of his own, reading. Wrapped up in a blanket, he'd found himself a spot under the rowan tree, his medical bag at his side. There were some rocks and loose stones there and one of the rocks was large and flat enough to serve as a seat. The tree, its dark red buds still clenched tight shut, offered something to lean against, but little shelter. Granda looked grey with tiredness and still shook with periodic fits of coughing. Hanna told him what she'd seen from the battlements and he listened in silence.

'Do you really think we will be safe here, Granda?' she asked.

'How can I know, my dear? It's all so much more complicated than it was – of our own making. Joseph sent messages with Elias to the bishop in Lincoln and the king's representative in London yesterday morning – but he will scarcely have arrived in Lincoln yet.'

So that was where Elias was galloping off to… Two days to Lincoln, if riding at speed, another two to London – and then the same back again. Could they wait that long? Didn't many castles hold out for weeks and months against their enemies? So long as they could make the food last…

'You must go to help your Ma and Muriel, Hanna,' Granda said. 'It's best to keep busy – and there's nowhere here for you to work with me. Our manuscripts are best left as they are – hidden away. We'll talk later, my dear.'

Hanna was required to help first in the kitchen and then keeping an eye on the children as they played outside in the upper bailey. She had to rely on the accounts of what was happening below given by the men who were now taking it in turns to keep watch – and they said little more than that the crowds were growing in number. The watchmen spoke to their wives, sisters and daughters rather than directly to her. Hanna didn't like it. All the others in the castle the same age as her were married. She sensed the other girls were steering clear of her and she felt an oddity here in a way that she had never been conscious of with Ma and Granda at home. She missed Ben more than ever, and she missed Will.

It was well past noon before she had a chance to return to the battlements where, if Will were to send her a letter with Jack, the bird would surely be able to find her. Caleb the butcher and Manasser were on watch duty but they were not alone. Gentill was there with Leo, Hakelin and Flo – and also craning over for a view were Levi, Uncle Joseph, Rabbi Yom Tov and Simeon.

'Come and see, Hanna, come and see,' cried Hakelin when he saw her. Levi, Uncle Joseph and the rabbi took no notice. Gentill made space for Hanna to take a look. Hanna sensed Manasser eyeing her suspiciously. She ignored him.

There were three, maybe four times as many gathered in the lower bailey now as there had been in the early morning. She thought she recognised Mary and the other women from the outside the bakery among them.

One figure in particular Hanna really wished she couldn't see: the monk in the dirty white surplice. He had set up a trestle covered in a white cloth. Some of the crowd were kneeling in front of it and the monk was talking and gesticulating at his 'altar' with his back towards his impromptu congregation.

On the near side of the bailey, others were building. They were using the timbers Hanna had noticed on arriving at the castle. They had constructed two large platforms, onto each of which they were now building a frame. They were being instructed by three men on horseback, one dark-haired, one red, the other white-blonde. All wore the dark blue and scarlet of de Malbisse.

Hanna screwed up her eyes to see. They weren't just wearing the colours of de Malbisse, it was Malbisse's squire de Cuckney, the young Scot Marmaduke Darrell, and the Beast himself. Always, those three. The Beast, who'd owed so much money to Uncle Baruch when he was struck by an arrow during the hunt (money now owed, like Marshall's and Darrell's, to Uncle Joseph); and de Cuckney and Darrell – leading the mob to burn down the homes of her friends in London, driving the loaded cart away from Spen Lane as the flames leapt up around the bodies of Comtessa, Cresselin and baby Baruch. Hanna's heart pounded and she felt herself suddenly hot and damp with sweat.

As they continued to watch, the white monk, his prayers done, came over to encourage the men doing the sawing, holding timbers steady for them, dragging new ones to be cut. He stood back as the men took one of the bigger timbers and manoeuvred it onto one of the two finished platforms to form a long, central arm.

'What are they building, Daddy? What is it?' asked Leo.

'I – I don't know, Leo.' Manasser looked across at Gentill.

'It's time to leave now, children. Say goodbye to your father now.'

'Are you coming, Hanna?' asked Hakelin.

'Yes, I'm coming,' she said, but as she turned to go her eye was caught by the sight below of a slim figure of a boy. He had a jackdaw on his shoulder and a dog at his side – Will. He had a tray of something – seed cakes? – hung around his neck which he was selling to others in the crowd. He glanced up at the keep every now and then. Could he see her? It didn't feel safe to wave.

She was distracted momentarily by a raucous shout bursting out from the gaggle of young men with the crosses on their backs gathered outside the brew house, jugs of beer in their hands.

When Hanna looked back to where Will had been, he was gone, and no sign of Jack.

'Come *on*, Hanna,' said Hakelin. He had come back to fetch her. With a last glance at the lower bailey, she took his outstretched hand and went.

Leaving Hakelin to play with the other children, Hanna went again to find Granda. Despite the chill in the late afternoon air, he was still sitting under the rowan tree. Uncle Joseph, Levi and the rabbi were with him. They were describing to him what they had seen in the lower bailey.

'They're like nothing that I've ever made,' Levi was saying.

'They're siege engines, I fear,' said Granda, quietly.

'What does that mean, Samuel?' asked Uncle Joseph.

'Giant catapults, with which to hurl rocks at this keep – if I'm right. I saw them in my childhood, as we fled Al Andalus – and Ranulf, our old sheriff here, he'd talk about them in his tales of battles and soldiering.'

'So you're telling us that they are building machines with which they will knock this tower down?' said Levi.

'Yes, I think so,' said Granda.

Hanna remembered the catapult slings and stones that she, Will and Ben had experimented with when running wild at Acaster. They had rarely succeeded in hitting anything with them – but these were enormous machines.

'We can't just let them do that,' said Levi. 'They've taken my wife and my daughter-in-law and all but one of my grandchildren – and I'm not letting them take my son and little Levi.'

'What do you propose we do, Levi?' asked Uncle Joseph.

'Abe and I have searched the keep for weapons and there are none,' said Levi, 'But I've my tools – we can go into the lower bailey once it's dark and destroy the machines.'

'How? You'll be killed before you can do anything to them. They're not just going to leave them there unattended overnight,' said Granda.

'And they can always build more,' said Uncle Joseph.

'Whatever, we must hold to the holy law,' said Rabbi Yom Tov softly, 'to abandon it is worse than death. Far better to die at our own hand –'

Granda opened his mouth to speak but instead began to cough uncontrollably. His body shook and he fought for breath, his face turning red and his eyes bulging.

'Granda, are you all right?' said Hanna.

'Go, child, fetch some water,' said Uncle Joseph.

Hanna ran to the keep, shooing the chickens by the door out of the way. She had never seen Granda this bad. She dipped a bowl into the bucket of water by the well in the kitchen.

But by the time she returned outside, walking so as not to spill the water, the coughing fit had ended. Levi and the rabbi were helping Granda to walk back to the keep, one on either side; Uncle Joseph followed behind. Talk of siege engines and castle defences and what it might mean to hold to the law was ended, for the time being.

The soup that evening was thinner and the pieces of bread smaller than the previous day – 'Tomorrow, we will make a special Shabbat meal,' Muriel said.

But the question on all their minds was no longer, 'Will the food last?', rather, 'When will they fire the first missile?'

Friday 28 Adar 4950 / 16 March 1190

Again, Hanna's sleep was broken by a nightmare revisiting Comtessa's bedroom at Spen Lane and once more, having slept in Ma's arms, Hanna woke free of its memories.

Leaning over the battlements in the cold, misty morning air, she scanned the crowd below for another sight of Will. The men on watch duty ignored her. Other than them, Hanna was alone.

Many in the lower bailey appeared to have spent the night there. The monk was already chanting and gesticulating in front of his table. De Cuckney and Darrell were standing by the siege engines and remaining piles of wood with a group of men, though none was yet sawing timber or wielding a hammer. The giant catapults stood tall with their central arms in position. There was a heap of what to Hanna looked like fishing nets piled up on the floor next to them.

Then Lord Malbisse himself arrived, riding proprietorially round the lower bailey on his magnificent white horse. Wraiths of steam billowed from its nostrils and merged with the mist as the animal snorted and tossed its head. With the harsh tug on the reins that Hanna remembered, de Malbisse stopped to speak to Darrell and de Cuckney. At once the men started work, busying themselves with saws and wood and nets. Hanna recalled, too, the Beast's pale, unsmiling blue eyes and the jagged scar that stretched upwards across his face from the corner of his mouth. She shuddered and felt sad for the girl who'd believed she had 'powers' and could defeat an enemy by sticking nails into a wax effigy even now contained in a bundle of clothes two floors below… What had ever made her think she had the power to change anything?

And then she started – there was Will! Will, with Jack and Beaumon, and the tray once more strapped around his neck. Each time he sold a cake from the tray he moved closer to the inner moat, the bird on his shoulder, his dog trotting alongside, and looked intently up at the keep.

Hanna kept her eyes fixed on him. He stopped, stock-still, staring in her direction. She was sure he had seen her. A woman came up to him, bought and paid for a cake. Hanna kept her eyes locked on them both. The woman moved away to rejoin her friends.

Will turned to speak to Jack who was still perched on his shoulder, then looked up again at Hanna. Keeping his eyes on her, he held his arm out so that the bird hopped onto his wrist. Will took Jack in his hands and was speaking to him. Then he threw the jackdaw up in the air and Jack was flying towards the keep. He flapped his wings and soared upwards, over the moat and the inner bailey wall and higher still towards the battlements. Hanna could hear him calling as he flew closer to her – 'Cy-aw, cy-aw.'

He landed on the wooden wall in front of her and she could see Will's letter tied to one of his legs with a thin strip of leather.

'Cy-aw,' he greeted her.

'Hello, Jack,' Hanna said. The fine white feathers that grizzled his head gave him an air of elderly wisdom. Hanna glanced again into the lower bailey but Will and Beaumon were gone. On the battlements, Caleb and his brother Aaron were talking to each other, and had apparently noticed nothing.

Jack remained still for her to untie the parchment from his leg. 'Don't go yet, Jack,' she said. He looked at her expectantly but, with no food on offer, he gave one more 'cy-aw', opened his wings and launched himself into flight. He was gone.

Hanna unfolded the letter. There were no words of greeting, simply: *The sluice gate is broken and I can bring the boat into the moat. I will wait tonight on the north-west side of the keep. Will.*

Throughout the keep, the women busied themselves and their children with preparations for Shabbat, as if it were quite normal for them all to be preparing together in the castle rather than at home. Some removed the clothes and bedding from the second-floor hall and the king's chambers above and took them outside to air. Others, meanwhile, remained to dust and sweep the hall and the chambers. Still others were busy in the kitchen below, plucking the chickens Caleb had slaughtered, kneading bread and leaving it to rise, chopping onions and the last of the carrots.

Hanna was glad to be outside airing the clothes and bedding, together with Gentill and Flo. Leo and Hakelin were with Manasser and the other men who, displaced from their chamber, had gathered to pray together on the far side of the keep. The sun was shining and a stiff spring breeze blowing, lifting the garments up into the air as the women shook them like so many colourful, waving flags. Hanna's spirits lifted with them as she felt the scrap of parchment in her pocket: *I will wait tonight on the north-west side of the keep...* She looked at the bailey wall – the rowan tree, she'd be able to use that to help her climb over.

Flo was gurgling with laughter as she jumped up to grab each garment shaken by her mother as it was tugged upwards by the wind. Then, tiring of the game, she toddled off to find her brothers and father. She was already disappearing round the other side of the keep by the time Gentill and Hanna realised that she'd gone.

'I'll catch her, don't worry,' said Hanna.

As she rounded the corner of the keep, the wind carried the mellifluous tones of Rabbi Yom Tov towards her.

'The Christians prowl like wolves at our gate. Their machines are poised to knock down this tower. So let us take our fate into our own hands. As Abraham offered Isaac in sacrifice to G–d, we must offer ourselves –' Hanna made a lunge for Flo just before she disappeared between the legs of the men.

'Got you!' she whispered into Flo's ear, turning swiftly to get out of earshot as Flo began her wail of 'Daddy!' – but still able to hear the rabbi continuing, 'We must offer ourselves, lest they defile us with their water, as they did our brother, Baruch, or burn us at the stake. G–d commands us to die for his law, my friends…'

Despite the sun and the warmth of Flo in her arms, Hanna found herself suddenly cold and shivering.

She handed Flo back to Gentill. The shaking and folding were all done now. She looked over at the rowan tree – Granda was just settling himself down underneath it, this time sitting on the blanket which the previous day he had wrapped around himself. The rock on which he'd perched the day before had gone, as well as the smaller ones that had lain near about it.

Granda looked thinner, older. He smiled at her as she approached.

'My dear, how are you?' But speaking set him off into a wheezy cough. Hanna couldn't wait for it to subside.

'Granda – Will sent a message – the moat is open – he's coming with his boat tonight.'

Granda forced the words out through his coughing. 'You must go, leave with him.'

'And you, you must come too, Granda.'

Granda shook his head. 'I'm too slow – my cough –'

'Hanna, can you help me take these piles of clothing back upstairs?' It was Gentill. Hanna would have to argue with Granda later.

She was halfway up the stairs to the second storey of the keep with her bundle, when she had to stand to one side to let two people pass, on their way down. It was Levi the carpenter and his son, Abe. They were sweaty and grimy, as if fresh from physical labour. They barely nodded to her as they passed.

When she'd helped stow away the bedding and clothes in the hall, Hanna stood on tiptoe to see from one of the windows what was happening in the lower bailey.

The central arms of each engine now had a net on one end and one also had a wooden barrel fixed to the other. A couple of the men were working on a second barrel. Others were unloading rubble and broken masonry from a hand-drawn cart which stood between the two wooden constructions. De Cuckney, Darrell and the Beast had gone, but the white monk remained.

'So this is where you are?' It was Ma. 'I was expecting you to join us in the kitchen.'

'I was just coming –'

'It's all right,' said Ma. 'It's all done for the time being.'

She squeezed next to Hanna to look out of the narrow window. The castle gate opened and another cart was hauled in. The monk hurried over to help.

'The rabbi wants us to kill ourselves, Ma,' Hanna said, as if it was something she said every day. What other way was there to say it?

The monk was helping to haul the lumps of rubble out of the cart, adding them to the pile that lay between the wooden engines.

'I know,' said Ma. 'Manasser thinks he's right – I've left Muriel arguing with him.'

'But the children –' Hanna began.

Ma interrupted. 'I can't do it, Hanna. I can't. Not when Ben and your Da may still be alive –'

'We can escape, Ma, go to find Ben and Da,' said Hanna. She spoke rapidly. 'The sluice gate into the moat is broken. Will is bringing his boat in tonight –'

But something was hurtling past the window, and then another, and another – rocks.

One fell into the inner moat but the others went further, landing the other side of the lower bailey wall, just short of the cart containing the rubble, and the men unloading it.

A couple of them looked around and up at the keep.

But another boulder was already arcing through the air, clearing moat and wall – and then the white monk was prone on the floor, his body at once obscured by those that gathered around him.

Other faces were turned upward towards the keep, with cries and shaking of fists. Hanna could hear shouting from the battlements above, too.

Hanna and Ma looked at each other. Hanna felt a brief flicker of pleasure, of relief, and then a deep sense of shame.

Mother and daughter turned to look out of the window again. They watched as the monk's body was loaded onto the empty cart, and carried away, through the castle gates.

'How is that going to help us?' Ma said.

Later, when the men came down from the battlements, none could say who had hurled the fatal rock.

The sun was fading. The final preparations for Shabbat were complete. The wall torches were lit, and loaves of bread set out on cloths arranged on the floor in place of tables; the rabbi's Kiddush cup stood brim-full of wine (Uncle Joseph and the rabbi had packed bottles along with the precious items from the synagogue.) Hanna queued in the bailey to wash her hands before entering, and now waited with Ma for the last to file in.

Hanna had tried to argue with Ma and Granda further about escaping with Will that night, but each was adamant that she should leave alone. 'I'm not well enough,' said Granda, 'I will be a burden to you.' 'I must be with your Granda, Hanna, to look after him for your Da – I will be here for you and Da and Ben when you return.'

They both dismissed Rabbi Yom Tov's talk of suicide. Granda was talking to the rabbi now, a little apart

– but each appeared to be listening respectfully to the other.

Hanna felt faint and headachey with hunger and tiredness. The siege engines were trained on the keep, their ammunition piled up alongside and ready, but it seemed the castle's attackers were biding their time. Hanna had heard drunken laughter and singing, regardless of the white monk's death. So she and her fellows would have one more night, at least, secure in their tower…

Muriel was to light the Shabbat candles. Traditionally, when they were all together the task had fallen to Anna, as the wife of Joseph, but then she'd fallen ill and now she was in London with their daughters. Last time, it was Comtessa who'd lit them… Hanna wished that it was Ma lighting the candles, at home, with Da and Ben, and Granda.

But she smiled affectionately at the air of self-importance that Muriel wasn't quite able to quell as, kneeling above the Shabbat candles on the improvised 'table' on the floor, she received the taper from Manasser. Muriel touched the taper to each wick in turn. Each flame first wavered then settled to a steady burn, illuminating her broad, kindly face with its high eyebrows and deep laughter lines. Slowly, three times she encircled the candles' light with her arms and murmured her blessings, Hanna and Ma and all the other women and girls murmuring along with her. Then they held their hands in front of their eyes and were silent in private prayer. ('Please G–d, let Ben and Da be safe. Please G–d, let us all be safe'.)

'Shabbat shalom!' said Muriel. 'Shabbat shalom' 'Shabbat shalom' the familiar, gentle syllables repeated softly up and down the hall. And then Rabbi Yom Tov picked up the cup of Kiddush wine and sang its blessing. 'Amen,' he said. 'Amen' everyone replied as they passed the cup from hand to hand. Then in turn he blessed the bread, tore it, and urged them all to tear and eat their bread likewise, and they did.

The soup was still thin, but tasted of chicken and had carrots and onion floating in it as well as globules of golden chicken fat. But Hanna did not feel full even when she had finished it and eaten her portion of bread.

The rabbi stood up again. 'Let the women and children leave us,' he said.

There was murmuring around the hall. Muriel and Ma exchanged looks. Muriel stood up. 'With respect, Rabbi Yom Tov, it's a matter a life and death, we all know it is, and you can't discuss it without us women. Let those who wish to leave with their children do so and the rest of us will stay. This is what my Abraham would have wanted, I am sure.'

Rabbi Yom Tov looked at Uncle Joseph, who nodded his head. 'Let the women stay, as Muriel suggests,' he said. Hanna could see the look of anguish mixed with defiance on Gentill's face as she left with Leo and Hakelin, holding the sleeping Flo tight across her chest.

The room fell silent again, all eyes on the rabbi.

'Tonight is our last night together,' he said. 'Our enemies will attack tomorrow, if not tonight, and if we fall into their hands we will die amidst their jeers. G–d is demanding our lives back – how much better if we return them with our own hands. Let us mock death and offer ourselves up, like a whole burnt offering on the altar of the Lord.

'We can't let ourselves or our possessions fall into the hands of the Christians. We must kill tonight our wives, our sons and our daughters and burn this keep and with it our bodies and possessions.'

Hanna looked at the faces of those around her. Joseph, apparently emotionless, was betrayed by the muscle twitching beneath his eye. Manasser was rapt. Ma's face was dark with rage. Granda was struggling to stand up. Seated with the other men, he was too far away for Hanna to help him.

The rabbi was still talking. 'Each individual martyr will receive a gold crown upon his head, in which are set precious stones and pearls, each shall be given a golden throne under the tree of life. We shall see G–d eye to eye, in his glory and his majesty. Each of us shall point to him and say, this is our G–d, we trusted in him and he delivered us; let us rejoice and exult in his deliverance.'

Levi was on his feet. 'I'm sorry, Rabbi, but I'm not having any of this. By my reckoning, we should live by G–d's commandments, not die by them,' he said. 'I've said it before and I'll say it again: they've taken my wife, my son's wife, and all but one of my grandchildren – and I don't intend to let them take my son and my one remaining grandchild, too. We have family in Lincoln, and that's where, in the morning, we plan to go. If it means we have to promise that we'll become Christians, so be it – it won't be the first lie that I've told in my life.'

The Rabbi began to respond. 'Let those who don't agree, sit apart –'

But now Granda was up and steadying himself with his stick. 'No, first let me talk, Rabbi.' Hanna willed him not to succumb to another coughing fit. 'There is another way, as Levi suggests.' His voice was quiet, but steady. 'It's the way that many in Al Andalus took at the time that my family fled those who wished to convert us to Islam. Many – with the blessing of our rabbis – simply gave the outward show of being followers of Mohammed.

'If any of us tomorrow decides to throw ourselves on the mercy of our Christian oppressors, we are not forsaking our faith in pursuit of wealth or status – but because we wish to bear witness to what has been done to us and our community.

'So long as a person is alive and is breathing there is hope. "Choose life, that you and your children shall live," isn't that what Moses told us?

'And, please G–d, there will soon come a time when the oppressors stop oppressing us and we can again live a normal life together, open in our faith.'

Caleb the butcher stood up, and his knife was in his hand. 'We should not be arguing against the rabbi,' he said. 'I have my knife here, free of imperfections –'

Hanna could stand it no more.

'I don't want to die – or any of us,' she said. De Malbisse is a murderer. I know – I was there the first time he tried to kill my uncle Baruch, and he's stirred up the crowds against us – I don't trust him to let any of us go' – a tide of voices was rising in the hall – 'it's true,' Hanna insisted, 'and I've no intention of killing myself – or of letting anyone kill me.'

She was aware of Ma's eyes on her and Granda's, and Joseph telling her to sit down and be quiet.

'We can escape – the moat is open – my friend Will is bringing a boat – he can't take all of us at once, but I'm sure he'd make more trips…'

She turned to Manasser and Muriel. 'Let me at least take Leo and Hakelin with me – and Flo,' she said. 'Let's ask Gentill. I will take good care of them.'

Manasser was on his feet. 'That Christian boy,' he said. 'We know all about you and that, that Will! Samuel, for all your learning, you should have ensured your family paid better attention to the rabbi here.'

Hanna was almost crying in frustration. People were talking among themselves. Would no one listen to her?

'Muriel, Ma, Granda,' she begged. She held her arms out towards those she had lived and prayed with all her life. 'All of you, come with me, please.'

The rabbi was about to speak, but before he could say anything else, Hanna felt her arm grasped and found herself being pushed towards the door.

'Come, my dear,' Granda said, pulling her out and onto the narrow stairs. The air was suddenly cold upon her face.

'No, Granda, no,' sobbing now, she struggled against his grip, trying to return to the hall, but he held firm.

'You must go, Hanna, you must escape with Will, go to find Da and Ben.'

'But Ma –'

'She'll be with us shortly. You go down the stairs in front of me – help me now, there are things I must give you before you leave.'

'Let those who don't agree, sit apart from us…'

The rabbi's voice followed them as they descended. Hanna grabbed her bundle of possessions from the women's quarters as they passed. Her sobs had stopped by the time they reached the garrison's quarters at the base of the tower. She lifted the torch from its bracket on the wall as Granda opened the door to the storeroom. He placed his medical bag that he'd been carrying next to the chests that had once had pride of place in his study. He let out a sigh as he caressed the script on the top of the pile.

'See, my dear, how beautifully you have written here. And what you have written…'

'Granda, I can't take any of this with me,' she said. 'How will I carry it, with my own things?'

'Inside my bag,' he said, as he attempted to roll the manuscript small enough to place inside – but his hands were shaking too much. He thrust it impatiently towards her.

'You can use it, Hanna – the medical knowledge it contains, you can use. You have a gift and you must not waste it. Come on, fold it, put it in the bag – you must go.'

Granda opened the other chest and took out two books. 'And take these, too,' he said. 'One is the original, in Arabic, containing the second volume that we haven't yet translated. You will find a way. And the other is the Torah from the shores of the Sea of Galilee – the rabbi gives his blessing for you to leave, on condition that you take it with you for you and others to read from it the word of G–d,' he said.

'But you will need them – your bag, your books…'

'No, my dear' – he held her gently by the shoulders and looked her directly in the eyes – 'I won't'.

Hanna nodded. She knew if she spoke, she would cry, which wouldn't help anything.

'Now go,' Granda said.

There was a noise on the stairs outside. Ma came through the door. Hanna flung herself at her, hugged her fiercely, felt hot tears on her cheeks.

'Ma, come with me, please. We can go by boat to the coast, to find Da and Ben. Make Granda come with us. Please.'

'Sshh, my love,' Ma said, stroking Hanna's hair. 'Shh. We can't. You know we can't. You will have a better chance alone, with Will's help. Your Granda and I – we need to be here in case Da and Ben come back before you find them.'

Hanna pulled away from her mother. She took a deep breath to stop her sobs.

'But you'll be killed,' she said. 'If you stay here, you will die.'

'We won't, Hanna, I promise you. Your Granda and I, we will be fine. Your Granda is sick, and I will take care of him, for you and for Da. We will pray, and we will pretend – tell them what they want to hear, and these bad times will pass. And when Da and Ben return – and you – we will be here. We will be together again. But for now, you, you must go, I don't want you to endure these bad times.'

Ma's gaze was unwavering, her voice low, even. Hanna wanted to believe her but –

'Come, my child, it is time for you to go,' said Granda.

He unbolted the door to the outside.

Ma held her arms out to Hanna once more, hugged her.

'Take care, my love,' she said. She looked at Hanna unflinchingly; she smiled. 'You must go now. We will be fine.'

Granda put the bag in Hanna's hand and pushed her out of the door.

29. UNSEEN

The night air was cool. Again, that feeling of numbness, of detachment. Ma would be fine, she'd said so. She and Granda would look after each other.

Hanna walked quickly across the bailey towards the west wall. She couldn't stop herself glancing back, but the door was already shut. The moon was hidden by thick cloud. There was rain in the air.

'I am invisible,' she thought.

She didn't let herself think about what might be happening inside the castle. She reached the rowan tree, trying to gauge its position in relation to where the sun had set that evening. The tree was at least on the side of the castle that Will had promised to wait and its trunk forked helpfully at about Hanna's hip height. Granda's bag bumped against her. She shifted it behind her and secured it and her own bundle by means her tunic belt around her waist so that she had both hands free. Then it was the work of moments to hoist herself up into the tree, from there to the top of the wall and then to ease herself down. The tricky bit was not at once to hurtle down the steep slope into the river below. She tugged the bag back around to her side and flattened herself against the wall.

Her eyes were by now accustomed to the dark. The river lay slick and black below her, but there was no sign of Will and his boat. She slithered down the wall onto her backside, and began to inch her way down the hill holding bag and bundle in her lap with one hand and grabbing hold of tufts of grass with the other to slow her descent. It was a cold night for a swim.

'Hanna – is that you?' Will's voice!

'Yes. Will, where are you?'

She was aware of a figure waving at her, some twenty feet or so to her right.

'Here. Hold on, I'm coming to get you.'

There was the soft splashing of the oars in the water and oily ripples in the black water, then she could see that he had positioned the boat directly below her.

'Here, I'll catch you,' he said and Hanna half-slid, half-jumped down into Will's waiting arms. The boat see-sawed in the water but they didn't fall in. They swayed together, held each other close.

'Thank you, Will,' said Hanna. They pulled apart, still holding each other's hands, looking into each other's eyes.

'Just you?' Will asked. 'What about the others?'

'They wouldn't come,' Hanna said. She dropped his hands abruptly and stowed bag and bundle out of the way of the oars. 'We must go.'

He sat down and took the oars. 'I'll tell you what's happening once we're away from the castle,' he said, as she sat down opposite him. 'We'd best keep quiet till we're out of the moat and back in the river.' He pulled on the oars, turning the boat back towards the lower bailey.

Beaumon wasn't there, nor Jack.

Hanna was suddenly overwhelmed with sadness, with missing Beaumon, her yearning eyes and wagging tail, only it wasn't really missing Beaumon: it was everything. She swallowed hard, shook her head as if to dislodge the feeling, like Beaumon shaking the water from her ears after a dip in the river.

In the dark, she felt the choppy waters where the moat met the river before she saw the bridge and broken sluice gate. No sound came from the castle; the oars splashed rhythmically in the water. She couldn't see Will's face, just the occasional gleam of his teeth and the shine of the white of his eyes.

They passed through the sluice gate and Will pulled hard to take the boat back into the river's main current.

Finally he spoke, his voice low and urgent.

'There's a barge sailing to Selby in the morning, taking wool. The captain is a friend of my father's, plus, your Da once treated his wife, and she's going with him, has family to visit.'

'He'll take me?'

'He will. You can trust him. Plus, I've told him you're good at dressing up as a boy. He's happy for you to act as crew.'

'But I've no clothes…'

'I've brought some of mine. Clean, mind. Ma got them ready for you.'

'But you're coming, too, Will, aren't you? To help me find Da and Ben.'

She still couldn't see his face.

'How can I, Hanna?'

'You could, easily. Your Ma and Da can manage without you for a while.'

'I can't leave them, Hanna. They've no one else. Who knows how long "a while" will be? I'd like to come… But you know I can't.'

'You could.'

There was a short pause.

'Listen, Hanna. Could you stay here – with me, once this trouble's over?'

'You know I can't, Will – I can't – for so many reasons.'

'And I can't come with you – for so many reasons,' he said gently.

Hanna sat at the bow of the boat and sniffed the air. Like Beaumon, she thought. Her head felt light from lack of sleep. The river opened out wide and grey in front of her, York was already far behind. The barge had caught the outward tide with perfect timing and had the north wind as well in its sails. The land on either side was densely wooded, the smaller trees a misty green, just coming into leaf, the oaks rising tall and bare above them. Granda's bag, with his book and manuscript, was safely stowed with the boat's cargo below. The coarse woollen tunic and leggings she wore felt rough against her skin, but they were Will's and comforted her. (With her own clothes in the bag that she'd left with him, a wax effigy lay crumbling and spells unread.)

Granda and Ma were tough. Of course they would be all right. Hanna ignored the feeling of sick dread in the pit of her stomach. Her skin still tingled from her pre-dawn wash in the cold river, and the broth that Jane, the captain's wife, had given her to drink was scalding hot and salty.

'Your da is a good man,' Jane was saying. 'So you're on your way to find him and your brother, are you?'

'Yes,' said Hanna. 'I am.'

EPILOGUE

So Hanna was spared knowing, for the time being, the truth of what happened at the castle that night and the following morning.

Those who chose to die with their rabbi first made a pile of their clothes and belongings and set fire to it, and also to the roof, so that their bodies would in the end be consumed by the flames. Then the men cut the throats of their wives and children, and Rabbi Yom Tov cut Joseph's throat before finally killing himself.

Those who chose life escaped the flames and waited below until morning, when they offered to their attackers to convert to Christianity. The crowd at first accepted their offer, but then, led by Richard de Malbisse, killed each and every one of York's surviving Jews there present.

After that, de Malbisse and his co-conspirators went to St Peter's where they demanded the documents recording their debts to Baruch and Joseph and then burned them in the middle of the church.

That was on 9 Nisan 4950 / 17 March 1190 (Palm Sunday, for the Christians).

King Richard's representative came from London after a week or so to investigate, King Richard being on his trip to retake Jerusalem. However, by the time the king's representative arrived in York, Richard de Malbisse and his fellows had fled to Scotland. They were given fines, but never paid them in full.

No other punishment was imposed.

ACKNOWLEDGEMENTS

The book of magic that Hanna 'borrows' from Granda and from which I have 'borrowed' several spells is based on *Sepher Ha-Razim* (*The Book of the Mysteries*, translated by Michael A Morgan), probably written in Babylon at some time during the early fourth or late third century CE. A Yorkshire monk, William of Newburgh, told the events set in train by the coronation of Richard I that culminated in York six months later in his book *The History of English Affairs* (available online at http://sourcebooks.fordham.edu/). Rabbi Yom Tov, Baruch, Joseph, Richard de Malbisse, Ranulf de Glanville and the white monk are all present there; John Marshall, Marmaduke Darrell and de Cuckney I found in the pages of Richard Dobson's *The Jews of Medieval York and the Massacre of March 1190*. (In an earlier version of the novel I attempted to incorporate Dobson's suggestions that de Malbisse's actions were part of a plot involving his Percy relatives and sanctioned at the highest level by the king's justiciar, former Bishop of Durham Hugh de Puiset – but this proved too complicated for my story.)

I'm grateful, too, to all the other historians who studied twelfth century legal and financial records to find out about the lives of Richard de Malbisse, and Baruch, Joseph and their fellow Jews - Joe Hillaby, Robert Mundill, Patricia Skinner and Hugh Thomas, as well as, earlier, Cecil Roth and, further back still, Joseph Jacobs. I based much of Rabbi Yom Tov's final speeches on those recounted by Robert Chazan in his study of suicides in Germany during the 'first crusade' almost a century earlier which are thought to have been written down subsequently by survivors. (But I also left out a lot that is interesting about the real Rabbi Yom Tov: a respected religious scholar from Joigny, the author of an elegy to the thirty-two Jewish martyrs put to death by burning in Blois in 1171, two of whom had studied with the same teacher as him – perhaps his friends?; and also the author of a hymn still recited today in many synagogues on the eve of the Day of Atonement.)

Muriel is largely inspired by the seventeenth century memoirs of Glückel of Hamelin – in particular, her business activities and relationship with her husband (see https://muse.jhu.edu). I also owe a big debt to the Jewish Women's Archive (https://jwa.org) for the useful information I found there.

Granda's life story is loosely based upon that of the philosopher-theologian-doctor Maimonides – though his family fled south from Cordoba to Fez and then Egypt rather than north as Granda's family did. Although Granda is not a philosopher or deep religious thinker and scholar like Maimonides, Granda's thoughts on reason and the way to reach G–d are inspired by him, as well as his views on choosing life over suicide (see, in particular, Maimonides's *Letter on Apostasy*). I am grateful to Joel Kraemer's *Maimonides – the life and world of one of civilizations's greatest minds* for his evocations of twelfth century Cordoba.

As a non Jew, for the rhythm of the Jewish year I relied heavily on *Burning Lights*, Bella Chagall's memoir of growing up in Vitebsk, Russia, at the very beginning of the twentieth century, as well as Hayyim Schauss's *The Jewish Festivals – A guide to their history and observance* – and am grateful to the congregation of Catford and Bromley United Synagogue for making me welcome there.

For information on medieval medicine, I owe a debt to *Health, Disease and Healing in Medieval Culture* edited by Sheila Campbell, Bert Hall and David Klausner; and on hunting to John Cummins's *The Art of Medieval Hunting: The hound and the hawk*, Richard Almond's *Medieval Hunting*, and Simon Armitage's rendition of *Sir Gawain and the Green Knight*.

I should also like to thank the various individuals and friends who commented on the manuscript or otherwise helped me: David Alterman, Ashley Brown, Barbara Chandler, Linda Cox, Rhona Green, Ruth Gripper, Edward Hayman, Martin Kemp, Galyna Levchenko; Kara May, tutor in creative writing at Goldsmiths College, without whose stern words I'd never have got under way, and Tejus Dasandi, Claire Hughes, Caroline Lambie, Lulu Le Vay and the rest of our fellow students who were such helpful and sympathetic critics; Sarah Richmond, Brandon Robshaw and David Stone. Any errors are, of course, wholly my own.

And my biggest thank-you of all: to Laurie, Stan and Eleanor.

FORTHCOMING

To Aleppo Gone

1191. Aleppo, Syria. Az-Zahir Ghazi, nineteen years old,
has ruled as Emir of Aleppo for five years. His court
includes his Kurdish uncle, a Jewish physician held against
his will, and a Persian mystic.

Meanwhile, Az-Zahir's father, Saladin, Sultan of Egypt and
Syria, is defending Jerusalem from attack by Richard I,
King of England and Duke of Normandy, Aquitaine and
Gascony. Among King Richard's entourage is a young boy
from York, whose medical skills are truly remarkable.

Hanna's story continues amid the struggle for control
of the holy places and riches of the east.